Seven Varieties of

Silence

Lewis Blair

Seven Varieties of Silence

The rickety iron lift rattled and shuddered and sang harsh metallic notes as it carried the pit 15 backshift from the bright daylight of the pit head down one hundred and seventy fathoms to the murky blackness of Main Dook Brae, where grainy white lights every ten yards did little to penetrate the satanic gloom of tunnels punched violently through the dark belly of the earth. The foreman wrenched open the barrier and it clanged against the lift shaft. The other seven men spilled out. They shouted their greetings to the bottomer, who had gone down on the lift before and was already clearing spilled coal with a wide shovel that scraped the ground with teeth-grating shrieks. The eight men tramped down Main Dook Brae. On their way they passed the early shift heading for the lift.

'Never fear, the back-shift's here!' shouted a sinewy man with a thick walrus moustache.

'Aye, well, the hard work's done, so you ladies can take it easy. As always!' replied one of the departing men over his shoulder, safely surrounded by his crew.

On they trekked, heavy boots on rough ground, their head lamps hanging loosely from their caps, little cans of oil attached by string to their caps, drops of paraffin oil dripping onto taut skin and cheap coats. The team traipsed down the tunnel alongside the parallel tracks where later they would wheel tonne loads of fresh cut coal. They came to the firemen's cabin and hung their coats and their dinner bags on wobbly pegs. The gaffer having given them their orders, they set off further north east into the working heart of the mine, the black abyss swallowing them up once again. Time passed strangely in the pit without the sun to signal the hours.

1

Half a mile away, a young woman tended to a steaming pot of broth. A hearty smell of carrots, ham and pearl barley rose from a heavy iron pot. She lifted the lid with a thick towel, stirred the simmering broth vigorously, and replaced the lid. She turned back to the slicing of a well-floured loaf of brown bread on a slab of grainy wood. Her gran had made the bread soft and springy. Her own efforts were usually hard and dense, only good for the ducks. She rested a hand tenderly on her swelling belly, and gazed out of the window.

Outside lay the cobbled main street, the only street of Mavis Valley. The street ran between two rows of terraced houses. The houses were modest, two rooms and a kitchen, but they were solidly built and kept the rain out. Smoke rose from chimneys and a thin breeze carried it east towards Jelly Hill. At the north end of the street lay the wilderness plantation, a long narrow forest no broader than a cattle field. Beyond the thicket lay the remnants of the Antonine Wall, marking the northern limit of the meaningful reach of the Roman Empire, though a grassy mound was all that could be seen now. At the south end of the road lay the Forth and Clyde canal, an artery for the village, and a barrier between it and the larger towns to the south. Some way west along the canal, there sat the steel swing bridge that heaved train carriages loaded with coal over to the south bank of the canal, for carrying onwards to the juddering, spluttering factories of Glasgow and the hungry fires of tenements and townhouses.

The village road was alive with the contented sounds of a Sunday evening in summer. A group of women gathered around a proud young mum with her tiny baby, giving gifts and encouragement. The young mother stood with the baby nestled in the crook of her arm, soaking up the attention. A few yards away, a man sat in front of his squat house, mending a crooked wooden chair with hammer in hand and nails between his cracked lips. His face was pale from so many days in the mine. A small shy boy stood a few feet away watching, keeping still and silent. The boy turned his head at the sound of the older boys and girls running up the road with wet faces and dripping hair, having plunged themselves into the still water of the canal with their legs looped around the girders of the swing bridge. They had been warned on pain of death never to swim in the canal, but no-one had said anything about drooping into it from the bridge. They carried on clattering up the road towards the plantation, the next adventure having been hurriedly agreed. The afternoon sank languorously towards the evening.

The dinners were nearly ready and the street had begun to empty when a high, harsh siren burst into life, the sound keening from one of the mineheads to the west. The adults, and those children old enough to understand, stopped what they were doing and looked west. A few moments later, a boy, no more than fourteen, came pelting round the corner from the canal path and into the village. Everybody knew him as one of the apprentices at the mine.

'Fire! Fire! There's a fire in pit 15! We need help! Come on! Any man off shift, we need a rescue brigade! The deputy manager said to call you in! It's a fire!'

The poor boy felt the burden of his role and his message and he banged aggressively on the doors that remained closed, shouting out his message, rallying the people and frightening the people. Whilst some gazed, slow to garner his meaning, others broke into running, conversations abandoned and dinners forgotten.

The people swept down the little road, the men's hard shoes clapping on the stone, the women hiking up their skirts to run at a pace. They rounded the corner onto the canal path, the strong young men pulling ahead of the others. The people ran and ran, silent but for their panting. Soon they were hurtling alongside the railway towards pit 15 and began to spill wildly through the wide iron gate of the colliery, tumbling in towards the pit head where the crowd was gathering, a shouting, shuffling mass. Beyond the people a thin snake of smoke was rising from the pit opening,

3

sailing and dissipating elegantly in the sky above the mine.

The young woman stopped sprinting abruptly at the edge of the crowd, her face crimson red and her chest heaving. She looked around quickly then grabbed the arm of an older man she recognised.

'What's happening Archie? Do you know? Have the men got out?'

The old man was staring like everyone else at the small coterie gathered around an off-duty foreman who was giving orders, pointing and gesturing, handing out rudimentary gas masks.

'I'm sorry Maggie. I don't know any more than you. They say there's a fire somewhere near the base of the pit head. Nobody knows how bad it is or where the backshift are.' He turned to look at her for the first time, and saw the terror around her eyes.

'Is Michael working tonight?' he asked.

Wetness broke from her eyes and her hand went to her mouth, smothering a pained cry.

1

Joe Miller's last client of the day lowered herself gingerly into the age-worn chair opposite him.

'My last therapist told me I was the most profoundly bereaved person he'd ever met,' she began.

Joe half-smiled, his eyes narrowing a little. He took a long breath, seeking fresh patience from the intake of air. The walls of the therapy room had heard and absorbed a thousand stories like this and they were indifferent, which Joe could not be.

'My daughter died 4 years ago, on August 22nd 1979. The anniversary is soon. I...I don't really know how to live without her. My doctor is very good, very sympathetic. He said maybe I should come here, get some help, see another therapist. The last one, I saw her privately, she... she just seemed to get it, you know? She felt what I was going through. Walked in my shoes. She saw how my life has been changed beyond all recognition.'

Joe shifted position to change tack. Alongside his sympathy, he felt his familiar irritation with the early signs of the heroic victim mode, and he nodded inwardly to the irritation, acknowledging it. And a little lift of anxiety about following in the footsteps of the idolised last therapist.

'Well Martha, I appreciate you being so open. Obviously this has been a terrible loss, and I can understand that it's hit you very hard.'

Martha nodded solemnly.

'And I would really like to hear more, perhaps today, and no doubt in future sessions. But is it okay if we backtrack a little? I guess firstly I should introduce myself. I'm Joe Miller, one of the therapists in the team here. We had a referral from your GP a few months ago, so I am sorry for the wait.'

'That's okay, I'm here now', she responded.

And not going anywhere, sighed Joe inwardly.

'So we're here to get started with some regular sessions, if that's what you're looking for.'

She nodded, then looked away towards the box of tissues on the small table between them, paused, then picked one out.

Joe continued listening. He made some notes as Martha narrated her story. He made some empathic comments, not so much because she needed any encouragement to talk, but almost just to prove to himself he was more than just a bland receptacle for her monologue. Martha told the story of her daughter's illness, the rapid deterioration, her building fear, and then the bitter end. She soaked up a few tears with the tissues. To Joe, the story felt rehearsed, well-trodden, and he felt guilty for thinking so. Eventually, he had to interrupt in order to give his regular spiel about confidentiality and boundaries and the nature of their respective roles in therapy, before bringing the session to an end.

After the session ended Joe shepherded Martha to the front door. Getting to the end of the day had lightened his mood a little and he ended the session with a little more genuine warmth for her. He watched through the porch window as she waved and turned right towards Westercraigs. Across the street lay the communal garden for the parallel roads. Three boys were racing from one white birch tree to another, the victor yelling with triumph and crowing over his defeated friends.

He turned back to the department. Having spent the day confined to one chair in one room he did not wish to return to it when finally he had a choice. He locked the door to his room and entered the main office on the opposite side of the hallway.

The office was empty save for Bernie, the secretary. She sat behind a broad oak desk which faced the doorway. On her desk was the typewriter which clacked and whirred for much of the day. On her left sat a bank of grey filing cabinets reaching along the wall towards the huge bay window. The terraced villas were reached by a few steps, lifting the houses up just high enough to evade the peering eyes of passersby.

Joe said a quiet 'hi' to Bernie, picked up the Glasgow Herald from a low coffee table, and sank himself into a tall luxurious armchair that always seemed out of place in an NHS office.

Bernie continued typing without missing a click but raised her bespectacled eyes to gauge Joe's readiness for conversation. He was looking seriously at the front page of the newspaper, his mouth firmly shut, and his nostrils flaring with deepening breaths. Joe liked to think he was hard to read but Bernie knew that look, the 4:30 look she called it. She returned her eyes to the paper creeping out the top of the typewriter and pressed on the foot pedal to play the taped letter she was transcribing. All the therapists had their rituals for the start of the day and the end of the day. At the start of the day Joe would come into the office and try to be friendly but it was obvious to Bernie that he was intent on getting a green tea and preparing in silence for the first client. By the end of the day, especially a full day of clients, he wanted the camaraderie and distractions of the main office. Bernie was a crucial cog in the workings of the department and she weathered the changing moods and needs of the therapists, as well as the phone calls and arrivals of all manner of clients. She was behind with the day's letters anyway so she carried on typing until Joe was ready to emerge from the intensity that the work rubbed off on him.

It was not long before Zara came in to the office, smiling wordlessly to Bernie, and carrying a black coffee. Zara Robertson glided more than she walked, her long skirt making her movements seem smoother and her soft soled shoes slipping quietly along the floor. She noticed Joe a moment later.

'Hello Joseph.' She knew he liked it when she used his Sunday name.

'Hi Zara.' Joe looked up from his paper and let it rest on his folded legs. 'How you doing? I've hardly seen you all day.'

Zara gave the impression of limitless compassion and Joe was always relieved when even she toiled and tired.

'I'm okay, thanks' she replied. 'Glad to get to the end of the day, I must confess. I just saw Mr and Mrs Davidson – you remember them?'

Joe did remember them. The family had attended the department in various combinations, the kids individually, the mother and the daughter together, and now the father and mother as a couple. All had agreed that Zara was the therapist most likely to remain compassionate but savvy in the face of the complex and narcissistic games played by the father. Their manager, Oliver, inevitably felt that he could probably bring about a miracle cure but he had already tried and by all accounts failed when he worked with the son.

'Ah, yes' said Joe. 'How's that going?'

Zara released a long breath, choosing her words carefully.

'I think there is a lot of fear in that family. Mr Davidson fears losing his role as the strong head of the family. So much so that he'll drive the others away without realising he's doing so. Mrs Davidson fears finding out that she doesn't actually need him, that she's stronger than she thinks. The kids have got the right idea moving out because they're afraid of being stuck in the endless micro-dramas that go on in that house. I really doubt whether I'll be able to find some decent leverage to convince the dad to release his grip. I'm not sure he's capable of seeing the damage he's doing because he has his own skewed rationalisation for everything that happens, and none of it is his fault as far as he's concerned.'

Hearing how pessimistic she sounded, she changed direction.

'But, you never know. Maybe there are some embers of genuine empathy and generativity that can be stoked. Again, though, I'm not sure he can let a mere woman do that for him.'

'Well, you can but try' Joe replied, too tired to conjure anything more profound.

Zara went on.

'I was also at a meeting at Eastfield Royal, about the closure of more of the wards there. It's barren up there I tell you. You'll notice it when we go up to do the group. They've known for some time they'll be closing these wards so they're not repairing anything. Have you ever seen the old dining hall? Beautiful arched ceiling, deep ruby and jade, ornate cornicing, wood panelling, just stunning in its hey-day. Now it's tired and ragged, paint peeling from the walls, weeds growing up through the floorboards. The windows barely keep the rain and wind out. Around the whole place floorboards are splintering, baths are rusting, pipes are bursting. The old nurses home looks like it's about to swallow its own chimney. The patients used to help with those beautiful gardens – the lawns, the vegetable garden, fruit trees and the herb garden. Now they're neglected and overgrown. The sooner we get those patients out of there the better.'

'Where are they all going to go?' asked Joe.

Zara's face brightened. 'Some of them are going into supported accommodation units. The council are funding two new places just for the patients coming out of Eastfield. But, you know, I think the medics are placing far too much faith in the new generation of antipsychotics. As if even the best medication could make up for so many years of disempowerment and institutionalisation.'

'Well, I think that's a pretty charitable view of the medics' thinking' replied Joe. 'I hope it's a better life for these folk when they move out of there. I had to visit a young guy up there last year when he was re-admitted, and I cannot for the life of me see how it would have been therapeutic for him there. Sure, they monitored him and kept him safe, but there was nothing meaningful for him to *do*. They all sat watching crap television, and making endless cups of tea.'

Zara smiled. 'This isn't really funny but did you ever read about the so-called pink spot? Researchers who were looking for some biological basis for schizophrenia got all excited when they found that schizophrenic patients in hospital all had this pink colour in their urine. They thought it must be evidence of a biochemical difference. Turned out it was just due to them drinking all those cups of tea in the wards.'

'I know what you mean' Joe said, 'it's funny and it's not.'

Almost on cue, Oliver Morrison, the department manager, came into the office. He raised his eyebrows and nodded extravagantly to them all.

'Hello, hello, hello' Oliver added.

Bernie, the consummate reader of needs, stopped her typing to give Oliver her full attention. Joe folded the newspaper that had remained on his lap and placed it on the floor. Zara was doing nothing she needed to cease in order to give Oliver the conversational space he needed to occupy.

'How are you all doing?' Oliver asked no-one in particular. As if anyone could then freely say anything other than 'fine.'

'How are you?' Joe replied with rehearsed politeness.

'Ah, busy, busy. You know how it is.' Oliver stood with hands on hips, tucking in his loose tan shirt at his waist. He wore one of his many checked ties, which hung too low. His accent was finest syrupy Kelvinside.

'I sometimes wish I was still doing more clinical work. All these meetings and interruptions. Too many people wanting my time. And the few patients I do have are all utter corkers. Too many borderlines and flaming narcissists, not enough time.'

These days Joe tensed with irritation and embarrassment before Oliver even started to speak. He often tried to limit Oliver's grandstanding by giving as little reinforcement as he could get away with. But Oliver had grown used to that lack of response and just assumed everyone was treated that way. He didn't notice that other people could elicit genuine interest in what they said. Or, Joe thought, perhaps Oliver believed his presence and conversation were so impressive that others were just intimidated into submissive silence. Oliver continued unabated.

'One of the junior psychiatrists at Eastfield wanted to consult with me about a patient in the wards. So she came over and we spoke for a while. I really do worry about the amount of psychotherapy training these junior doctors get. Honestly, they think after a few lectures and reading some Karen Horney and Harry Stack Sullivan that they're ready to analyse any Tom, Dick or Harry. At least they have the good sense to consult us sometimes.'

As so often, Joe didn't know how to respond wisely to Oliver's attempts to drag others into a collective narcissism. Judging by Zara's pained smile she was thinking the same thing. And Bernie either believed in Oliver's skill completely or she was the best at hiding her true feelings, for she didn't even flinch.

Oliver moved to the pigeon holes and inspected his for any further proof of his importance. He pulled out a letter and scanned it.

'Oh yes, I was to bring this to everyone's attention. It came up at the management group. I've to reiterate the importance of security – filing cabinets, doors, et cetera. An office at the MacAdam Centre got broken into. The secretary came in one morning to find a broken window and a filing cabinet forced open and case notes out on the desk. They got fingerprints. Turned out that the mother of a patient had broken in to read what her daughter had been saying about her in therapy. Actually they didn't really need the fingerprints. The daughter's case notes had been tampered with – Tippex over all the disparaging mentions of the mum. Including the therapist's suggestion that her mum was 'over-involved.' I guess the mum lacks a sense of irony.'

The others were intrigued. The business of therapy was rarely that dramatic.

'It's funny, isn't it?' Zara said. 'Family members are often so curious about what's being said about them. I guess she must have had a hunch that her daughter was talking about her in her sessions.'

'Yep' said Joe. 'Mine often try to convince the client that it would be in their interest for me to hear the family's point of view.

Usually they want their own catharsis but don't want to be seen to be the one asking for help.'

'Yes, well, check and double check those locks, ladies and gentlemen. And be diplomatic in your notes lest the family should ever see them,' added Oliver. He swished back out of the room letting Joe and Zara get on with finishing their days, having injected, he imagined, a welcome shot of confident colour into the grey emptiness of their lives.

2

Joe left the department behind and headed towards Duke Street. The air was cool for July and the white clouds looked harmless for now. The train was quicker but Joe felt like the walk to town instead.

He headed west along Duke Street and crossed Bellgrove Street. The faint smell of dead cattle from the abattoir mingled sickly with the scent of hops from the Tennents brewery. Men were streaming out as the shift ended, some heading straight for a pint at The Ladywell opposite. Joe passed the brewery and the Cathedral came into view up the hill, its fine stone blackened by smog but its Gothic grace unblemished. The Royal Infirmary stood alongside, no less smeared sooty black. Joe passed The Great Eastern though he remained wisely on the opposite side of the road. Several old men sat smoking on the front steps and from one of the open windows Elvis was pining for a lost love. The building was grand but its reputation was fierce, filled as it was with homeless drunks, a vast cacophony of defeated and diminished stories. Although he had seen some clients from The Great Eastern, Joe had never been inside. He knew he'd be treated like a jumped up social worker in those dirty halls with his ironed chinos and leather elbow patches.

He moved on up the gentle slope towards the High Street, the oldest part of the city, and carried on west onto West George Street and down towards George Square, the pulsing heart of the city. As he approached the square, Joe could hear a loudhailer, a man's voice, a political voice. He passed the grand carved doorways of the Royal College building where students of Strathclyde Uni spilled out, many heading for the square. Joe found himself walking behind three girls. They wore tie dye and neon colours with hair dyed pink and purple and fixed wild and exciting with hairspray. One began singing softly 'This land is your land' whilst her friends began unfurling a rainbow coloured flag with the CND logo emblazoned upon it. They danced lightly across the junction to the square, carrying the flag across their backs, whilst Joe carried on west. Their youth and energy and femininity were mingled and Joe felt a kind of corduroy drabness about himself.

The girls joined a growing crowd on the tarmac and grass of the square, surrounding the statues of great soldiers and statesmen. Joe slowed to a halt to look over, as others around him were doing. On a small platform a gaggle of men and women drew the attention of the crowd. Many of the protestors carried banners and flags: CND, Trident Ploughshares, the Scottish Socialist Party, Christian CND, and the Labour Party. Two gangly men carried high a replica nuclear missile of cardboard and plywood painted black and red and they shook it up and down whenever the crowd cheered. Some wore brown paper bags over their heads, sour and simple faces drawn on with black marker. Mothers fitted them over their children's confused faces.

'Thank you for showing up today!' shouted the speaker. 'Thank you for caring enough about the safety and very survival of our world to be here today! To show our neighbours and our leaders that we are not all asleep with apathy but that we dare to protest against the insanity of nuclear weapons! Thank you for standing against the futile arms race of the so-called great powers!' and the crowd shouted and applauded.

'We cannot stand by and let this madness continue, can we?'

'No!' shouted back the crowd.

'We do not want nuclear weapons in this country or any country, do we?'

'No!' shouted back the crowd.

'And we will continue to speak out for peace, sanity, and brotherhood, won't we?'

'Yes!' came the loudest yell.

'We must demand more humanity from our leaders – much,

much more. We deserve better. The world deserves better. Peace, brothers and sisters, peace!' And the speaker departed the stage.

A tall pale woman addressed the crowd solemnly.

'And now, brothers and sisters, it is time to remind the watching world what nuclear weapons can do. Here and now, we die symbolically, to show the world what a nuclear attack could do. Spread out, give yourselves space, and let us spend two minutes in death.'

The people in the square began to lie down on the cold damp ground. Bodies lay flat, some curled up in a protective shape, others flayed out as widely as they could stretch. Some lay on their backs with their mouths wide open and their eyes staring at the sky. Many wore white mock protective suits. Some of the young women and men had painted death on their faces, their mouths bloodied with harsh red lipstick and their eye sockets blackened with mascara. They lay still on the ground, soft cheeks pressing against hard concrete, clothes taking dampness from the ground, cold seeping into warm flesh. Young and old bodies lay prone and overlapping. More spectators stopped and stared. A few journalists took photos and a helicopter could be seen above the rooftop of the city chambers. The pigeons that usually colonised the square hung back at the edges of the strange tableau.

Eventually an air horn punctured the uneasy silence and the bodies began to stir. People rose to their feet in silence that was both solemn and self-conscious, and began to slip away. The spectators got moving again and the cars and buses came back to life on the surrounding streets. It was Friday night and the pubs were filling up on Queen Street and St Vincent Street. Joe stood for some minutes, staring. He felt like he believed in their cause, and he didn't think it was right to do nothing as the superpowers built these ludicrous weapons. And he admired their passion and the single minded intensity of it all. But Joe's compassion was fatigued and his dad had given protest a bad name. After some moments in observation he headed towards Central Station for the train home.

3

Joe got home as the rush hour began to die down. Home was a first floor flat in a sandstone tenement in Pollokshields. His place on the long row on Shields Road looked out to Victorian villas opposite and an unused church on the corner. The wide road was lined with big old lime trees on its westerly side bursting gradually through the weak concrete, mighty roots rippling the pavements. The mildly moneyed denizens of the south side had been some of the first to embrace the sandblasting trend of the seventies. Decades of smog and dirt had laid a matt black mask over most of the city so that even though TV and photos had gone colour many years before, the world they captured in Glasgow remained a mixture of black and nearly black. Only after the wild winds of 1968 brought dozens of crumbling buildings down did the city realise it had a problem with its buildings that knocking down would simply not solve. Rather than razing the tenements, as the planners were then advocating, they began to adapt them, adding internal bathrooms and blasting away the collective black lung of the industrial century, revealing beautiful red stone and sandstone, the warm colours emerging, blinking, in the sometime sunshine. By Joe's time, tenement flats had gone from crumbling inconveniences to fashionable assets, affordable to young singletons and couples, with big enough lounges for parties and the shared space letting strangers hear the wonderful groans and sad delights of a neighbour's life, the dancing at midnight vibrating through ceilings, the leak of a roof uniting the tenants unwillingly, the back court an impromptu stage with an audience of hundreds.

Entering his flat, he picked up some inconsequential post and laid it on the pile on the hall table. His silver Sturmey Archer stood in the hallway, dirt on the tyres and black grease on the gear cogs, reminding him how long it had been since he'd been out on it. Joe went to the lounge where the windows let in good light from the sun falling in the west. He stood for a few moments looking down onto the cars passing by, before heading to the kitchen. He took a batch of vegetarian chilli from the fridge and spooned a thick clump into a pot to re-heat. As he waited for the food to warm, he stared at Edward Hopper's Nighthawks, admiring and pitying the solitude of the cafe patrons.

He ate in a distracted state at the table in the kitchen alcove. A book of short stories by Hermann Hesse rested in his free hand but he was not taking it in. The faces and voices and stories of his clients swirled around his head, jockeying for attention. He tried to listen for what was most dominant in the tangle of memories and feelings from the day. Each person was so much. Each of these people surveyed the dramatic terrain of their own enormous lives. Each of them was formed and endlessly reformed by their very own slow motion tornado of endings and beginnings, hoping and flailing, wishing and avoiding. The distant husband, the dream job, the sagging weight of family shadows, the crisp pain of death. Their fortunes and misfortunes were grand in their own eyes, just as Joe's were to him. Everyone is I. Everyone swims in the vast sensory treasure and detritus of their own deep immersion in the world. Joe thought about the conceit of empathy, the delusion that we could truly get into someone else's phenomenological world, to experience it as they experience it. That a listener, a lover, a therapist, could magically lay aside their own fused on lens to see through the alien lens of the other. And he thought of how experience is lonely and how consciousness is both universal and utterly stranded on these islands of but one inhabitant. With what little success could Joe truly find his way into the subjective inner vantage point of another human being. Despite the bridge of language and the common understandings of what our senses carry to our souls, there was a distance, always, and he felt acutely his inability to span it.

The chilli was losing its heat in the bowl as Joe dragged his attention back to the present. He scooped it up with hunks of crusty bread, wiping the chocolate brown sauce from the sides, mindful of leaving mess for himself to clean. He thought about Martha and her splendid grief. He wondered again why the grandiosity of suffering irritated him in quite the way it did. He believed that suffering was not a competition between people but perhaps at the felt level he resented someone else asserting their credentials of sadness so brazenly. But then, if that was the case, surely he wouldn't be doing this job? No, he thought, it could not be as simple as that. It must be something about the dramatising of one's suffering, the holding up of it like a trophy, baring the wound for the pity and admiration of others. It is one thing to be sympathised with, another thing to actively seek out sympathy, to pull and draw it from others like a leech.

And then how was he to work with Martha? Would he always be irritated by her grief-as-trophy? Perhaps. And perhaps, he reminded himself, it was useful to notice his reaction. It was all grist for the mill. What she triggered in him might be what she triggered in others. What if others found her expression of grief boastful and irritating but didn't communicate it, or even understand their irritation? He might be the one person willing to bring it to awareness, to lay it out like a map on the table and examine it together like collaborative cartographers of the psyche.

But would he actually do that? Or was he kidding himself? Was it worth the risk? Perhaps she should be allowed to wallow in the grandeur of her grief for now. Perhaps she would come out of it when she was ready. Maybe Joe was being too harsh. Looking for an issue to tackle that might resolve itself anyway. But then, what was she wanting from him?

His thoughts continued to swirl around - questions posed but left unanswered, hypotheses generated that would not be tested. Joe felt then that his tired mind could not be wholly trusted with these questions of therapeutic judgement and the torrent of questions would soon reach a kind of intellectual panic. He looked for something to do. He turned on the tap at the kitchen sink and watched the water slowly begin to give off hot vapour. He watched closely, willing his attention to one thing at a time. He watched as the fairy liquid gave rise to bubble after bubble after bubble, the lather expanding into a green froth that undulated and spread over the rising water. He held the dirty plate upright and let it sink under the cleansing water. He washed the plate deliberately, slowly, watching the russet stains slip magically from the glazed clay. If only emotional stains could be washed away like that. He lifted the clean plate out and held it as still as he could above the water, watching the pale green bubbles careen down the surface and around the rim, meeting at the bottom and forming a curved triangle where drips plunged into the waiting water below. Joe gazed and waited, gazed and waited, willing gravity to pull the last few drops down off the plate. He stood the plate carefully on the drying rack and washed the pot and the fork in the same manner. He let some more cold water into the basin and sank his hands under the water until the green lather lapped at his black Casio. The heat spread through his skin and quick electric tingles jumped around his wrists and arms. His mind started to quiet, the cogs turning more slowly and deliberately, like a heavy steel locomotive slowing and losing momentum as it approaches its last station. He stared out of the window to the back court, where two pigeons nosed around the bin shed, and the solitary slim conifer shimmied noiselessly in the breeze. Joe dried his hands with a tea towel and took a Grolsh from the fridge.

Now he did not want to produce, nor did he want his insight to be tested. He settled for a video of All The President's Men, familiar and untaxing. He lay down, unfolding on the long sofa as he watched, rubbing his tired eyes under his glasses. His body sank gratefully into the soft cushions and the sunlight fell more weakly through the wide windows. The film's recurring motif of typewriters and the night-time scenes and the lovely unfolding of the whole foolish saga eased his conscious mind towards a dissolving mush and Joe descended into sleep without a fight.

In his dream, Joe was at a beach, familiar but alien in that peculiar way only dream places can be. The sky was hazy pastel blue and the breaking waves combed pebbles up and down the beach, playing a slow dignified rhythm of sifting percussive swoops. The smell of hot sand hung everywhere. Joe was walking away from the beach and a woman (a stranger? a wife?) was by his side.

To leave the beach they passed under an elevated railway line which ran parallel and close to the water line. The single railway track sat on wide low arches built of red brick, and the sand from the beach spilt onto the rough concrete floors of the tunnels. Joe and the woman passed through one of the arches where the glaring sun gave way to a cool darkness. As Joe walked out the other side of the arch, he momentarily caught sight of someone shadowy standing on the edge of the railway line. In that brief moment it looked like the person had been lowering something into the water on the end of a rope. A moment later, they were gone, if they had been there at all, and Joe almost dismissed it as a trick of the light. But unease was upon him and he left the woman's side to climb up the embankment.

The steep embankment was covered in grass and sand and he slipped back a little on each step. He reached the top of the mound and stepped gingerly over the steel track. At the water side of the track, one end of a thick rope lay carelessly on the sharp rocks. The rope hung off the side of the embankment and disappeared into the water. Joe picked up the rope and began pulling it. At first nothing showed. Then a pink object came into view, blurry at first, rising in the water. Joe pulled further on the rope and saw that the other end was tied around the neck of a small baby. He lifted the rope until he could cradle the baby. He looked on its still face and felt his own face contort with horror.

Disturbing as it was, he sensed the baby had not been long in the water. He loosened the wet rope from around its neck, and laid the baby on the ground. It was wearing a pale pink dress, and the sodden cotton clung to the little body. Joe looked around and could see no-one. In the distance the headlights of a train were approaching slowly from the west. Not knowing what else to do, he began pushing gently with two fingers of each hand on the baby's chest. He repeated this crude effort a few times, and a few moments later the baby spluttered, spat out some water and opened its eyes. Almost immediately she was alert but silent and calm. Joe knew he had to find a hospital for her.

In that manner of dreams he found himself instantly somewhere else, coming off a train into an unfamiliar city, carrying the baby in his arms. He expected he could quickly find a way to a hospital. But as he stepped off the train, he saw that many people had been shot, some killed. Some people stood around, dazed, but it did not seem an option to ask them anything. Joe walked without direction and the baby remained silent, breathing softly against his chest. The city looked now like Edinburgh but different, and deserted. Everywhere was a vague colour of sallow regret. He knew there was a children's hospital, and a doctor friend worked there. But he walked the gridded streets and could not find it. He found himself abruptly at work, where his colleagues were meeting together. He told them what had happened and they were sympathetic to the baby's plight but they couldn't help.

Helplessness rose in his chest and then he was falling through the disintegrating landscape and then with a jolt he was awake. His eyes were pinned on the thin shaft of light that fell between the curtains of his room. A painful thud pulsed in his chest. He caught his breath and touched the wooden bed frame. He lay back down, his body heavy, stared at the ceiling and wondered a while about the meaning of the dream, before his weariness pulled him back into a fitful sleep.

4

The mezzo-soprano keened and lamented through the slow and patient building of the Lento-Sostenuto Tranquillo ma Cantabile. The first movement of Gorecki's 3rd symphony floated through Joe's consciousness as the Walkman turned the spools of tape, and somehow this lifeless electronic manuscript was transformed alchemically into waves and wafts of delicate sound and intricate movement and swells of emotion. Joe stared dumbly out the window as the bus huffed its way through Pollokshields and Dumbreck. He got off at Mosspark Boulevard in front of Bellahouston Park and the drizzle began to smudge his glasses. The wide open grass sloped up towards the Pope's Wall and the dog walkers and joggers traipsed the criss-cross of paths. He always took the bus one stop further than he needed to so he could walk a little on the boulevard, where fine sturdy elms, unnaturally spaced, spread strong wide foliage and dappled shadow across the path. He remembered ten years earlier, cross country runs through February gloom, Mr Hackett barking them towards the looming hill, calf muscles stiffening, thighs heavy, Glasgow-white skin reddened by frigid rain, and thin white cotton vests plastered to wiry teenage bodies. He remembered the gallus ones, the Ibrox Tongs, sneaking out of sight for a short cut when the thick bushes hid them from Hackett's suspicious attention. And the glorious moment when back at the school they changed into dry clothes and fizzing sensations returning to numbed fingers and a sugary hot chocolate could be had from the vending machine in the dining hall.

Joe crossed Dumbreck Road and arrived at his parents' place, a stolid grey semi they'd bought new in 1964. His sister would have waltzed straight in but ever since he'd moved out Joe had rung the bell and waited to be invited in. Ingrid Miller greeted him at the door. Her hands were floury and her cheeks flushed from the kitchen's heat. They hugged lightly, with a little shyness. Joe handed her some rough oatcakes and Orkney cheddar from her favourite deli in Pollokshields.

'Your dad's in the living room. I'm just finishing the tea.'

Joe could see through the frosted glass door that the television was on. He opened the door and his dad got up, pushing himself out from the armchair onto his bad left leg.

'Hello son, come on in, grab a seat.'

'Hi dad. How are you?'

His dad muted the television, and folded up the newspaper. Joe saw the familiar red top of The Morning Star. His dad kept his eye on the TV, where Thatcher was giving a press conference about the latest miners' strike. Grey men in black suits backed her up with serious expressions and stern posture.

'That bloody woman,' Joe's dad said. 'I cannae stand the sight of her. Her and her upper class cronies.'

'Why are you watching it then?' asked Joe.

'Cause she's the bloody prime minister. And the rest of us have to live with the consequences of her decisions. I tell ye, that blinkin' war has emboldened her no end. She beat the Argentineans for a worthless piece of rock, so now she thinks she can beat the miners. And she probably will, judging by how things are goin.' Anyway, what's new with you?'

Joe was surprised that his dad had kept the rant to a minimum.

'Not much' said Joe, sighing. 'Work's work, you know? Ach, that sounds bad. It's alright. But sometimes it's a lot of wrestling for not a lot of progress.'

Alastair nodded, his gaze still towards the television.

'How's that boss of yours? The one with his heid up his own arse.'

Joe smiled. His dad had latched onto his stories of Oliver, finding smug people even more irritating than Joe did.

'He's the same as ever. I could see him fitting right in with

Thatcher and Heseltine and the like. He'd probably be a Tory if he took any real interest in the world outside himself.' Joe didn't particularly like slagging, even Oliver, but to do so was one of the few ways to connect with his dad, so he often found himself joining in.

'Aye, I know the type. Ah well, he'll be pretty lost when the workers revolt,' his dad replied, looking as if he was only half-joking.

He continued watching the press conference. As the silence between them lengthened, Alastair turned the volume slowly back up with the remote control. Joe watched out of the corner of his eye as his dad gradually got drawn back into the television, forgetting Joe's presence. At first he groaned and grunted and sighed at what he was hearing. Soon, his body sunk lower into the sofa and his eyes began to grow heavy.

This was often the way of it and Joe was conflicted about his dad's detachment even as he tried to understand it. Alastair no longer worked in the shipyards and that work had been his joy, his social standing and his circle of friends. He had worked until his early fifties when the pain in his joints became too searing for him to drive rivets or turn a wrench. In the yard he'd been a shop steward, passionate about the working man's rights. He'd been tolerant of the managers, mostly, but it was the politicians for whom he reserved his finest ire. Thanks to them, the work had been drying up since the second world war, though more quickly so in the seventies when Alastair should have been at the peak of his power.

When Thatcher came to power in 1979, something in him heaved a deep sigh and prepared for the worst. The heavy industry that made Glasgow great also made Alastair great, and made great all the riveters and the joiners and the painters and the welders. The ships they built with their bare hands and their seasoned tools were roaring around the oceans, bearing the names of Browns, and Harland & Woolff, and Fairfield. The oily blood and greasy fingerprints of Alastair and his comrades were halfway around the world now. Their welded steel and iron and copper kept water out and cargo in, kept pistons firing and turbines rotating. Their legacy drove outward from the ports of the Clyde, and it was real and honest. He took pride in what these men had built together in these yards. But when he had to leave on account of his pain and weakness, it hit the man hard. The industry was slowly dying, whether one faced that fact or not. As its power waned, so too did Alastair's, and he felt both keenly.

He had found other work, slowly, falteringly. He tried at first in teaching but he did not have the patience. He thought of setting up in business, but he did not have the capital. By 1983 he was a technician in the science department of a secondary school in Paisley. He took some pleasure from the physical work he was able to do, and he dearly wanted to inculcate in the pupils a sense of their responsibilities and rights in the labour movement. But aside from the odd loner who hung around the classrooms at lunchtime to avoid the bullies, none of the kids listened to what he had to say. The teachers gave him his tasks, and he was mostly invisible to the pupils. Occasionally he could reminisce with a teacher about shipyard life, but mostly the rigour and pride of his industrial credentials were of no interest. Partly for this reason, Alastair made sure to take the bus every Friday night to the Queens Bar on the Govan Road. A few of his old compadres would meet him in the smoky lounge to drink and toast and hope the receding tide of dwindling contracts would turn soon. There he could glory in the old days and with every empty glass that hit the bar the metallic sounds and pungent smells of the yard would come more alive again in his greying imagination.

For Alastair, sitting stagnant in a comfortable semi watching politics from a safe distance, rather than in it up to his elbows – that was a slow death, a lonely relegation to the lower leagues. But he could not go quietly, for there was anger to be transmitted and blame to be assigned. So Alastair read and re-read the red press and muttered at the TV and bored his family with rehearsed sonnets on the past glories of the Scottish working class. The steely reception Lloyd George received when he addressed the unions at St Andrews Hall on Christmas Day 1915, the great strike of 1919, the Red Clydesiders sweeping into Westminster in 1922. In his sepia perspective, Alastair remained a guardian of this rich heritage but he squandered its real dignity through boasting and preaching and tired old anecdotes. Today, though, the indignant energy had given way to lethargy.

'I'll go and see if mum needs a hand,' said Joe quietly as he got up to leave the room. Alastair seemed not to notice.

In the kitchen, Ingrid looked up surprised when he came in.

'He's falling asleep,' Joe explained. 'And more interested in the TV.'

Ingrid glanced away, a little ashamed that Joe did not get his dad's attention for longer. She tried not to think too much these days about the change in the shape of their lives and the twist in her gut she felt for Joe.

Ingrid had met Alastair at a ceilidh for the entire staff of Brown's, the managers, the trades, the typists, the cleaners. She was bold in her approach then, a typist in the offices by day and a free and flighty teenager by night. Her mother wanted her to wed a professional man, to keep her from the poverty of the life they had tried to escape by moving to Glasgow from Orkney in the thirties. But Ingrid had quiet passion in her bones and she was at an age for ignoring her parents. Alastair had the gumption of a leader in the making and when he danced her firmly through the quick skips of a Schottische and the slow slides of a St Bernard's Waltz, the die was cast and parents be damned. They wed in 1951 and honeymooned by the bright lights of Largs with what little money their families had left from the waste of the war.

Isobel arrived two years later, soon followed by Joe. The children grew while Glasgow shrunk. The safety Ingrid and Alastair took from the hugeness and pre-eminence of the Clyde's yards began to shake under its own weight. The communities where whole economies and histories balanced on the industry began to feel the nagging signs of decline, and fear was both felt and despised. The children grew with the natural optimism and enchantment of a good enough childhood and the slow leaving behind of the dark wonder of war, but Alastair and Ingrid could only provide for so long what they did not truly have. In Ingrid's determination the children were to thrive regardless, so she kept silent from them the crumbling of Alastair's world and his retreat into quiet despair. She threw herself into the schooling and culturing of her kids and marvelled at the ever surprising uniqueness of their emerging personalities.

Now she looked at Joe, trying to measure his thoughts. She saw he was now a man himself, and certainly an adult about his work, but still a son of a father with a son's needs. And he had learned somewhere along the line to hush down his feelings and keep quiet counsel, so even now, especially now, she did not trust she knew his needs. His chosen medium was reflective talk so she tried to approach him on that plane.

'What would a therapist make of your dad, eh?' she said, unable to resist softening the intensity of her curiosity with humour. She continued chopping a pile of green chives with a wide knife. Joe looked at her face whilst she avoided his gaze and he wondered where this was coming from.

'Depends on the therapist,' he responded, then felt ashamed of his evasiveness. He tried again.

'No, but, really, you don't need a therapist to figure him out, do you? You know him pretty well. You understand him probably better than anyone.'

'Well maybe so but even that's not much.' She turned away, emptying the chives into a bowl of salad. 'He doesn't tell me much more than anyone else.'

'He certainly loved that job, though, didn't he?' Joe said.

'Well, aye, in hindsight perhaps. At the time he grumbled about

27

it like any man does. Always a fight to be had. Always a manager being incompetent. And he was never fond of getting up at 6am on the winter mornings, working in the freezing cold. He'd moan about that alright.'

'But,' Joe replied, 'you'd think from the way he talked now that it was all glorious camaraderie and noble production. And the thrill of the launch made everything worthwhile.'

'Aye, and maybe that was all true as well.' Ingrid said. She checked the potatoes that were baking in the oven, piercing them with a fork, releasing little flurries of steam. Outside the Paisley train rumbled past down the embankment beyond the end of the garden. Joe stood and went to the window. The garden was neat, neater than when he and Isobel had been kids. He remembered the rope swing that his dad had hitched to a sturdy branch of the thick cherry tree at the bottom of the garden. And the makeshift hut in one corner, with corrugated plastic roof and old railway sleepers for a floor. He remembered Isobel stealing a box of weetabix from the kitchen cupboards and the two of them crunching on it in the concealed safety of the hut. Back then they'd been too scared of their parents to steal anything more luxurious. And he remembered barbecues in the garden, his dad's one day a year of cooking, while his mum tried not to hover suspiciously.

'Remember when Isobel painted the tree?' Ingrid's voice broke in.

'She painted a tree?'

Ingrid smiled with the memory. 'Aye, you were young, maybe three. Every branch she could reach she painted a different colour. Dragged an old set of wooden stepladders from the garage and found the old pots of leftover paint. The trunk was one colour, the first branch another. I must have been watching you. Took me a while to notice she'd been too quiet. I found her sitting up the tree, a paintbrush in her hand, covered in blues and greens and magnolia and the tree looking like something out of a Dali painting. She was so proud of it. She was sat there grinning when I came out. And then the rain came on. And she cried her eyes out, knowing it would wash away her handiwork.'

Ingrid's eyes were lively as she stared out the window.

'So she came running in and grabbed two umbrellas, trying to stop the rain. Then she stopped crying and she threw away the brollies. She saw all the colours blending into one another as they washed forlornly down the tree and then she was delighted by the mess of it all, and she put her wee bucket at the base of the trunk, trying to catch the bleeding colours. The trunk of the tree looked like a tie-dye totem pole. And then she starting chucking anything colourful she could find into the bucket – rose petals, clumps of grass, a dead bumblebee, the yellow ribbon from her hair. She dreams in colour that girl.' Ingrid stopped, her hands planted on her hips. She sniffed and sighed and returned to the hob.

'That's a good story' Joe said, and then their silence returned. The old seeping silence that clouds over the guts of things like smog. Joe set the table and Ingrid returned to her cooking. Joe felt the beginning of tears at the back of his eyes and he kept his back to his mum. He stalled when the table was set, stood for a moment staring at the salt and pepper pots in the shape of chickens that had stood in the middle of that very table since 1964. He knew his mum would be avoiding his gaze too, both paralysed by closeness and concern that neither could articulate. Joe slipped out of the room, closed the door softly, shifted his glasses higher on the bridge of his nose and went back to the front room to sit with his dad.

Alastair was asleep and the television filled the silence for them. Outside the street was quiet, save for a tiler perched on the roof of the house opposite and Mrs Williams digging compost into her herbaceous border. Joe watched Alastair in his uneasy rest and noticed for the first time his stubble turning a little grey and the flesh of his jowls showing gravity's pull. In deference Joe looked away. He listened to his mum pottering in the kitchen and Alastair snoring softly and Joe clasped his hands and stared at the floor.

5

At Carntyne station, a smattering of passengers waited on the westbound platform. A teenage girl sat on a bench, her jaws gnawing a hunk of pink bubble gum. She wore headphones with thick black foam pads under tacky pink plastic. The loud beat of an Adam Ant tune was irritatingly audible to those standing near her. A young boy wearing a strawberry red body warmer ran around his mother, thwacking the ground with a leafy branch ripped from a nearby tree. The train pulled up, braking, hissing noisily, coming to a rest. The doors opened and Joe stepped out, still holding a second-hand paperback of Jason and the Argonauts in which he'd been engrossed right until the train stopped. He paused on the platform to open the buckles of his brown satchel and placed the book into its usual place, being careful not to bend the bottom corners of the pages.

Fifteen minutes later he was knocking on the door of Hunter House, a heavy hunk of solid oak, with a semi-circle of stained glass at eye-height. From inside he heard footsteps and Mary opened the door to him. She was young, new to the job, and still had a nervousness about her smile. She dressed herself in the bright sweet colours of the Woodstock era, all willowing dresses and straightened hair.

Ruth came out from the huge living room and greeted Joe. He had been assigned the clients from Hunter House since he started the job three years before. Ruth had made him welcome and showed interest in his work. She knew all the clients well and had a keen eye for their welfare. She seemed to have a soft spot for all of them. It was Ruth that had made the referral for Walter, and she ushered Joe into her office.

'Thanks for seeing Walter' she said. 'Do you want me to tell you some more about him?'

'Thanks but no, 'Joe said. 'Other than what I've got in the referral letter I'd like to go in with a blank slate. 'Does that make sense?'

'Like being the first one to step in freshly fallen snow' she said.

'I guess so. Is he expecting me?'

'Yep I believe so. I'll get Maggie to track him down.'

'How're things with you?'

'Aye, fine. The house is getting back to some normality after the escape from Alcatraz.'

'Sorry?'

'One of our more determined and, shall we say, flamboyant residents – he managed to get out and go AWOL.'

'How?'

'Well, the door alarm was getting replaced. So, for about fifteen minutes the door alarms weren't working whilst the sparkie switched the alarms. During that window of opportunity, Sandy 'Houdini' MacInnes managed to sneak out the side door. He then proceeded to dander down to the main road dressed in his full kilt regalia then hitched a lift back to his old house in Carntyne. It was only when he tried to pay the kindly driver for the lift with three shilling notes that the good Samaritan began to wonder about his state of mind. She phoned round the local residential homes and hey presto, two plus two was four.'

When Ruth smiled her fulsome cheeks bulged and pimpled and glad crow's feet formed at her eyes.

'Aye, well, good on him,' Joe replied. 'Hope I've got that kind of chutzpah when I'm his age.'

'I'll be long gone from this place by then so you can run riot round here if you like.'

'Thanks. I'll bear that in mind. I better head up to the room. See you later.'

'See you later Joe.'

Joe had been going to the house intermittently for some time so he had probably clapped eyes on Walter before, but he could not picture him and had no prior knowledge of him.

They were to meet for the first time in a small quiet room upstairs in the care home, away from the noise and occasional drama of the communal areas. Joe arrived first and let himself into the room. It was well-kept and for that he was thankful. The room was set aside for therapy in all its forms. There was a folded up massage table in the corner, a selection of acupuncture books on a small set of shelves, and two comfortable armchairs for talking therapy. The chairs had belonged to the house a long time. They were of sturdy mahogany, with cushioned seats and backs covered with a simple and dark tartan. A small round oak table was squeezed between the chairs and on the table sat a white ceramic lamp with a soft pink shade and hanging tassels. On one papered wall was a predictable reproduction of a deer on a hillock. On the opposing wall was the original fireplace, complete with black grate, neo-Gothic tiles, and a wooden surround with swirling patterns carved lovingly into the wood. A small vase of dried flowers punctuated the wide mantelpiece. In the alcove stood a tall mahogany bookcase filled with books of crossword puzzles, local history, spy thrillers, and biographies of Frank Sinatra, Ginger Rogers, Charlie Chaplin and the like.

Joe put down his bag and the locked briefcase and hung his coat on the hook on the back of the door. He unlocked the briefcase and took out one of the two files it contained. Walter's file had been newly made up by Bernie, containing the referral letter from Ruth, some blank clinical notepaper, and a copy of the typed letter which had been sent to Walter to confirm the date and time of his first appointment.

Joe had already read the referral with interest when Walter had reached the top of the waiting list, and he read it again now. Afterwards, he laid the file down on the table, stood up and looked out of the window. The house had been built with a great plot of land around it, and the gardens were well-established and neat. At the back left corner there was a garage which had been turned into a workshop by Grant the handyman. Beside the garage Grant was digging in the vegetable patch, shovelling compost into the soil. On a bench sat an older man, watching and talking to Grant. Soon the old man checked his watch, stood up with his walking stick, and headed towards the house.

Joe moved the chairs so that they faced roughly towards each other but not quite head on. He sat down again and poured water from a glass jug into two disposable cups. He opened the file to the first blank page and clicked the top of a silver Parker pen. He wrote Walter's name, address and date of birth at the top right of the page. In the left margin he wrote the date. Then, he laid down the notes, straightened his back, placed his hands on his thighs palms facing upwards and closed his eyes. Thoughts and physical sensations and memories and plans popped into his awareness like fizzing bubbles breaking the surface, crowding each other out in turn. He remained internally still and resisted the urge to pay attention to any of them. The mental events started to quiet a little as he sat in silence. He brought to mind his priorities for meeting any new client – establishing rapport and trust, openness to experience, and non-judgemental curiosity. These ideas were redolent with meaning and a sense of calling. They reminded him of why he'd chosen this work. They took him into the mature part of himself. The moment became peaceful. Joe was temporarily but fully present to the moment, a brief pause in the traffic of history.

There was a knock at the door, and behold, the traffic was moving again.

Joe rose and opened the door. There stood the man whom he'd seen in the garden with Grant. Walter looked about 5'8" though he would have stood two inches taller had he not been bent over slightly to his left where he leaned on his stick. Age had smoothed and rounded the shape of his face, and he was clean shaven. The top of his head was bald and his white hair was a narrow band around the sides and back of his head. His ears had lengthened and the lobes were magnificent. Walter's eyes were faded blue-grey but alert and nimble. He wore a red and yellow checked shirt under a blue sleeveless cardigan, fastened with large ivory buttons. He wore comfortable beige corduroy trousers and well-worn loafers on his feet. His stick was a rich russet colour and the varnish shone pleasingly when the light caught it right.

'Walter?' Joe asked.

'Yes, I'm Walter. How do you do? You must be Joe Miller?' Walter's voice was mid-pitched with a little rough rasp.

'Come on in. Grab a seat.' Joe held open the door and moved out of the way for Walter to enter the room.

'Which seat is yours and which is mine?' asked Walter, standing in the middle of the room.

Joe beckoned to the chair nearest the door. 'Why don't you take this one? That way you get the view out of the window.'

Walter sat down, using the arms of the chair to lower himself down, and stood his stick against the adjacent wall. Joe sat in the other chair and they faced each other.

'Help yourself to water if you wish' said Joe, gesturing to the cups on the table. 'So. I'm Joe, one of the therapists from the therapy team at Dennistoun. But I sometimes come out here to work with some of the residents here. Ruth had made a referral to us for you. Were you aware she was going to do that?'

'Yes, she discussed it with me. I didn't know this was available,' he said, gesturing vaguely to the room. 'But I told her, well, she sort of found out something was wrong. I've been having nightmares, and they announced themselves to anyone who might be passing my room during the night. Like the night shift, obviously. Ruth asked me about the nightmares, whether anything was wrong. At first I played them down. I didn't want to make a fuss. Dreams are just dreams, after all. And I'm not a boy any more. But they've been getting … stronger. And I don't think they're random. So I talked to Ruth more about it. I think she didn't want to pry too much, you know? But she mentioned counselling, suggested it I suppose. She didn't pressure me, but, well, you know, women have a way of suggesting things without suggesting things, if you know what I mean.' Walter made a wry smile.

'I'm not really one for talking about this kind of stuff,' he added.

'Sure,' said Joe. 'I appreciate you telling me that – it's helpful to know.' Joe felt Walter trusted himself to say what he was able to say, and he did not feel the need to prod him along very much. He often took some of the terror out of the first session by being more active, setting the scene, guiding. But often the client had been storing up their story for a long time and they came ready to tell it. The last thing they needed then was the therapist forcing a direction on the session. So he held back, verbally at least.

'Shall I tell you about myself then, my life story?'

'Yes, if you're happy to do so. I'm really interested to hear more about you.'

Walter seemed to take this at face value.

'How long have you got?' he smiled, as did Joe.

'No, really,' Walter added, 'how long is a … meeting?'

'Usually about fifty minutes to an hour' Joe explained. 'I keep an eye on time for us.'

'Alright. Where to begin, where to begin...' Walter focussed on a distant point out the window.

'Well. I was born in Auchinairn in 1914. Before the war started. Before Europe erupted into murderous rage. My father had worked in a mine near the Forth and Clyde Canal. Before I was born he and my mum had both lived in Mavis Valley, which was a small village near the mine, mostly miners and their families. Not there anymore. It was never the same after the fire. That was in 1913. A bad fire in the mine. Twenty two men died, including my father.'

Joe was doing the maths in his head and must have looked puzzled.

'My mum was pregnant with me when he died,' Walter explained.

'I see. So you never met your father.'

'No.'

'I'm sorry to hear that,' said Joe.

'Thank you. I've lived with that fact my whole life but I appreciate it's an unusual story for other people to hear. It's hard to burden others with sorrow, even your own. Anyway, after that, my mum's family moved from Mavis Valley to the new hooses they were building in Auchinairn. I guess the mine and the village held more bad memories than good by then.' Walter lapsed into some silence. Outside they could hear the faint whirr of a lawnmower. Down the hall a door closed and footsteps carried from the stairs.

'My mum must have been heartbroken when my father died but she never really spoke about it, to me at least. There was something ... complicated between her and my dad, and the families. It was maybe the sectarian thing. She was protestant, he was Catholic. Or maybe her family disapproved of him for some other reason, I don't know. There was never a good time to ask. Anyway, I'm sure we'll talk more about that in due course.' Joe made a mental note.

'She married Peter a year later. He was a decent man. He worked a barge on the canal most of his life, transporting timber from the factories at Kirkintilloch and Kilsyth. He knew my mum would have struggled without a working man's wages, but I think there was genuine love there as well as charity. After they married, my wee sister Annie arrived, all blond curls, mischievous eyes and dramatic flair. Then, a couple of years later, Sandy. She was the apple of my step-dad's eye, and who could blame him. She smiled like a cherub from a few weeks old and grew to be a fount of joy for a great many of us. And now she does the same for her children and her grandchildren.' Walter had a beatific smile on his face.

'So there we were, the three of us. My sisters followed me everywhere! When we were wee, Annie would walk beside me holding my hand and I'd be pulling Sandy in a rickety cartie we'd made with old pram wheels and a fish box. On a Saturday we'd tour Auchinairn with Sandy smiling sweetly and by the time we got home the cartie would be filled with hard boiled sweets, pieces and jam, and a few shillings.' Joe savoured the dose of vicarious nostalgia.

'Ach, but I'm painting it as if it was all sweetness and light. Things have changed a lot now. Those were hard times as well. My mum took great comfort in the girls coming along, and she had a decent marriage with Peter. But I knew from a young age that Peter wasn't my real dad and that my dad had died in the fire. My mum felt I should know as soon as I was old enough to understand. Though she wasn't the first to tell me. But once I knew, it made sense. My mum had these times when she'd be very quiet, and very private, and no-one could reach her. I found out later she visited his grave but only ever in secret. And once, there was a fire in a house along the road. No-one was hurt, and they put it out quick. But I remember she was white as a sheet and she couldn't eat for two days. Peter was especially gentle to her then.' Walter finally paused for some moments, and the lines along his forehead became more pronounced.

'What about your mum's family? Who was around?'

'Aye, well, she was from a big family alright. Three brothers and four sisters, and she was the eldest. I think that's where she learned never to complain. Her parents were pretty stern, you know? Hard-line protestant, at least on the level of public adherence.'

'Can I ask what you mean by that?' said Joe.

'Well, I don't know your persuasion, and I'm not asking you to tell me. But you must know the type. In my experience, those who are most bothered about the trimmings and the politics and the formalities of the worship, and why everyone else is wrong, they tend to be the ones for whom faith is a badge of honour, not a personal journey. They're more focussed on the container than the contents.' For the first time, Joe saw some irritation in Walter.

'Anyway, my maternal grandparents were kind to us, and gentle in their own way. But their home was never a place a child could relax, and they wore their religion like a well-pressed overcoat.'

'What about your step-dad? Did he have any family around?'

'Aye, to an extent. Peter's dad had died of TB not long before he married my mum. Another miner. His mum was good-natured and timid, you hardly got a word out of her. Peter had three brothers. They were all six-footers and the mum was a totie wee thing. No wonder she didn't stand up to them much. It was actually William, one of Peter's brothers, who told me about the fire, before my mum did. He was older than Peter, and he knew about my father and my mother. He told me all about it when I was twelve, over a bottle of home-brewed beer, down by the Gadloch. I was a little bit in awe of him, cause he was the only person I knew who'd been as far south as London, working on the trains for the North British Locomotive Company. It was a great big secret to keep from a young boy. No wonder he couldn't keep his mouth shut.'

'What was it like to find out about your dad?'

Walter stared out of the window a long time and rubbed at an eyebrow.

'It was strange. I think I had a suspicion before then that something wasn't right. I don't even know what, just a feeling. So when William told me, it opened a whole can of worms but it kind of answered some questions as well. Then of course I wanted to know more. But William didn't know that much. He knew about my dad but didn't know him. He couldn't really give me a sense of the man. He'd heard my gran say something about my dad's family being poor papists and about keeping my mum on the right side of the tracks. But there was kind of a reverence for the dead as well. The men who died in the fire – they all had a kind of black mystery about them. It was well known about.'

Joe wondered how far to push at this stage but sensed robustness in Walter.

'So what do you know about the kind of man your dad was?'

'Well, that's the million dollar question, isn't it? You want to know what quarry you're strewn from, what kind of yard you were built in. Really I know very little about what he was like. I mentioned it earlier but I think they had fallen out – my mum and dad. I think he left her. Perhaps the pregnancy, too young, the family difficulties, I don't know. And then he died.'

'You seem like you're not sure?'

'No, I'm not. It's all hints and rumours and strained silences. I've had to piece it together from fragments. Not a lot of straight talk about that stuff.'

'Would you have liked to have known more? About your dad? About their relationship?'

'I don't like the idea that my dad left a teenage girl pregnant. I don't like the idea that he gave up on her because of whatever was going on in the families. I would have preferred to believe that he was a decent hard-working loyal man. Doesn't the whole world want men like that - fathers like that? I would rather know that's who I took after, rather than someone who couldn't commit, who gave up.'

Walter paused, perhaps looking for some response from Joe. Joe felt a pang and knew roughly where it came from.

'How has that affected you then? If you believe your dad gave up on your mum too easily, how have you approached relationships?'

'I haven't,' Walter replied. He smiled wanly and covered his mouth with his hand. Joe suddenly questioned whether he'd gone too personal too quickly - again.

'I'm sorry Walter. Perhaps that's me probing too much. We don't need to go into that just now.'

'Naw, naw, you're fine. I guess you get paid to ask the awkward questions.'

'Well, maybe so. All the same...'

'No, it's a fair question. I knew a girl once. Nearly got serious. She was keen. So was I, mind you. We had been stepping out, courting you might say. I was about twenty. There was no good reason for me not to marry her. But I got scared. I got scared that there was too much of my dad in me and I wouldn't be able to stick with her through sickness and health and all that. If my dad had given up on a pregnant fiancée, what might I do? In my stupid hesitancy I thought the noble thing was to not take the risk of hurting her further. Better to end it then than further down the line, with a ring on her finger, or kids around. I didn't trust myself to see it all through, even though I loved her dearly. I tried to explain it to her but she didn't get it. She thought I was fobbing her off.'

Joe had an image of a twenty year old Walter, his hair slicked back with brylcream, braces and boots, the young gent. And then he pictured him calling it off with the girl, trying to tell her why, and the heartache and the anger and the confusion. He felt another strong pang of pity and not a little identification. Perhaps wanting to dial back on the emotion, Joe caught sight of the clock. It was approaching the hour, and even Joe was surprised anew at where the time had gone.

'Walter, I appreciate how much you've told me already today. We will need to finish soon, I hope that's okay. It's particularly interesting the phrase you used about William, that he couldn't keep his mouth shut. I'm guessing there are things you *have* kept your mouth shut about. But maybe you've decided they've been kept packed away too long.'

'Yes, I think so, something like that.' Walter breathed out loudly, and gazed at the carpet.

'If you're happy to pick up next time from where we've left off?' Joe asked.

'Aye, aye, that would be fine thanks. How often do we meet?'

'Weekly, if possible, at least to begin with. I could meet you at the same time next Tuesday if that suited you?'

'Yes, thank you, that would be fine.'

'Will you remember that or would you like a note of the appointment?'

'Aye, you'd better give me a note. My memory's better than most of the folk in here but just in case.'

Joe wrote on a pale blue note and handed it to Walter as they stood up together. Walter gathered his stick, and Joe held open the door for him.

'Thank you very much for listening,' Walter said, and shook Joe firmly by the hand. 'By the way, I'm an Aberdeen fan. Did you know Joe Miller is their right winger?'

Joe's face lightened. 'Yep. It's been mentioned,' he said dryly.

Walter raised his free hand as he left the room and said, 'Cheerio.'

Late that night, Walter dreamt. In this dream, like others before, he was scrabbling around in the dirt of a field. The field was immense and he could see no boundaries of hedgerow or fence. Far away there were low hills, devoid of features. Long stalks of wild grass surrounded him, and no wind disturbed them. The sky was hazy blue and bright, but he could not locate the sun. He needed desperately to find the hole in the ground he knew was there somewhere. He was a boy, and below his slate grey school shorts his knobbly legs were gathering grazes and wet blood and dry dirt, as he pulled and lunged around on his knees. His hands grabbed aside tall, thick bunches of coarse grass, and his small palms swept the dry soil in vain. His fingers clawed the dirt, and his nails were chipped by stones and blackened by soil. He looked up over the top of the grass, fear and desperation rising in his chest. Sickening thick smoke was rising from all over the field, building and building, gathering into a canopy which filtered the yellow sunlight into silver grey shafts. He knew he must find the hole where the smoke was rising from the great fire in the mine. The smoke seemed to come from everywhere but he could not find even a rabbit-sized hole. He did not shout for he knew he would not be heard. No-one else knew of the fire, no-one else could help. It was up to him to find a way down, to slice through the impassive crust of the earth, to rip wide the roots that held the strong ground together, to break its hold on the men below.

He stood up again abruptly, turning around, scanning the field frantically. He ran a few feet, where the lifting smoke was thicker, and dived down, fighting his hands through the green stalks, certain there must be a hole where the smoke was escaping. Panting sobs began to erupt from his mouth, out of his control, the fluids of panic flooding his body and twisting his throat. And still the smoke rose from every sweat pore of the field, and there was no hole nor tunnel, no way down to the cavernous spaces under the earth.

And he stood up, and began stamping his foot brutally on the solid ground. He lifted his knee high and drove his foot crunching against the ground. And no pain erupted from his foot and he drove his foot hard and mercilessly against the soil and the stems of the long grass. And the sound of his stamping built and built until it reverberated against the near hills, a colossal, cavernous sound from the stamping of his feet. And still the ground would not give way.

6

Joe rang the doorbell at his sister's house then opened the door for himself.

'Uncle Joe!' came a yell from the top of the stairs as the kids came spilling and rollicking downstairs to meet Joe in the hall. Joe beamed at their welcome and hugged them tightly, little Rosie getting squashed in the scrummage.

Isobel lived with her husband Frankie and their three children. Isobel was three years older than Joe, and strewn from a very different quarry. She had the self-effacing humour and resilience of her paternal aunts. She bred in her three children a ferocious curiosity and a wildness of creative thought. She had in fact many of the qualities that their father had known and celebrated in better years. She'd studied art and design at college, smearing her dungarees in oil paint and wet clay for three years. Her father had wanted her to study nursing or teaching but she was as bolshy as he was and she could defy him daily and still have fight left in the tank. In the college scene she had met and joyously fallen in love with Frankie. Although Frankie was Canadian, he had cousins in Shawlands and he'd come over to Glasgow to study and to search out his roots, as so many North Americans did. Frankie was a big man and broad-shouldered in temperament. Together, he and Isobel created a home life that was a gift to their children, free and expansive and hopeful.

Their children found adventure everywhere and all life was a canvas for their painted hands and febrile imaginations. Sarah was seven, the leader of the troupe, the originator of the most elaborate of their schemes. She had blond hair which never stayed long in its pigtails. Her muscles were lithe and wiry from endless handstands and tree-climbing. Where there were sticks, Sarah saw a den to be built. Where there were worms and snails and beetles, she saw an etymologist's lab to be constructed. She entered each day with a new batch of plans and the energy to bring at least some to fruition.

David was five, the perfect middle between the two girls. He shared Sarah's energy but channelled it into forms and patterns and order. Sarah's explosions of imagination were fine with David as long as he could systematise them, give them some parallel lines, impose some right angles, make a list. David saw patterns and puzzles in the raw material of life, and found great contentment in making order out of chaos. He was precise and efficient with even the movements of his body, making him seem older than he was.

Rosie was last, three years old and two pigtails wide. She came into a family where the rules were already set and the norms established. She was wise enough to be flexibility personified, and smiled her way into a place of contented teamwork. With huge brown eyes Rosie looked first to Sarah, then to David to concur. And then, if both these wise souls agreed, she was happy to tag along. She would happily explore the big rooms of their home and the lanes and tunnels of their overgrown garden as long as Sarah or David could be heard and called upon.

On this particular day, Joe had arrived before his parents, and was welcomed into the chaos. His sister's home was brimful of books, records, paints, plants, musical instruments, photographs, models, maps, and inventions. The furniture was bashed and shaped by kids' bodies and upstairs the kids' rooms were always a carnival of puppets on swings, Lego men in castles, dens hung from bunk beds and comics splayed on the floors.

Joe released the kids from the bear hug.

'Uncle Joe, are you staying for lunch?' David asked.

'Well, if you'll let me. Would that be okay with you?'

'Of course!' David replied. 'I'll put your name on my list, and now Rosie will give you your welcome present.'

Rosie looked up at David for confirmation, who nodded and nudged her with his elbow. She rummaged in a plastic Safeway bag she was holding. She pulled out a blob of plasticine, green and blue and vaguely resembling a figure, and handed it to Joe.

'Thank you Rosie, that's wonderful' said Joe, admiring the figure as Rosie looked from it to him with a proud grin.

'Dat's you Unca Joe!' she proclaimed.

'I've written the menu!' David announced. Sarah rolled her eyes.

'Okay,' Joe replied. 'What's on the menu today?'

'Hold on!' David shouted, and sprinted through to the kitchen. He appeared again a moment later with an A4 sheet of paper. 'We've got two types of soup - soup number one and soup number two. Then you can have a ham sandwidge or a tuna sandwidge or a egg sandwidge. You tell me what sandwidge you want and I'll put a tick beside it.'

'Well, what a great choice! I'll have a tuna sandwich please. What kind of soup is soup number one?'

Sarah leapt in for her opportunity. 'Soup number one has got worms, snails, conkers, bird feathers and grass.' Rosie burst into laughter, and David began scribbling on his menu.

'In that case, I will have soup number one. Lots and lots of it' said Joe.

Sarah screwed up her face and said, 'Yeuch!'

Frankie came downstairs two at a time and greeted Joe with a handshake. He wore a flowery shirt, denim shorts and sandals almost all year round.

'Hey man, what's up?' said Frankie.

In the kitchen, Isobel was tending to soups and breads and homemade lemonade and arranging the table, but happy in her occupation. She was dressed in denim dungarees and wore a yellow floral apron. Her long hair was held back from her face with a red bandana. Joe greeted her and sat down at the big wooden table.

'Joe, would you get the fruit juice from the fridge?' The tall fridge, with the help of many magnets, was a gallery of rainbows, self-portraits and animal scenes.

'So, how's the job Frankie?' Joe asked. Frankie was an English teacher who appreciated English literature much more than Canadian.

'Yeah, you know, not bad. Got some new classes this year. It's the usual set up. About a third of them are genuinely interested. Another third are not too fussed but they get on with it. The last third take up most of your attention. They're the jokers, the slow ones, the bully and his crew.'

'I don't know how you do that job. At least the people I see have chosen to come, they want to get better. How do you cope when some of these kids don't even want to be there or don't want to learn what you're teaching them?'

'Maybe I like that challenge,' Frankie smiled. 'Don't you get some patients who don't really want to be in therapy?'

'I guess we do in a way. Often they're ambivalent – half wanting to be there, half hating that they are. Not wanting to think they need it. Not wanting to open up. But when they are ready and motivated, it's a great thing. Depends what they're after. Some of them want you to be a landfill, somewhere to dump their rubbish so they don't need to look at it anymore. It's better if they want you to be a recycling facility, to do something together to transform their garbage in some way.'

Isobel brought two big pots of soup and sliced bread to the table. The kids caught the smell and started to pinball their way to the kitchen.

'Plenty of kids in my classes that could do with some help like that,' said Frankie ruefully. 'I guess it's not always the parents fault but bloody hell - some of these families. It's a wonder some of these kids get to school at all, never mind with a packed lunch in their bag and clean clothes on their backs. I've got one wee dude, looks after his diabetic mother, dad's nowhere to be seen, he's the oldest, so he gets home from school and cooks the dinner for them all, tidies up, helps the younger kids to bed. Then we expect him to do homework as well.'

There was a loud knock at the door as Joe's mum and dad arrived. The kids caterwauled their way through to the hall and flung themselves at their grandma and grandpa. Even Alastair on one of his grey days could be reached by the exuberance and joyous hugs from the grandkids. Ingrid breathed in their joy and stored it up in herself.

'Come on through, lunch is nearly ready,' Isobel shouted whilst Frankie got up to greet them.

The family gathered and squeezed around the table. The kids got their aprons tied to them like straightjackets, though they would still manage to spill soup on white and pink t-shirts. Isobel surveyed the seated family and brought the last of the food to the table. Her mum kept her peace whilst Isobel led the offering and the pointing and the ladling. Frankie cajoled the kids into accepting a perfunctory helping of sliced peppers and cucumber. Joe watched how the kids carved out their own identities even in the way they ate their meal – Sarah barely able to keep her backside on her stool with nervous energy, David arranging his food in geometric patterns on the plate, Rosie eating slowly and mindfully and watching how the adults dipped bread into their soup, watching with fascination as the bread magically changed colour. Ingrid watched Isobel most of all, thinking how the girl was now a woman, and her own woman at that. And with that a guilty pang of envy. Alastair laid into his food with the long habit of answering real hunger after a morning of work in the yard. Isobel felt the responsibility of growing more into her role as family glue, and with that security came also the freedom to ruffle things up. It was in the air that someone had to bring up the topic Alastair was avoiding, and Isobel felt most able to do so.

'So, dad, when are we gonnie clear out gran's house?' Isobel asked.

Alastair made a show of chewing slowly the food that was in his mouth.

'What's with the "we"? Your mum and I can manage it just fine.'

Isobel stared laconically at her mum, who returned the look.

'I've no doubt you could, but will you ever? How long's it been? Nearly two months?'

'Ah'll get round to it,' said Alastair, and began prodding wee Rosie's cheek with a carrot stick for distraction.

'The stuff's gonnie get dusty and mouldy soon.' Isobel was the ringleader when it came to prodding Alastair, and the others sat back and waited for the predictable game of 'yes, but.'

'Frankie and me and Joe will help. How about two weeks today?' and she looked to the others for their nods and mumbles of assent. 'We'll get someone to watch the kids. The five of us – we'll get a good chunk of it done together. No problem.'

'Ach no, you don't have to do that. Your mum and I will do it, won't we love?'

'Izzy's right, Alastair We'll no get round to it less we get a wee kick up the backside.' He looked disappointed at her taking the other side. 'I know it's not easy, going through their stuff. All the reminders. But we've got tae do it. Don't want the rats chewing all that good furniture to bits. Your mum wouldnae want it going to waste.'

'But you kids won't know what stuff to keep, what to throw out. Naw, I'll do it myself one weekend.'

'Naw you won't,' said Isobel, and she stared him out. 'Well, are we all decided? Two weeks today?' The others grinned and Alastair sunk his head further towards the soup he was intently eating. Joe marvelled again at Isobel's way with their dad.

The topic was ended and the meal was eaten and enjoyed and Frankie and Alastair hoovered up the scraps. The kids began angling for the visit to the park they'd been promised, an escape from the boring grown up talk around the table. So the table was cleared and the dishes dumped in the sink for later. Isobel packed a couple of rugs into a rucksack and Frankie found the frisbee and the football in the wild corners of the garden. The family set off at a slow dander to Queens Park.

The park sat on a steep hill where three centuries earlier Mary Queen of Scots had met her match against her half-brother's army. The park was busy as the peoples of Govanhill, Crosshill, Mount Florida, Langside and Shawlands all tumbled into its broad grass fields. The sky was cloudless and the sun cast gentle heat and light at the people and the grass and the slate grey tarmac paths and the shallow pond where toddlers reached tantalisingly for green-billed ducks.

The adults sat on two thick rugs on the warm grass whilst Sarah and David threw a frisbee between them and Rosie tottered around in her own wee world. A man and his boy kicked a football clumsily to and fro, the boy with more gusto than the man. A group of teenagers in denim and leather drank cheap beer under the shade of a wide oak. Alastair watched an excitable dog run from its owner and scatter wildly around the open space. The owner, a young man in jeans and a vest, stopped to light a cigarette, gazing listlessly at the dog between scanning for sunbathing women. The Doberman panted and woofed around the Millers rugs, searching for scraps of food and sniffing impetuously at their bodies.

'Shoo! Away wi ye!' shouted Alastair He looked for the owner but the man was talking to a couple of girls lying on the grass fifty yards away. Isobel opened a bottle of home-made lemonade and handed plastic cups of it to the others. Frankie's face screwed up as he gulped a glug down.

'Did ye no sugar it enough?' asked Ingrid. 'Your poor husband looks like a cow sucking vinegar off a thistle.'

Isobel blushed. Alastair turned back to keep an eye on the dog which could not handle its freedom. Sarah and David were chucking the frisbee nearby when the movement caught the attention of the dog. It leaped its way towards them and jumped for the frisbee, missing it by inches. David picked up the frisbee and threw it back to Sarah who caught it cleanly with great delighted. A second later the dog was at her side and grabbed the frisbee in its flailing mouth. Sarah let out a squeal of delight and played her part, tugging at the frisbee whilst the dog tugged back. For a few moments the tug of war continued. Then the dog took a stronger aggressive lunge backwards and snatched the frisbee from her hands, growling slightly through its clenched jaw. Alastair, watching the dog's behaviour with some concern, got to his feet. Ingrid saw him move and saw the furrowing of his forehead and looked towards the kids. Joe saw her gaze change and watched his dad pace towards the kids.

Sarah, a wide smile on her face, made to grab the frisbee again and as she did so, the dog lunged upwards, dropped the frisbee from his dripping jaws, and sank its teeth into Sarah's forearm. Sarah screamed, a rich and terrified scream and the whole park turned to see. She sank to her knees with the dog's weight on her arm and tried to tug her arm back from the frenzied creature. They wrestled as the blood began to spill from her arm and the dog growled low. An instant later the charging Alastair was upon them and threw his big frame around the dog, wrapping an arm around its hairy neck, roaring as his face contorted in rage. Suddenly Joe was upon the vicious creature as well, trying to get a hold of the writhing body.

'Grab its jaw – get the jaw open!' Alastair yelled.

Without a thought Joe grabbed the dog's jaw with a hand on each side of Sarah's slender arm. His fingers felt the hard bone of the jaw and the soft gums and the thick saliva and he pressed his nails as sharply as he could into the flesh of the dog's mouth. Joe stamped a foot on the dog's tail and it wailed with pain. Alastair squeezed viciously on the animal's neck and Joe tried to prise open its jaws. Now Frankie was there with his arms around Sarah. Joe pulled hard and felt the force of the animal's jaw straining. Sarah managed to pull her arm free, red with blood, and stumbled into the arms of her parents who pulled her clear. By now the owner was running over and yelling and others were gathering around. Alastair forced the dog under his body and twisted at its neck. Joe was lost in fury and did not feel the sharpness of the teeth against his vulnerable fingers. He saw the glaring eyes stare fear and evil as he sank his fingers further into the dog's mouth, to pull harder on its straining jaw. The animal let out a ferocious cry as Joe pulled harder and harder until there was a sick crack. The mouth lolled open and instantly the body collapsed, the muscles sagged and the noise dropped to a shrill wheeze and then stopped. For a few moments time hung loosely in mid air. A solitary cloud moved slowly over the sun and a chill came over them all.

Now Alastair and Joe heard each other panting and looked at each other's ashen faces. They looked at the stricken body between them and felt the power they had exerted. Alastair's full weight was still on the body and he moved away with disgust. Joe let go and stumbled backwards and sank heavily on the ground, staring at the bloody mess of the dog's face now stone still on the green grass, its mouth jarred open at a sickening angle and its eyes wide open. He wiped his hands roughly on the ground leaving streaks of blood.

'What have you done?' the owner shouted from a few feet away. Alastair turned his head and breathed in heavily. Frankie and Isobel pulled and shielded the kids away. Alastair got to his feet jerkily, lifted the limp and bleeding dog by the back legs and started swinging it wildly at the owner, the dog's head and dangling front legs striking pathetically at the owner, splattering him with blood and saliva as he yelled his pathetic indignation and self pity. The owner tried clumsily to grab the dog from Alastair as it flew around the space between them and it was all a fumbling mess of limbs and flesh. Alastair finally let go of the dog and the owner picked it up in his hands and stood staring at it with an anguished expression. Alastair smashed his fist hard into the face of the owner and the man careened backwards, falling heavily with the dead dog still in his arms. He sat dumbly on the grass, his nose dripping blood onto the broken face of the dead dog. Joe watched his father and then he looked at Sarah, whimpering quietly in the tight arms of her parents, and then he stumbled to his feet and kicked the dog's body hard through the hands of the owner, breaking his fingers and eliciting another howl of anguish. The owner looked around at the gathering crowd for any kind of support as he huddled over the dog and cradled his crushed hands. No-one moved. The owner began to cry pitifully. He gingerly got to his feet, glancing quickly between Joe and Alastair He held the lifeless body of the dog and walked unsteadily towards the gate. The people standing by stared as he went by, and he avoided their gaze as best he could.

Alastair came out of the spell and went to the huddle around Sarah. Joe joined them hesitantly. Sarah was sitting on Isobel's knee, crying and trying not to. She looked at the bloody mess of her arm, the soft peach skin marred and ripped red and she looked away quickly, yet her gaze kept getting drawn to the compelling strangeness imposed on the familiarity of her own body. Her legs were shivering and she burrowed her head forcefully into the crook of Isobel's neck. On her green Scooby-Doo t-shirt, Shaggy was obscured by a dab of blood. Isobel held her firmly and soothed soft words in her ear, her own eyes brimming with tears. Frankie held the younger two in his long furry arms and eventually unshielded their eyes. He passed the two kids to Ingrid's hugs and he stood up beside Alastair and Joe. The three men stood loosely together. Frankie's eyes were red and the muscles of his wide jaw worked and trembled. He looked away from Sarah to the men.

'Alastair, Joe, thanks. Thanks. I um, I feel terrible that I didn't see it coming. I should have been there to help her. First I mean.'

Alastair responded quickly.

'Ach, Frankie you couldn't have really prevented it. I was worried about that mutt but even I didn't get there in time. It's the bloody owner's fault, not ours. Should have had that thing on a leash, or train it right. How's the wee one doing?'

'We're going to take her round to the Victoria – the A&E.'

Joe wanted to contribute.

'Do you want me to run to a phone box and get an ambulance?'

'Naw, man, thanks for offering but it's just as quick to take her round there ourselves. I'll carry her.' And indeed it was right that the father should carry the wounded child. The others stood back as Frankie gathered Sarah into his large arms, able at last to do his part, and she wrapped her good arm around his thick neck. Isobel touched Frankie lightly on his back as he moved off and they drew concern and strength from each other. Alastair offered his shoulders to Rosie, and David clambered onto Joe for a piggy back. Ingrid picked up the rugs and the bags where they'd been abandoned and the family set off together. The whole park watched as they headed towards the gate at Victoria Road, walking close together, watching their steps. An old lady in a green dress joined up gently alongside their walking and spoke quietly to Isobel, handing her a twenty pound note.

'For some ice creams for you all after ye get her seen to. Whit a terrible thing.'

Isobel thought first to decline out of politeness then remembered that the greater politeness would be to accept the gift and the spirit of it. The woman peeled off from them, her deed done.

The family continued their sorrowed walk to the hospital, each of them processing in their own way this rite of passage and affront to innocence. And for Alastair and for Joe, the colours of sorrow and sympathy bled into colours of anger and potency and they both wondered at the strange strengthening they had taken from the expression of their rage.

Up on the men's shoulders David and Rosie looked at each other. For them both, David piped up.

'Grandpa, will the police come and arrest you and Uncle Joe?'

Joe looked at his father with a little of his nephew's curiosity.

'Us?' said Alastair 'Come to arrest us? No, no, no, not us, no way. Why? Because we killed the dog?'

David nodded.

'Look son, that was a horrible thing that happened. The dog shouldn't have bitten Sarah. The owner shouldn't have let it run around like that. But we did what we had to do. That dog, once it had gone bad, it would've stayed bad. It might have bitten other people, even other children. Once a dog goes bad, it can't go back to being good.'

David contemplated this from Joe's shoulders, and Rosie listened intently.

'They're not like people. Sometime people do bad things but they can become better again, and do good things. Dogs like that, once they've gone bad like that, they have to be … stopped. If we hadn't killed the dog, the police would've.'

David lapsed back into silent thought and Rosie followed his lead. In front, Frankie carried Sarah as she began to shiver and became light-headed. She felt both chilled and clammy, like her body could not make up its mind about the temperature around her. She kept replaying the flash-bulb image of the dog lunging for her arm, though she dearly did not want to. Her mind was trying to integrate that unreal moment into the running storyline of her life. She looked at the drying blood and the deep cuts on her arm and her brown freckles showing through the pink stain and felt the searing throbbing pain. She clung to her father's neck and she felt the solid muscles of his chest and arms as he carried her. She remembered being younger, three, four, being lifted from the car after a night time journey into the house and into bed, half-asleep and droopy, the grownups taking care of everything. Her muscles and Frankie's muscles remembered this now She blushed a little at such a tender memory of a more helpless time.

Soon the hospital came into view. Its size, its age and its authoritative red signs comforted them. Here were the people who can work magic on mauled arms. Here was safety and care. Here was antiseptic and clean water and fresh sheets and clinical air, to neutralise the dangerous mess of spilled blood and toxic infections and hidden killers. Here were the sorcerers and sages who can deconstruct the myriad mysteries of the human body and its ills. Here were the artists and technicians, confident and dependable. The family spilled through the swing doors into A&E and were swallowed up into the benign machinery of the infirmary. Outside on Grange Road, the veins of the city carried on pulsing. A street sweeper stopped his cart beside the main hospital entrance to sweep up the cigarette butts around the bus stop. A young couple, her arm in a sling, flagged down a black cab. A bus of Celtic supporters trundled towards Hampden, green and white scarves and flags drooping from the windows. And at the crossroads with Battlefield Road the traffic lights switched unwavering through their choreographed sequences, on and off, on and off, on and off.

7

'Have I told you yet about how a pile of horse dung broke my leg?' Walter asked with a twinkle in his eye. They had been meeting weekly, Tuesdays at half past one. This particular Tuesday was drenched with summer rain, a sticky and sleepy day. Walter took Joe's silent smile as encouragement and continued.

'I was working as a telegraph messenger for the Post Office. I'd been doing that from the age of 14. After school, weekends, scooting around Glasgow on a bike delivering telegrams here, there and everywhere. When I was 17, they brought in a battalion of motorbikes to replace the bicycles. All about speed, you know? So I got a 125cc BSA Bantam. What a buzz that was when I first got let loose on it. That's the way to make you feel like a man. Until of course I crashed it. I was tearing round the corner from Queen Street onto St Vincent Street, when I skidded on an enormous pile of horse poo. That thing must've been the size of an elephant to crap like that. Anyway, my back wheel skidded on it, I tried to right it, thought I'd got it under control, but then wobbled my way smack bang into the side of a number 54 tram. Broke my leg in two places. And the horse got away scot-free. I managed with a bit of a limp from then on, but the leg got worse as I got older, hence the stick and living in this place a bit before my time, if I do say so myself.'

Walter was smiling into the distance.

'And did you know, they only finally abolished telegrams last year? Remarkable.'

'How long did you do that for?' Joe asked.

'I guess until I was about 20, 21. Aye, that's right, cause then I got a job as a junior reporter for the Evening Times. I cannot swear that my memory is entirely dependable on this but I remember reporting on a cart horse that had dropped dead in the street. The policeman who was first on the scene dragged the horse ten yards round the corner onto Crow Road because he couldn't spell Balshagray Avenue!'

Walter erupted in childish hysterics at his own joke.

'I also ended up a doorman at the Locarno Ballroom in the years when Glaswegians discovered dancing in a big way That was a blast as well.'

When Walter talked like this of his younger days, Joe was transported to an earlier time that seemed simpler and more noble. He knew nostalgia could be deceiving but if he was honest, he enjoyed the illusion. So many of the stories he usually heard were dark and dismal and dominated by pain. Though they were getting towards Walter's troubles, his story carried grace-notes of good cheer, and Joe let himself be salved by them.

When Walter lost momentum with his stories, silence invited depth.

'Walter,' Joe began, 'I recall last time that we began talking more about some of the dreams you've been having. And we agreed we'd perhaps come back to that today. What are your thoughts about that?'

Walter was silent a little longer than usual before responding. 'Yes, of course, we should. I suppose I'm a bit reluctant but maybe that's to be expected. I've gotten used to pondering these things only in the privacy of my own thoughts.'

Joe nodded. He could readily empathise with that, though he reminded himself that similar experience did not equal empathy.

'I respect the fact that your preference, or just the way you're wired, means that you're not used to sharing such private material with someone else.' Joe did not feel he had to persuade Walter to go deeper, but that it was enough to acknowledge the ambivalence.

Walter began.

'I've been having these vivid dreams for the last few years. On and off. Some of them are obviously about my dad. Some are maybe about ageing. Some are just really weird and I can't make head nor tail of them, but they all seem to have the same intensity, the same … flavour. So maybe they matter as well.'

'You said that you've been having these dreams over the last few years. Why just in the last few years do you think?'

'I have wondered about that. I don't know. Nothing significant has happened in recent years, as far as I can tell. Maybe you'll tell me otherwise,' Walter grinned.

'Maybe,' said Joe. 'Maybe we'll work that out together. Could you tell me about some of the dreams?'

'There's one I've had a few times. It seems fairly straightforward. I'm in a field and I know that underneath the field is the mine where my father worked. Smoke starts coming out of the ground and I'm trying to dig a hole in the ground for my dad to escape from the fire. I start to panic, I can't find any way for him to get out. Time is always running out in that dream. Oh, and I'm just a wee boy in the dream.'

'What kind of age of a wee boy?'

'About 7 or 8 maybe? Certainly I feel small and vulnerable. There's no-one else around and there's a terrible feeling of loneliness and panic. I get desperate, trying to find a hole or dig one.'

'It sounds really distressing, especially for a young boy. I get a sense from you of the desperation of it, and your fear for your dad. Given that you know what happened, is there perhaps a sense of inevitability about it at all?'

'Yes, I think that's right. All along, I know he's going to die. And there's nothing I can do about it.' Their eyes met briefly then both looked away. Walter's brow furrowed.

'Do you know,' Walter continued, 'that's just reminded me of another dream. But one I had many, many years ago. I haven't thought of it in a long time.' Joe tried to read the expression on Walter's face but it was odd.

'I only had this dream once. I'm pretty sure of that. I was in a building, not sure exactly what it was. Maybe a hospital, maybe some kind of factory or chemical works, or something like that. I was led along a long corridor. It was very bare, clinical you might say. The walls were sky blue, I remember that. Then I was being led down a narrow flight of stairs. I don't know who was leading me, an adult anyway. I must have been a boy in this dream as well, though maybe a little older than the other – twelve, thirteen maybe. At the bottom of the stairs we came out into some kind of forest. It was thick with trees and very, very quiet. The ground was mossy and the whole place was ... succulent. I can remember there were rich smells, forest smells, you know. There was a small river we could see through the trees. The person guiding me pointed and there was a man in a white hospital gown sitting on a tree trunk throwing stones in the river. Although I couldn't see his face, I knew it was my dad. The hand on my shoulder pushed me gently toward the river. I felt incredibly shy, incredibly unsure of myself, really not sure what to do. We got to the river, a few yards upstream from my dad. The shyness was overpowering, the nervousness. My dad was facing the other way, he hadn't seen us yet. I looked away, expecting him to turn round at any moment. I bent down and started picking up some of the stones on the little shore of the river. Whoever was beside me pushed me gently towards my dad. I put the wee stones in my pocket. This mysterious guy was encouraging me to go to my dad. Nothing was said but I seemed to hear, 'This is your chance to love him.' My feet were pinned to the spot. And still he hadn't turned round and seen me. And I remember thinking, 'How can I love him when I know he's going to die?' And then I woke.'

There was a strong, weighty silence in the room. Both men were breathing deeply. Walter felt a tide of emotion in his chest. Joe was captivated, and fearful of breaking the spell.

'Thank you for telling me that. How do you feel at the moment?'

Walter looked at the tips of his fingers, which were joined in an arch. His fingers slid past each other until they were interlaced.

'I feel surprised that I haven't thought of that dream in so long. Surprised that it still makes me feel like a bit like a lost child. As if I'm still mourning for my dad all these years later.'

'Maybe you are,' Joe said.

Walter's mouth drew in. His front teeth pushed into his lower lip. His eyes tightened and his gaze was on the floor.

'Isn't that a bit … odd, though? After all this time?'

'Well, is there a timetable for grief?'

Walter pondered this, glancing briefly at Joe. Joe's expression was one of curiosity.

'I see. I see what you're doing. I would have to say, yes, I think most of us believe in an unwritten timetable for grief. But I guess you're getting me to question that.'

'And it's not just a matter of grief, is it?' said Joe. 'Perhaps it's a lifelong process of living without a father, and living with less … natural, less automatic access to the deep masculine within you. That which perhaps your father could have passed on to you had he lived. And yet, despite never having that formal father figure and the male energy that can come from that, you do have a real generative father energy about you. A *grand* father energy. I think, as a younger man than you, I sense some of that from you. I wonder if it might be important to you to pass something on, some kind of life, some kind of fatherly wisdom or gift.'

There was a further silence.

'I don't know, Joe. I think you might be barking up the wrong tree.'

Joe was surprised, disappointed.

'Hmm. Well, okay, perhaps. What tree do you think we should be barking up?'

'I still think maybe I'm right. That my dad was kind of weak-willed, and that's what got passed onto me. That maybe I made the right decision to not get married and not hurt someone else.'

'Okay, well let's say that's true. What do you want now? Why are you having these dreams? Why are you not satisfied with that explanation of who you are?'

'Maybe the dreams don't mean anything. But I want to stop them. What can I do about them?

'I don't think you can do anything with the dreams. Maybe the dreams are doing something with you.'

8

The sun was five hours high in the sky when Zara and Joe took a left turn off Baldrennan Road towards Eastfield Royal Hospital. From the main road, a long driveway parted the trees for a hundred yards. The driveway then took a long curling loop around the front lawn before slicing through the suite of crumbling Victorian buildings. Webster House, the largest and oldest of the buildings, commanded the wide open lawn. It stretched almost the width of the grounds and stood four stories tall, red sandstone worn pale pink in places, high wide windows, squat chimney stacks like turrets and a grand arched doorway. Zara drove them past the north wing, along the main artery of the sprawling hospital grounds. Built away from the city, the hospital had been sited with therapeutic space and stigmatic separation equally in mind. Beyond Webster House a squat red brick building had been the old nurse's home. An overgrown football pitch separated the nurses from the old ECT ward. On their right was Baxter House, a miniature of Webster, and behind it a slim ribbon of forest shielded the grounds from the dairy farm beyond. Zara parked in one of the small car parks dotted around the place. She and Joe stepped out. Even the fresh air felt old in this place where the anguish of countless souls had swirled for decades amongst the corridors and common rooms but were sucked down into silence by the space between the sanctuary and the city.

On Baxter House the tall windows faced south, reflecting the sun onto the wide round lawn. Chimneys punctuated the long roof and crumbling gargoyles adorned with streaks of moss framed the dark porch where Zara and Joe went in. Inside, the entrance hall gave way to long corridors left and right. Stone busts of Dr Ewan Baxter and Dr Archibald Watson, long-dead psychiatrists, stood proud on wooden plinths either side of a marble staircase which led to the upper floors. The varnished pine floor and the thick stone walls made every footstep echo. The rehab ward occupied one half of the ground floor, reached through wide swing doors on the left of the entrance hall.

Rehab was an ambiguous word in a place like this. Many patients had been in the Royal all their lives. Many should never have been there in the first place but it had been a convenient catch all not only for men and women in emotional pain, but one might also find in its quasi-medical captivity an old woman sent there as a pregnant unmarried teenager, a veteran of war with combat fatigue, an otherwise fit young man with club foot, an epileptic, a drunk with half his brain drowned in gin, a woman made destitute and homeless by divorce, an anguished novelist driven wild by the great novel he couldn't write. The Royal was an institution, a village, an industry, a sub-culture, an experiment, a museum.

In the rehab ward, rooms of four beds each ran parallel along the sides of a dark corridor. Glass panels in the doors revealed beds with starch white linen, curtains drawn round some, patients in grand wooden high-backed chairs. On the walls of the corridor hung black and white photographs of the hospital in the late nineteenth and early twentieth century's. Patients running races on the front lawn in white shorts and vests under the watchful eye of stern looking doctors swathed in black despite the sunshine. Women in the workshop, sewing dresses on huge Singer machines. The huge brick chimney being built, clothed in scaffold, men with fine moustaches and black waistcoats perched at height.

Sister McGeachie greeted Zara and Joe. The staff nurses had prepped the patients for Zara's group. She had wanted for some time to set up an outdoor therapy group as part of the rehab treatment programme. With some difficulty she'd convinced the medics that they could and should run an outdoor psychotherapy group in the grounds of Eastfield. Zara knew the medical staff were sceptical about it. A step too far, they thought, into the psychobabble that emanated from the humanistic hippies of California and the psychoanalysts of New York and Vienna. But Zara had argued that the grounds were beautiful and therapeutic, and that the men who'd built the hospital would have wanted their well laid paths and carefully chosen birches and oaks and Douglas firs to be enjoyed and appreciated. Some of these patients would soon, in theory, be leaving the hospital to live back in the urban sprawl of Glasgow, so they should enjoy the 30 acres of gardens whilst they could. She also had a theory that human beings were not made for buildings and certainly not buildings which had absorbed years of anguished cries and a thousand public nightmares. She guessed that patients might find more peace outdoors and a sense of vocational purpose clearing the overgrown edges of the grounds, pruning and shaping, and watching new growth emerge. In her hopes, the patients would take solace and symbolism from the perennial cycle of nature's death and resurrection.

The group of five patients were waiting in the common room, sitting in a huddle of armchairs near the door. They looked suspended in their waiting, not here but not yet elsewhere either. Olga was Georgian and had fled her country under the threat of 're-education' under Stalin. Her thin black hair was iron-straight and flopped over her face to conceal as best she could the pockmarks of old acne. She was sitting alert and stern in a high-back chair, a long black leather jacket wrapped around herself. TJ was tall and fair and wore his girth like a tool belt. He smiled widely for approval at Zara and Joe. Jackie wore the double denim of her country music idols. She liked Joe a great deal and so she had worn her brightest reddest lipstick. Quintus was the eccentric uncle of the ward. He had his nose in a book as always so it was the bald top of his bowed head that greeted the visitors. And lastly was Adam. Only twenty-three but already a regular presence at the Royal. He sat with his legs crossed in a wide spongy armchair, his hands clasped under a baggy grey sweater and his head upturned to the intricately corniced ceiling, his mind turned always away from the prosaic in favour of the elegiac.

Outside a light breeze whistled through the trees from the west, the Gulf Stream buffeting and cleansing the west coast as always. Zara turned to Jackie.

'How are you feeling about moving out of the hospital Jackie?'

'Ach, alright. They've got me a flat in Sandyhills. No far from ma ma. I've been in here too long. Want to buy a fish supper whenever ah please. Want to play my Clash records loud and proud.'

'Aren't you scared at all?' Quintus asked.

Jackie stared at him as she thought about her reply.

'A bit. Mostly about the voices. But they're pretty quiet the now. Hope ah can pay my bills and don't get chucked oot,' and she laughed abruptly, a strident whoop.

They turned off the tarmac path onto a grassy path which led away from the buildings towards the wilder parts of the grounds.

'I get nervous about it, I must say,' Quintus said quietly. 'My mum used to cook for me. Before she died. Having all those meals cooked at the hospital – I like that. I fear I might live on beans on toast.'

'Where will you be living Quintus?' TJ asked.

'I don't know yet. They haven't found me anywhere yet. I saw the psychiatrist on Friday. He's put me on a new medication, Chlorpromazine. Is it Largactil, the other name?'

'Ooh, better be careful with your dose,' Jackie chipped in. 'Makes you wander around like a zombie I've heard. The Largactil Shuffle they call it.'

TJ kicked Jackie lightly on the back of her leg.

'Whit?'

TJ nodded towards Quintus whose face was a frown and whose head was down.

'Oh, aye, sorry, never mind me,' she added quickly. 'Ah just talk shite a lot. Just jealous, really. I only get Haloperidol.' TJ gave her a smile of approval.

Around them the big bushy holly shrubs crowded round downy birches, hazel and rowan. The air smelled of sap and wild raspberries and the manure the farmers were flinging upon their fields. Zara hung back as the group fell into silent wandering, the soft fascination of the forest textures and colours stilling the need to talk. Even Joe's inner monologue had quietened down.

'Has anyone seen Adam?' Zara asked. No-one else had noticed that Adam was no longer strolling amongst them. Shoulders were shrugged and heads shook.

'Adam?' Zara called out. There was no answer. Both Zara and Joe knew that Adam lived in a kind of unfettered freedom charged with grandeur and mystery and could wander off in an oblivious daze. He could also suffer the electrical storms deep in his brain that sent his body into violent convulsions.

'I'll have a look around for him,' offered Joe. They were near an open field which would not offer much in the way of exploration opportunities so Joe went the other way, deeper into the woods. Layer upon layer of dead sticks and leaves carpeted the forest floor as Joe took some steps into the darkness of it.

'Adam?' he called, his voice soaked up instantly by the trees and the soft moss and the furry lichen.

'Up here!' came Adam's voice from almost directly above him. Joe looked into the thick canopy of the trees and for a few moments could see nothing but branches reaching out from ruler-straight trunks, each a radius and each with its own subsidiary system of branches, and a blanket of greenery, lit from above by the morning sun. Then a part of one tree shook, a twig fell down through the tree, and Adam shouted again. Now Joe could just make out the blue of Adam's jeans through the thick interweaving of branches. Joe marvelled at how he'd managed to get so high so quickly.

'Come on up!' shouted Adam. 'It's amazing up here!'

'Thanks for the offer Adam but no, I think I'll stay on solid ground. I don't think it's very safe up there.'

'Safe? Safe? Never mind whether it's safe. It's majestic! It's wonderful! You can see for *miles* up here. Come on up – you'll love it.'

Joe felt a pang of envy for Adam's pioneer spirit but felt also his responsibility for him.

'Adam, that's great, I'm glad you've enjoyed it up there. But can you come down now please? I'm a bit worried for you up there.'

There was a long silence from Adam, whilst the tree rustled thinly in the wind, whispering its secretive lisping language. Zara and the group walked over to Joe. Zara wore an expression of bemused curiosity.

'Joe! Come on Joe Miller! You must have climbed trees before. Come on up! Show us what you can do!'

Joe smiled wanly at Zara, beginning to feel a little stupid. Her look was non-committal. Adam continued yelling from the tree.

'Joe? If you come up here and join me, then I'll come down afterwards. Just for a wee minute. Come and see the world the way I can see it!'

Despite himself, Joe looked at the tree with fresh eyes. The lowest branch was reachable, and thick enough. The ascending branches were at nice gaps from each other. The inner parts of the branches were mostly bare so there was little green growth to impede a climber. And the part of him that was proud protested that of course he could climb it if he chose to. He was only a few years older than Adam. He glanced around at the others. He wondered what kind of example he wanted to set them. Weren't they asking these patients to take risky steps out into the unfamiliar? And why should it always be the staff telling the patients what to do?

Joe felt his pulse quicken as he gripped his hands around the overhead branches, got his left foot into a hollow knot, and pulled his weight upwards. His Doc Martin squeezed into an acute angle and he reached for the next limb with his other foot. He looked up, dam could see he was trying. He moved gingerly, y, planning each step carefully. The bark was cool and rough against his hands and a layer of sticky sap began to form on his soft skin. Now he was twelve feet off the ground and he tried not to look down. Zara said nothing. Quintus wore a look of fatherly concern. Olga crossed herself and looked away. Joe felt a rational fear that was never there when he had done this as a child. His adult body felt suddenly heavy and cumbersome, as if he could feel the waves of gravity pulling at it, taunting him to fall. He stayed close to the trunk, hugging it, stopping at each stage to gauge his progress. He stopped where the trunk split into two distorted and twisted beams and he kneeled awkwardly in the narrow space between them, his sweaty face rubbing against the velvety leaves that surrounded him. Now he could see Adam closer, his body half concealed by the lush green roof of the canopy. Adam poked his head down out of the greenery and shouted with delight.

'Joe! You made it halfway! Good on you! Come and see the view. I'm nearly as high as the buildings!' Adam shook the thinning branches around him and the whole top of the tree swayed and rustled, sending leaves and bark raining down on Joe.

For a moment Joe's muscles remembered what his mind could not. The muscles revived what it was like to reach and strain with a growing quickening body. The splendour of isolated absorption in climbing, daring, gauging the probable safety of each branch, lithe limbs looping around tree limbs, shifting weight, sinews and tendons holding fast as the body works as one glorious fluid ensemble. His body and not his mind dug up from a buried place the wonder of reaching the top, a nervous mother on the ground forgotten, the scent of waxy leaves and thick skin of bark squeezing honey sap sickly from its folds.

Then the weight of his adult body felt gravity's pull stronger and the corporeal nostalgic kick was gone and his self-consciousness returned.

'Alright, Adam, steady on,' Joe said. 'I think that's enough for now. That's a great achievement. For us both. Can we go down now? I'll see the view another time.'

Adam looked with pity at Joe in his awkward pose, his flesh mashed into the V shape of the tree, holding tight to branches, white knuckles protruding through pink skin, his long fringe bedraggled and his glasses squint on his face.

'Alright,' Adam relented. 'You first.'

Joe manoeuvred himself out of his perch and gratefully let his weight pull him down from branch to branch. Above him Adam looped and swung with confidence as he descended and Joe felt the rocking of the tree as it resonated with Adam's exuberance.

Nearing the ground, Joe's breathing was heavy and he smiled sheepishly as the troupe watched him droop from the last branch to the sanctuary of solid ground. Adam meanwhile had waited patiently for Joe to get out of the way and when his turn came he swung wildly on the last branch.

'Ladies and gentlemen, the great Trapezio!' And with a final flourish of his swooping long legs he threw himself far from the tree and landed on his feet, teetered backwards for a moment then righted himself to stand tall and triumphant. TJ and Jackie clapped and whooped. Zara smiled quizzically at Joe and could not read his expression.

The noise fell away and the forest was serene again. The group shuffled a little. Zara looked around at them all.

'What was it like up there Adam?' she asked.

'Yeah, amazing, fantabulous, otherworldly. I love it when your face pokes through the last of the leaves and all of a sudden you're above it all and you can see everything! By then you're on really thin branches, and it's all moving and swaying like a real living thing. But the branches are like a hug around you! You know you couldn't fall too far without a branch grabbing you.'

His eyes were alight and he kept his gaze on Zara.

'And when you look around, wow, what a sight. I love the way the Campsies rise up out of the ground, like a green wave. And being able to see the farms and the canal and the river. And all the time the tree is swaying you about. It's a living breathing ladder to the sky!'

The group smiled and breathed in Adam's joy. Joe felt a pang of shame at his dry fear and his blandness, as if the colour he saw in so many others was bleaching out of him, a little at a time.

The group moved on in a kind of slow and ragged waltz through the still woods. Something scurried amongst the nettles and ferns, little paws crunching on crisp leaves. The air smelled of drying pine cones and juniper berries.

'Oh my' said Quintus, who was crouched near the base of a willow. He appeared to be looking at the ground. Zara moved towards him and he turned towards her holding a small chaffinch in his cupped hands. He tenderly stroked the small dirty wings, which were beginning to stiffen. Quintus held it up at eye level to see its tiny face, and his expression was solemn. The eyes of the bird were open, their look of alarm frozen there forever. The delicate legs and feet looked utterly fragile and the body did not yet have the weight and substance of age. Quintus looked upwards into the tree and saw a small ragged nest high in the branches.

He sighed.

'Its first flight,' he said.

Zara gazed around the group to gauge their reactions. Jackie stepped forward, her borrowed green wellies crunching the twigs underfoot. She stood alongside Quintus and caressed the stricken bird.

'Its first flight,' he said again. 'Poor thing never made it past its first flight. Can you picture it?' he said towards Jackie. 'Nervously wondering whether it was ready to fly. The parents prodding him out, thinking he was ready. He wasn't. He wasn't ready.'

Jackie nodded.

'We used to find dead birds in my garden,' she said brightly. 'But it was the cat. Sweet little kitty cat inside. Vicious wee bugger

70

outside.' Quintus grimaced a little and to his relief Jackie moved away.

TJ moved over, taking his turn. He stood beside Quintus, a full foot taller and heavy-chested but gentle with it, and he watched with quiet respect as Quintus gently pushed at the tiny spindly legs of the bird, exploring it in a way he never could had it been alive. He rewarded TJ's patient attention by cautiously passing the precious object into his waiting hands. TJ could wrap his big wide hands easily around the dead bird, enclosing it, protecting it too late. He felt the almost weightlessness of it, the vulnerability of it. TJ held it in one hand, bent down, and lifted some dead leaves from the ground and placed them on the bird like a blanket and the crinkling sound of the dry leaves cracked the silence. Quintus smiled a little. TJ noticed his smile.

'Do ye want to bury it?' TJ asked him.

Quintus looked up at him quickly. He could see TJ was quietly serious. Quintus looked at Zara and she nodded and smiled. Quintus looked back at the bird and thought of its fragile flesh and feathers and bones withering away and being gnawed to nothingness in broad daylight by the cruel army of nature's carnivores, its form and shape slowly wasting to raggedness and then to nothingness. And he thought then of men in the great war, men he'd read about in books, men dying in the ditches and the trenches and the forests and who were never buried but were left to disintegrate and decay in the sick mud. And he thought of his grandmother whom they lowered gracefully into the ground in a shiny oak coffin lined with white silken cotton when he was thirteen years old, him holding the black cord with great concentration, her descending box etched in his memory as he encountered the permafrost of death for the first time.

'Yes,' Quintus said, 'yes, I think we should.' He looked again to Zara for her confirmation and she nodded kindly again.

'Where do you think would be a good place?' she asked.

Quintus looked around.

'Maybe not too close to here. If the parents are still in the nest, you know?'

Quintus walked a few paces further into the forest, stopped, kicked at some fallen branches, and began smoothing a patch of ground with his hands. He picked up a thick branch in one hand and began scraping it through the rough dry soil. He scraped at the ground with the stick and lifted the disturbed soil with his other hand and built a little mound. He dug the hole slowly and with reverence as the others watched on. He dug out small stones from the hole and laid these in a separate pile. Then the stick broke on the hard packed soil so he laid it aside and dug simply with his hands, his fingertips and ragged nails scrunching through the soil, and he felt the cool succulent soil crumble through his fingers and he rubbed the larger chunks down, ground them down to finer soil and laid it on the mound. Eventually he decided the hole was big enough for the body to be gently absorbed back into the earth in dignified privacy.

Quintus waved TJ over and he walked carefully, cradling the chaffinch in his cupped hands, careful not to let the blanket of leaves fall off. TJ knelt down beside Quintus and made to hand him the bird but Quintus mouthed 'You' and motioned to the hole. TJ smiled sheepishly and ceremoniously laid the small body in the hole. Quintus arranged some of the dead leaves under and around and on top of the body, and finally covered it up completely. They both picked up handfuls of the soil and sprinkled it over the shroud of dead leaves and in the quiet forest the patter of soil on the leaves was crisp and clear. TJ stepped back and Quintus lifted the rest of the soil into the hole until there was a little mound rising above the level of the ground. He packed it down and placed the little stones on top, like the cairns he'd seen once at Clava. Quintus stood up, waited a few moments, felt a little breeze on his face, and then it was done, and he walked away to join the others.

Again they stood in a huddle, waiting for Zara's direction.

'Shall we head towards the burn?' Joe suggested. No better

ideas were offered, and they began to follow Joe along a lightly worn track.

'It's sad when things die,' said TJ. 'Sad and lonely. Sad and maybe confusing. Maybe the right time, maybe the wrong time. It sinks you down doesn't it? Sinks you down into here,' and he laid his hands on his fat gut. 'Sinks you down like a weight, like when my uncle had a cat and it had too many kittens, and he got a big sack with bricks and...' He saw Quintus grimace and stopped. 'It feels like balloons shouldn't float so easily, or carnivals should stop. And it always has to happen eventually, doesn't it?' He seemed to be speaking to the trees around him. 'My mum died last year. Not like that bird, out in the open and alone. She was wired up with tubes and bandages and all that stuff. It was like we were all trying to hold her up in life with ropes and safety nets. But she untied the ropes and she slipped through the nets anyway, didn't she? It was time. The right time. We weren't meant to hold her up with ropes and nets any longer. It was time.'

The group walked slowly, following TJ's pace, marching behind the drum major.

'TJ, what did you feel when you held that little bird in your hands?' asked Zara.

TJ stopped to think with his hands on his hips and his face screwed up a little. The soft wind rustled the ageing leaves as the forest waited with utter patience for his reply.

'I felt huge, for one thing. I felt so much bigger than this tiny delicate thing. Felt like a giant, but a good giant, a kind giant, you know? It was so light and flimsy. Sad. Sad that there was never a chance for that wee body to explode into movement. It never had a chance to fly and swoop and glide in the air. It never had the chance to do its own thing, be independent, find its own food, make its own nest, discover its favourite place to sit and watch life go by. I wish she'd had a chance to taste more of life.'

'My people, too much death. Way, way too much death,' said Olga. 'Death dripping from the fingers of every government bureaucrat.' She flicked her fingers towards the ground. 'Every family lost someone in the purges, the wars, the gulag.'

For Olga, the ward felt a little too much like the imprisonment she had escaped in Georgia. Out here though was different, and she trusted Zara.

'Quintus,' she continued,' you got to bury that little insignificant bird. You gave it sweet, pretty funeral. We lost loved ones, mothers, fathers, children, and sometimes we never even got their bodies. Left to rot in a filthy shed, or out in the trenches.'

'Surely what the Germans did was worse?' asked Quintus.

'Maybe yes, maybe no,' replied Olga.

Jackie was stopped, squinting through the thin rays of sunlight that pierced through the thicket of trees. She held one hand above her eyes and pointed loosely with the other.

'Look, what's that?'

She wandered off the path in the direction of the boiler house with its huge chimney. Down a little slope she had spotted a square of brick emerging out of the long grass, half-hidden by overgrown dandelions and chickweed. The ground sloped down towards an opening, where soil and branches and dead leaves had gathered.

'Is this a bomb shelter?' Jackie asked.

'Think so,' replied Zara.

Jackie scrambled down the slope and peered inside the gloom. She stepped over a pile of debris at the opening and disappeared inside. She stood still a few moments whilst her eyes adjusted to the darkness. To the others watching from some yards away it looked as if she had been swallowed up into the dank darkness of a cave. Inside, Jackie sat on one of the wooden benches built into the side.

The others crowded round the entrance then went down into the soft gloom with Jackie, all except Olga who sat on the grass outside, picking daisies. In the shelter Jackie was raking around at the far end. She reached down and pulled at something in the dirt, then spun round excitedly.

'Look at this!'

She had found a gas mask, straps hanging loosely and caked with thick dust, the buckle rusted, the filter canister covered with muck. TJ took it from her, examined it, handed it on to the others. Jackie returned to her forage and pulled gingerly from under the bench a faded yellow tabloid and a hospital gown that had once been white. The gown was deeply grey and rotting but a large brown red stain was discernible on one sleeve. And Joe saw suddenly the blood and spit and teeth in Sarah's arm, the bloody mess on his hands as his fingers grappled with the flailing mouth of the dog. He tried to banish the image from his mind, but it stayed draped over his awareness, tendrils of it dripping blood and wrath and disgust.

Jackie rummaged more and found a copper model aeroplane. Its rusting bolts were still held together and the colours of the Air Force were crudely painted onto the wings and fuselage. Quintus took the newspaper out into the daylight and sat beside Olga. The date was 17th March 1941. Two days earlier the Luftwaffe had ripped audaciously across the North Sea, across Fife and Stirlingshire, guided by fires lit along the route by German spies, and had pummelled Clydebank with wave after wave of incendiary bombs, searing missiles ripping through beautifully made boats and bodies. The newspaper headlines were muted, perhaps by shock or by British reserve.

Quintus read out a few paragraphs.

"An amazing rescue of a 15-year-old boy from a bombed tenement more than two days after the property had been partly demolished in Thursday's raid on Clydeside took place yesterday.

An 11-year-old girl was also extricated from the wreckage of the tenement by the tireless efforts of the rescue squads. She had been trapped for 36 hours, but was still conscious when brought out.

The boy is believed to be named Stanley Ewing. Clad in his pyjamas, he was found in a concealed bed. His rescuers heard his voice long after it had been assumed that no one in the pile of debris could be alive.

When they reached him the rescue party found that he was uninjured and fully conscious. By a remarkable stroke of luck a bag of sugar had been thrown into his bed from a cupboard when the house collapsed, and during his long imprisonment he sustained himself with the sugar."

'Is there anything in there about the Soviet Union?' Olga asked. Her voice was low and her chin down at her chest. '1941 was the year of Barbarossa. The Nazi devils. As if Yezhovshchina had not been evil enough, the purge, the terror.'

Quintus scanned the ragged and dirty pages, peering at the small print, turning it over like it might disintegrate in his fingers. He shook his head for Olga. She moved slowly away. Jackie tried on the rusted gas mask and the others gathered around Quintus and the newspaper. In the paused stillness, Joe peered into the gloom of the shelter, breathing in the scent of a time he could not imagine.

Zara drew alongside Olga, deliberately but gently. Joe noticed then that Olga was breathing quickly, her shoulders rising and falling like slow pistons. Zara placed a hand on her back. Olga began muttering quietly, shaking her head, then gazing at the enveloping canopy of trees and shrubs around them. Joe saw Zara speaking quietly to Olga, gazing at her face. Olga began to speak more loudly and clearly.

'I remember bombs and danger. Bombs, bombs, always. Leningrad, Smolensk, Sevastopol. Always danger. And after, it was not safe. In your country the war stopped when it stopped. In my country, one evil moved out and another one had already moved in. I was young. My brothers and sisters – we were all so young. And innocent and beautiful. And here – this place is beautiful too. It is peaceful yet I cannot find peace. These beautiful places. Krasota. The sweet flowers. The birds and the deer – I saw a deer last night!

I cannot be this. I cannot. I am no longer beautiful like this place. I was once – you must believe me. I show you photos. This place - it dies but comes back new and young and beautiful each year. Me? No. I never get young again. I cannot save my beauty for tomorrow.' She gripped her face, squeezing her cheeks, and ran her thin fingers through her thin hair.

'And these! These horrible marks on my face! The bites of the moskit! Why they not go away? Why these ghost bukashka keep marking my face that was once so beautiful?'

She began to wail and keen, loud and mournful. Zara continued to stand by her side, an arm around her, telling her it was okay, that she was okay. But Olga was entirely caught up in the flood and very alone.

The rest of the group had all stopped, and stood loosely around. Beside Joe, Adam was watching closely. He moved slowly over to Olga and Zara. Joe watched, unsure of whether to stop him. The others watched with curiosity. Adam came to Olga's side, Zara on her other. He kept his hands clasped in front of him and his head was dipped like a monk. Joe could see Adam's lips moving and could make out only a tender tone and small lilting musical movements of pitch. Zara was watching him closely, hesitant but patient. Olga was crying softly but her head was tilted towards Adam, lowering her moans to hear him. Adam stopped speaking, laid an arm on her shoulder, lifted his head, and looked around. Behind him he saw a path through the trees to an open field. He held out his arm to Olga and she snaked her arm through his. He led her slowly down the path. Her crying quietened further. Joe and Zara exchanged glances and followed at a distance with the others. Adam led Olga along the path and into the sunlight which had not yet gathered warmth into its glow. Adam stopped and looked around again. He went to the grass near the trees where there were still shadows. He knelt down in a smooth movement, the knees of his jeans wetting quickly in the dew. He laid his large hands flat on the grass, and moved them in circles, soaking his skin with cold dew. He stared straight ahead into the forest for a few moments, still as a rock, then stood and went to Olga. He whispered to her, and she stared at him. Adam turned up his palms, showing them to her. He whispered again. Hesitantly, she pointed at a place on her face, high on her left cheek, and pulled her finger away quickly. He raised his left hand and touched the place on her skin she had shown him. She flinched a little, but stayed where she was. He asked again. She pointed to a place on her chin that was dimpled and rough. Adam lifted another finger and slowly stroked the place. He asked again. She pointed to a patch of dry skin near her widow's peak. Adam gently rubbed the place with his fingers, spreading the dew on her skin so it glistened with tiny embers of the soft sunlight. The heaving motion of her quick breathing began to diminish and her shoulders which had been tight around her neck began to let down their guard.

Adam whispered again to Olga and she looked at him now, was still for a few moments, and then nodded. Adam walked towards Quintus, who was standing a few feet away, his hands joined behind his back, his head tilted to one side like a curious bird. Adam put an arm on Quintus's back, and brought him to the shadowed and dewy grass. Quintus looked quizzically at Adam, who nodded encouragingly and knelt down, gesturing to the grass. Quintus stared for longer and glanced briefly at Olga. She had her eyes closed and her face turned upwards a little towards the sunlight. Quintus bent down and laid his hands flat on the grass, lifting moisture from the ends of the grass stems and rubbing it delicately over his hands. He moved in a dignified stride towards Olga. At his approach she opened her eyes and met his gaze. She stretched out one arm so her leather jacket was pulled halfway up her forearm skin of her wrist and forearm was visible, harsh pockmarks dotting the pale skin. Quintus laid his hands gently on her arms, his own fingers shaking, his first tender touch with a woman in a long time. Jackie came and put a fleshy arm around Olga's shoulders, whilst the others stood back, patient and paused.

Meanwhile the crickets jumped amongst the long grass and the squirrels scampered up trees stashing nuts in their nests. A lilting breeze danced around them and carried on out to the fields of rapeseed and wheat.

9

It was the seventh time Walter and Joe were to meet together. Joe arrived at the home and Ruth met him in the hallway, a mug of sweet tea in her hand.

'You're here to see Walter?'

Joe nodded.

'He's expecting you. He's out at the garage with Grant. He's happy for you to go out and meet him there.'

Joe looked hesitant.

'If I go and meet him there, Grant will probably know Walter's seeing a therapist. If he hasn't told Grant that, my going out to meet him there may breach his confidentiality.'

Ruth grinned.

'He already thought of that. He said it's fine. He reckoned Grant won't give two hoots whether he's seeing a therapist or not.'

Joe tried a smile and turned to go.

'Joe,' Ruth asked, 'you okay?'

'Yeah. Yeah. Why d'you ask?'

'Mm. You just seem a bit...sombre. A bit serious.'

'Well, I am a serious kind of person. Can't really help it.'

'Well I know. Serious is fine. But maybe serious becomes more than that. Maybe burdened is a better word. It's a very responsible job you folks do.'

Joe was unfamiliar with being pinned down like this.

'Well, I kinda see what you mean. I'll have a think about that.'

Ruth looked unconvinced but pushed no further. Joe went out the back and headed for the garage. It was built of red brick and had a grey tiled roof past its best. The front of the garage consisted of two broad oak doors, which were wedged wide open with flat bottomed rocks. Joe paused to look whilst he remained unnoticed.

The garage was lined on its back wall with high racks of shelves. On the shelves were pots of paint, paint trays, varnishes, motor oil, boxes of nails and screws, empty plant pots, packets of seeds, bottles of fertiliser, green netting, barbecue coals. On one wall tools hung neatly on hooks and nails. A rake, fork, spade, edging shears, hacksaw, panel saw, felling axe, splitting maul. All had their place, fitted horizontally or vertically into their niche. Another wall was clear except for a high wooden worktop fitted against the wall. In front of the worktop was a garden bench in progress, waiting only for the back and armrests. In the centre of the garage was a heavy, squat workbench. It was solid rough pine and looked like it had been salvaged from a school woodworking department. There were four royal blue metal vices, two on each long side. One vice held a long slim beam of red oak, with pieces of leather protecting the wood from the grip of the vice. Grant was bent over the vice, shaving the edges with a silver block plane, so that curled ringlets of shorn wood gathered on the floor.

Grant looked early twenties. He wore pale denim dungarees and a red checked shirt, the sleeves folded up to the elbows, showing taut and freckled forearms. His hair was long and held in a ponytail. He wore his sideburns long and furry. Grant moved smoothly left to right over and over, shaving layers of the wood, softening the edges of the beam. A lock of his hair hanging loose from the ponytail was the only inefficiency of motion. Grant's face was set to the task, his gaze fixed on the wood.

Just inside the garage on the right hand side, Walter sat on a tall three-legged wooden stool. He held a plastic cup in his hand, and Joe noticed on a small metal table a bright red flask of tea. Walter sipped his tea whilst he watched Grant work. He looked at home in this place and Joe wondered how often he came out here. Grant appeared engrossed in his work and unselfconscious of Walter's presence. He stopped his planing, stood straight, put down the plane on the bench, and rubbed his lower back with both hands. Walter looked around and noticed Joe.

'Ah, Joe Miller, the Aberdeen winger, hero of the European Cup Winners Cup final,' and he raised a hand in salute.

Grant turned around quickly, first confused then realised the quip.

'Have you two met?' asked Walter.

'No, not properly' said Joe. 'I'm Joe, the visiting therapist.'

'Pleased to meet you. I'm Grant, handyman, gardener, general dogsbody. I've seen you around occasionally.'

'That looks like a satisfying job' Joe said, nodding to the unfinished bench. 'I'm impressed.'

'So you should be,' said Walter. 'That's very patient work. He's a real craftsman is our Grant.'

Grant looked down, smiling and trying not to.

'And look at this. Have you ever seen a neater garage? I love the way everything has its place.'

'Yep. There's something very appealing about that,' answered Joe. 'I sometime wish my job could have that kind of order and neatness about it.' He regretted this suddenly, wondering if Walter might take it as a criticism of him and other clients.

'What I mean is, therapy's never complete. It's never neatly tied up at the end. People stay a bit tangled up, bits out of place, a work in progress.' Walter was surprised. He'd never heard Joe talk about his work in general terms, only in relation to Walter.

Joe hesitated, wondering how to steer the conversation towards going inside for the session.

'Grant very kindly lets me watch him work sometimes.'

'I don't mind. You know when to keep quiet and when to talk.'

'High praise indeed,' said Walter to Joe with a wink.

'Are you wanting to stay here a bit longer?' Joe asked Walter. 'I can always go and get a cuppa with Ruth.'

Walter looked at Grant, who was sweeping the wood shavings into a neat pile.

'Well, if you want to go and drink tea with the women-folk inside rather than be with the men and the carpentry outside …?'

Joe blushed and the taunt was illuminating.

'No, I would rather be out here, of course. I just don't want to impose on Grant.'

Grant rescued him.

'There's another stool in the back corner there. I get lost in the work anyway. After a while I'll forget you're even there.'

Joe said thanks and fetched the wooden stool from the corner. He placed it alongside Walter's, swept a little dust from it, and sat. Walter said nothing. Grant had a copper shovel and a hand brush with stiff bristles, and was gathering the shorn wood into the shovel, before heaping it into a black plastic bin beside the door. He replaced the brush and shovel in their appointed places. He turned the vice anticlockwise with one hand, holding the oak armrest in the other. The wood came loose and the leather rag settled in the vice. Grant turned the wood over, covered the sides with the leather, and began tightening the vice on the wood again. The smoothed edges of the wood were now on the underside. Grant took a short pencil from his shirt pocket. Starting two inches in from one end, he drew a slow curve along the wood, about six inches long. Bending over, on the opposite side, he drew an approximate mirror image of the curved line. He looked again at both sides, adjusted the pencil line on the near side so they were as closely matched as he could manage freehand. Walter and Joe sat side by side, watching closely.

Joe felt a slight shudder at the enormous mystery of the other. Each person a rag tag bag of half-told stories and snippets of memory and longings and fantasies and simmering fears and secret ambitions and the deluge of the senses and the silent stillness of the deep self. And each self balanced upon the rope in the tug of war between being known and being private and the tug of war between wanting normality and wanting specialness and the tug of war between freshness and familiarity. In the small corner of himself that was wise he gave thanks for all of this, and for the chance to study it like an amoeba and tend to it like a garden.

Grant took a mallet hammer and a one-inch chisel from their hanging places on the tooled wall. Where the curved line met the edge of the wood, Grant placed the chisel edge. He looked from the side, checking the angle at which the chisel would penetrate the wood. With the chisel in his right hand and the mallet in his left, he began thudding the handle of the chisel. He held tight to the chisel, channelling the force along the pencilled line. The chisel burrowed no deeper than a quarter inch into the flesh of the wood as it inched its way along the length of the arm. When the chisel reached the apex of the curve, Grant removed it. He moved the chisel to the opposite end of the curve and began again there. In a minute, the two cuts met in the middle and with the last cut, the sliver of wood detached and fell to the floor. Grant returned to the first end, placed the chisel, and started the second cut.

From the corner of his eye, Joe looked at Walter. He was very still, his eyes following Grant's movements, and his breathing seemed slow and quiet. Joe looked back to Grant's work. He felt the passing of time. There came to his mind the thought that he should get on with his session with Walter - that he should not be wasting his time out here. But the thought sat there whilst Joe did nothing with it and he let the time pass like a slow river.

Grant shaved off five layers of wood with the chisel. He stopped and inspected the roughly cut curve. He replaced the chisel and the mallet in their places. He lifted an electric sander from one of the back shelves and plugged it in. The sander erupted into buzzing life. Grant held the vibrating machine against the developing curve. The shrill whine of the sander deepened a few tones as sawdust began spurting into the air around him, enveloping him in a golden cloud, and the sawdust sank slowly, coating the floor and the shoes and trouser legs of the watching men. The sound became a droning. The rising and billowing and falling of specks of wood took on a mesmeric quality and the two spectators watched in a quiet reverie. And the minutes passed by. And then, it seemed, the therapy session was over.

10

It was late on a Sunday night and all was quiet on Joe's street, save for the occasional band of teenagers teasing and impressing each other. Joe was caught up in reading James Baldwin, and didn't feel like sleeping yet. There was a sliver of pale ale left in his glass and an empty packet of dry roasted nuts on the floor. He sat in his one armchair which faced the bay window. A floor lamp cast enough light to read by. As his eyes began to ache behind his glasses, he admitted defeat and put down the book. He downed the last of the Belhaven, stood and stretched. He had forgotten to draw the curtains and anyway he liked the warm orange glow of the street lights coming in through his window.

As he pulled the curtains together, he saw a man and a woman across the road, walking towards the abandoned church at the corner. She was striding away from him, legs moving quickly, handbag clenched under her arm, shoulders hunched, and her high heels echoing loudly. He grabbed her hand and she pulled it angrily from his grasp. Joe could not make out the words but the tone was angry. The man ran ahead of her, and stood with his arms apart, a wide grin on his face, then grabbed her around the waist as she tried to go past him. In the street light it was hard to see but in the confusion of bodies it looked like she slapped him. At this he seemed to give up and stood still with his hands on his hips as she walked away. She walked a few yards then turned right into the grounds of the church for a shortcut through the corner. Joe grimaced a little at her choosing to go through there alone in the dark, though it looked like the drama was over.

Joe was about to turn away from the window when movement caught his eye. The spurned man had burst into a run towards where the woman had gone, and he ran through the same gate into the church grounds she had just disappeared through. Joe felt a surge of fear and anger. He feared making a fool of himself by over-reacting but his decision was already made as he grabbed his keys from the hall table and ran out the door, down the three flights of stairs, and out of the tenement. He ran diagonally across the road and got to the church a few seconds later. He stopped on the path just inside the gate. It was so dark in there, his eyes had to adjust to pick out the path and the shapes of the shrubs and trees. He could not hear anything at first. Then, a low, threatening sound, and a muffled attempt at sound. Joe looked around his feet, and picked up one of the grey rocks there to mark the path from the shrubbery, confused about what he might actually use it for.

For a few seconds, he was struck dumb. What do you say in a situation like this?

'Hello?' he eventually shouted. 'Is anyone there?'

The tiny muffled sounds again.

Joe was afraid, and ashamed of his fear.

'Do you need any help?' he shouted, realising it was a ridiculous question if his reading of the situation was right.

Joe moved further along the path and his footsteps crunched on the gravel.

'Hello?' Joe began to wonder if he'd got it wrong, and was wandering around dark church grounds with a rock in his hand for nothing. He stepped off the path into the high thick shrubs. He pushed through damp leaves and branches, and a bramble stem jagged his neck.

'Hello?' he said, trying to sound bolder than he felt. Then there was a spurt of noise from ahead - 'Bastard!' screamed the woman's voice with pent up fury. Something tore through the bushes, stamping and shoving violently. Suddenly the man was thudding past Joe just a yard away, out of nowhere. Joe grabbed at him, a clumsy reflex, catching hold of denim, spinning round, trying to grab the shoulder with his other hand. The fabric was yanked from his grasp, and the shoulder slipped from under his right hand. The man slammed into a tree trunk, staggered right, and thrashed through a rhododendron. Joe ran after him, and found himself rugby-tackling the man's waist and thighs. They both fell to the ground, the stranger flailing his legs wildly, Joe trying to get up on top of him. In his fright he had dropped the rock, and now he punched the back of the man's head. The man jerked over suddenly, pushing Joe sideways onto his hands, his hand twisting on the exposed roots of a tree. The man scrambled to his feet and this time got through the undergrowth before Joe could recover. Cradling his hand with the other hand, Joe got to his feet and squeezed through the tangled bushes. He could hear the man running on the gravel path. He momentarily thought about chasing him again, but now he remembered the woman.

Joe turned back through the bushes. His breath was coming in quick pants and only now did he notice his heart thudding.

'Where are you?' he asked gently into the darkness. Quickly he had to think about how this woman might be, and about what to do next for her.

'Over here.' Her voice was shaky but hard.

'Okay,' said Joe, feeling his way towards her voice. 'He's gone, by the way, it's just me. You're safe.'

A light appeared in the dark. The woman was sitting on a low bough of a tree, holding up her lit cigarette lighter.

'Thanks' said Joe. He stood some feet away, not knowing how near to approach her.

'I'm Joe. Joe Miller. I live across the street.'

The woman was silent, but Joe could hear her breath coming in quick gulps.

'I'm sorry I couldn't stop him from getting away. He ran away. He's gone. I don't think he'll come back now.'

Now the woman used the lighter for a cigarette, inhaled heavily, then put away the lighter, and only the red rim of the cigarette pierced the grey darkness. Her breathing began to calm as she sucked the smoke deep into her body. Joe stood still, not sure whether to look at her, to speak further, to take a lead. A car passed on Nithsdale Road, the noisy exhaust ripping open the silence then fading into distance. Joe looked at the woman and saw she was not looking at him but staring into space. He could see more now despite the dark and he scanned her quickly for any visible damage. She looked ruffled and her face was blotchy, but her clothes were where they should be. She held her left arm tight across her belly and her right hand rested on the shelf of the left arm, keeping the cigarette close to her lips.

Joe felt deeply uncomfortable being in this hidden place, a man with a woman who'd just been attacked by a man. He did not want them to remain there much longer. He felt he shouldn't push her to decide what to do, but needed to. He tried to speak slowly and gently.

'Listen, I don't know what you want to do next. I'm not trying to push you to come out of here before you're ready. But I live just across the road. If you want to come over to my flat, or wait outside if that's more comfortable,' he added quickly, 'I can call the police from there. Or an ambulance. There's a middle aged lady in the flat below mine. I'm sure she'd be more than willing to sit with you until someone comes. I guess I'm just thinking that you might not particularly want to be around a man just now.'

Joe knew he was rambling but they were things he had to say.

'We're not calling the police,' she finally spoke. Her voice was sweet, almost patronising. 'We're not calling the police and I don't need an ambulance. Thanks for your help but you can go now. I'm fine.'

Joe pulled back his head and shoulders in a jolt. He did not speak for a minute.

'Have I misinterpreted what just happened? I assumed he was...' Joe searched for the words, 'trying to assault you. And hurting you. Was that not the case?'

The woman sighed. 'No, you didn't misinterpret it. That wasn't some kinky fantasy we cooked up.' She left him hanging again.

'But he needs to be punished for this, surely.' Joe did not hide his incredulity. 'Do you know who he is? It looked like you knew each other.'

She waited another two inhalations from the fag.

'Yes I know who he is. Not well, but I know who he is.'

Joe's mind was fighting to understand.

'Okay. I understand that some women don't necessarily want or feel ready to report this kind of thing. But you know who he is. And I'm a witness. I'll gladly tell the police exactly what I saw. Whoever he is, he won't get away with that.'

She was silent again. Joe watched her narrow eyes. She finished her cigarette and dropped the stump into the ground.

'He will get away with it,' she said now. 'He will get away with it because they always do. The police wouldn't take it that seriously. I mean look at me, he didn't even manage to get any of my clothes off before you came along. I'm a bit drunk, it's a dark path – a stupid place for a woman to go herself. And I'll have no proof, just my word. The woman's word against the man's is never good enough in court.'

'But I said I would be a witness. I'll happily stand up in court for this. Surely that'll count for something?'

'You won't, though, will you? You're sayin that now. But when push comes to shove, you're a man. And the men stick together,' and for the first time she looked at him properly.

Joe felt like a cannon ball had hit him in the guts. He couldn't look at her then. He shuddered at her veiled anger, her dismissal of what he was and what he had done for her. He couldn't yet think outside of his own pity and his thirst for justice for this woman. She was clearly hurting and shocked, and needed to put it down to the nature of all men, rather than one bad man. It pained him that this pathetic embarrassment to his gender might get away with this, and perhaps do the same again. It pained him that he was being lumped in with this kind of guy, his individual conscience and values ignored. It pained him that she was barely grateful to him for rescuing her. For the first time he noticed the pulsing throb of pain in his wrist.

Whilst Joe was still mired in thoughts, she got up and began walking through the shrubs towards the street she had been taking the short cut to.

'Wait! At least let me call a taxi for you.'

She stopped and half turned.

'Alright. I'm gubbed anyway,' she relented.

'Alright,' Joe said. 'I'll go up to the flat. Would you at least wait on the other side of the street, so I can see you until the taxi comes? I want to see that you're safe until then. After that, you can do what you want.'

'Alright.'

They both walked back to the Shields Road side, and without any further words, Joe crossed the road and headed for his flat.

After calling the taxi, he went into the living room and turned off the lights. He stood back from the window so that he could see her but where she could not easily see him. He felt under her judgement. She sat on a garden wall, and looked up only once towards Joe's window in the ten minutes it took for the taxi to arrive. She got in and the taxi drove away and the street was again quiet.

In the dark room, Joe stood a little longer, staring at the wall where the woman had sat. He wondered where she was going, would she tell someone what had happened? Would she drink herself to sleep? Would she change her mind about him later on? He saw that he would never know. There was anger in him, but nowhere to put it, and sadness which made his whole body feel gravity's pull. It pulled him towards the bedroom, and he sank heavily into the bed. The street remained quiet and Joe slept weighed down.

11

The next morning Joe was awake in bed at 8am. His body could have slept longer but his mind was awake with the strange drama of the previous night. The sick shock of being mistrusted had faded a little but the sadness underneath it was pervasive and Joe had spent his dreams chasing and being chased by faceless dangers amongst bush mazes and thickets of thorny forests.

There was a quiet double knock at the door. Joe had not heard the intercom buzz or the close door slam. A neighbour perhaps. Or someone had foolishly let in the Hare Krishnas again. He tiptoed across the hall, stood at his door and peered through the spy hole. The landing was empty. Then he heard a meow. Joe opened the door a few inches and looked out. The landing was indeed empty except for Mr Scruffles, the plump bellied cat belonging to the Selby's who lived across the hall.

Mr Scruffles was docile and patient because he had to be. Mrs Selby should have been spending her retirement writing puppet shows or dressing dolls for a shop window. Instead of doing those things to discharge her creativity, she doted and experimented in equal measure on Mr Scruffles. In return for his obeisance, he feasted on the best of cat food three times a day, along with regular helpings of fresh salmon, coconut oil and full fat milk.

Mrs Selby lived in a tenement flat so she could not really lay claim to pretensions of grandeur. Instead she projected these onto Mr Scruffles, defending whilst bemoaning his preference for all things luxurious. Joe had gone into their flat one time to fix a leak under their sink. In the cupboard under the sink he found eleven milk bottles filled with sand. When he politely enquired about the sand, Mrs Selby told him that Mr Scruffles would only, could only 'have a private moment' in genuine beach sand. Therefore each time the Selby's visited the beach at Troon or Largs, they returned with their bags weighed down and their Wiseman's bottles filled with the west coast's finest.

Today, Mr Scruffles was standing on his doorstep wearing a red bow tie and lilac ear muffs around his head. Joe bent down to take a closer look. There were drips of cream on Mr Scruffles whiskers, evidence presumably of the bribe he'd innocently accepted before this latest humiliation. Tied to his collar was a red polka dot ribbon which trailed behind him to a Lurpak tub. Joe pulled on the ribbon and the tub slid noisily towards him across the concrete landing. He heard a muffled high-pitched snigger, and saw that the Selby's door was slightly ajar and wobbling. Playing along, Joe took the lid off the butter tub and found six glistening flapjacks with a note saying, 'With cordial good wishes, from Mr Scruffles.'

He chuckled despite himself, untied the tub from the ribbon and took it into his flat. He emerged a few seconds later wearing a flannel blue dressing gown. He carried the empty tub in one hand and lifted Mr Scruffles' ribbon leash with the other to lead him back to Mrs Selby's. Mr Scruffles rubbed his body against Joe's ankle and followed beside him. Joe knocked gently on the Selby's door. He heard footsteps which started close, moved away, and then came back again to the door. Mrs Selby opened the door and tried desperately to keep a straight face.

'Thanks very much for the flapjacks, Mrs Selby. I'm impressed by how well you've trained Mr Scruffles.' She grinned and gazed fondly at Mr Scruffles as she spoke, her fulsome cheeks bulging and her eyes crinkling.

'Oh yes, he's the cleverest cat in all of Pollokshields. At least!' Her voice sang.

'At least,' Joe said.

'Who's that, Maggie?' came the voice of Mr Selby as he came into their hallway. Mrs Selby stepped back so he could see Mr Scruffles in his regalia.

'Och Maggie, in the name of Keith Harris and Orville, what

have you done to that poor cat now?' She looked at him with wide eyes and a bashful smile, knowing she could melt his exasperation.

'The poor wee guy must think he's living in cabaret,' Mr Selby said, but his tone was kindly. He lifted Mr Scruffles and held him against his chest, examining his face for any signs of embarrassment. 'Hello Joe, what can we do for you this fine misty morning?'

Joe did not want to embarrass Mrs Selby further by mentioning the businesss of the flapjacks in a tub brought by Mr Scruffles to his door, so he quickly changed tack.

'Um, well, I just hoped that the noise last night didn't disturb you too much.'

Mr Selby answered for them both.

'I don't think we heard any noise, did we Maggie? We take our hearing aids out at night. We'd sleep through the Blitz these days. What was the noise about?'

'Ach, nothing much. Nothing important.' Joe was relieved. 'Just a couple having a bit of a barney out in the street.'

Mrs Selby's face had furrowed. 'I just don't understand why people have to shout at one another. I think they must enjoy it, secretly.'

'I think you've got something there' Joe replied. 'Anyway, don't worry about it. I better go and get dressed.' He turned towards his own flat. 'I'm popping down to the shops. Do you need anything when I'm there?'

'No thank you, Joe, but thank you for asking,' Mrs Selby said. 'You're a good boy.'

A few hours later, Joe and Walter were back in their familiar chairs. Walter had entered the room with a Tesco plastic bag. Before Joe could begin speaking, Walter started.

'I hope you don't mind but I thought today I might bring some of these bits and pieces to talk about.'

'Sure,' said Joe. He often encouraged clients to plan for the session and set the direction, but they rarely do so. He was pleased that Walter had. He wondered about the timing of the bringing but that could wait.

'So, what have you brought?'

'Ach, just some photos, mementoes, stuff to help with the old memory, you know.' Joe reckoned there wasn't much wrong with the old man's memory - it seemed sparky and vibrant.

Walter laid it all out on the small coffee table between them. There was a pile of photos, mainly black and white, a large wedding photo in a frame of white card with a decorative trim. A report card from secondary school, written in beautiful spidery ink. A pair of silver cuff links with pearl tops.

'Ah, now, I think you might be especially interested in this.'

Walter reached into the poly bag and pulled out the last item. It was a stone, about the size of a fist. It was wrapped around with a cord of some kind of welded metal, like a ribbon around a gift. Walter gazed at it for a few seconds. He lifted it to his ear, looked quizzically at Joe, then shook it. Something inside rattled, and Walter raised his eyebrows. Joe was suitably intrigued as Walter handed him the stone. Joe took it in both hands and began to examine it. He saw now that the stone was cracked roughly into two halves, which were held together by the welded metal. The ends of the lengths of metal were soldered together where they joined on each side of the rock. The metal looked aged, and the rock was a little orange where the rusted metal had rubbed against the stone.

'What's inside it?' Joe asked.

'I don't know,' Walter replied.

Joe tried to peer between the two halves of the stone but it was bound so well that he couldn't prise them apart at all. He shook it. He thought the rattling object could be something metallic but it was hard to tell. The stone itself was rough and ordinary, dirty grey and inelegant.

'What's this about? Where did this come from?'

'Joe, I've had it for nearly fifty years now and I still don't know the answer to either of those questions.' They were both leaning forward now, looking at the stone as Joe passed it respectfully back to Walter.

'Well, come on, put me out of my misery. At least tell me how you came by it, or why you've brought it today.'

Walter pulled a slip of paper out of the bag and gave it to Joe.

'I found it on my windowsill one day when I was about fourteen, with this note attached to it.'

Joe looked at the note. The paper may have been white fifty years ago but it was yellowy-grey now and creased with fold-marks. It felt like a stray breeze could rip it in two. The ink was faded almost to nothing but Joe could still make out the short message in simple spidery handwriting - *This belonged to your dad when he died. Thought you should have it*.

'You found this on your windowsill?'

'Yep.'

'When you were fourteen?'

'Yep.'

'Was your window open or closed?'

'Open.'

'And you don't know who put it there?'

'Nope.'

'And you don't know whose writing this is?'

'Nope.'

Joe put the note on the table. Walter placed the stone beside it.

'Do you have any idea who might have left it there for you?'

Only now did Walter pause before answering. He stared over Joe's shoulder out the sash window to the grey sky beyond. He rubbed his hand up and down his bad knee.

'I guess maybe someone who knew my dad. A family member, a miner, who knows.'

'But why leave it there anonymously?'

'I've asked myself the same question a thousand times.'

'Okay, maybe a question you can answer – why have you brought it here today?'

'This is the only physical thing that connects to my dad. If it actually was his.'

'Do you have doubts about that?'

'It would be a pretty strange hoax, don't you think? A lot of trouble to go to.'

Joe did not convey yea or nay.

'Did you ever ask anyone about it? To try and find out more?'

'No.' Walter stirred restlessly. 'You'll probably find this really strange but no, I never mentioned it to anyone. I knew with my mum not to go there. She was getting over my dad's death in her own way. I didn't want to risk upsetting her. And, as I said before, we didn't really see my dad's family after we moved away from Mavis Valley. So it felt like it was destined to remain a mystery.'

Joe took this in, took a few slow breaths.

'Someone thought this was significant enough to give to you. Fourteen years after your dad died.' Joe was just beginning to recognise the many questions the stone evoked, whilst Walter had lived with them most of his life. He waited patiently while Joe began to catch up.

'Aren't you curious about what's inside?'

'I really didn't know what to think. Whoever it was obviously knew where I lived, which was a bit disturbing. I was really curious at first. I had so little to remember him by. So even this strange ugly thing was loaded with significance. I wondered at first whether my dad had placed some message for me inside. He worked in the mines, with stone and metal and machinery. So I guess he could have created something like this. But then, he didn't know he was going to die. Or maybe my dad got it from somewhere else and kept it. Maybe the mystery man assumed it was significant but maybe it wasn't. My dad could have found it randomly for all I know. Or been given it by someone else for some reason.'

'Did you think anyone else might have known what its significance was? Your mum perhaps?'

'I thought about that long and hard. She might have known. She might not. Either way it would have brought up something she didn't want to talk about. Something had gone wrong between her and my dad. I never got to the bottom of it. It was only hints and awkward silences. But something had soured their relationship. Something to do with the families perhaps, I don't know. Some things you don't ask about, you know?'

Joe thought that yes, he did know, and nodded.

'Time just passed. I lived with those questions, turned them over in my mind, laid them out sometimes like a papyrus then rolled them back up again to go back in a dusty cupboard.'

Joe thought before speaking.

'But Walter it seems a bit strange to me. I think of how important your dad's absence has been throughout your life, and here you had possibly an opportunity to find out something about him, to open up a new branch of the story. I'm really curious about why you haven't cracked it open to see what's inside, or looked for someone in your dad's family to ask them about it, about him.'

'Well, I'm not sure I considered my dad's absence to be so important until you emphasised it. Plus it was different times then, Joe. I think it would have been considered disrespectful if I'd looked up my dad's family without my mother's blessing. I know it's the nature of your job for people to crack everything open and rummage around inside but the outside world isn't always like that, especially back then. People kept a lot in. Or kept it in the family.'

'I know. You're right. I'm forgetting that the world is not the therapy room. Maybe I need to get out more. What about now, then, how do you feel about not knowing what the stone's about?'

'I think I've just gotten used to it.'

'Do you have any fear about what you might find it you opened it up?'

Walter pursed his lips.

'I guess that, just now, I can imagine what might be in there. I can speculate. But what if I open it and I'm none the wiser? What if there's nothing but a broken screw in there? What if I find out that actually it was of no real significance to my dad? Then the possibilities will be dead. That would be so disappointing. At least just now I can imagine. I can wonder. I can sort of appreciate the mystery. I don't want to kill the mystery.'

'Well, did you ever come close to cracking it open?'

'I knew you were going to ask that. Do you know the answer already?'

'Based on your last answer, yes.'

'I did go through a period when the curiosity was unbearable. I had joined the army in 1939, national service you understand. Me and half the human race it seemed like. All under the command of a bunch of madmen. Anyway, my battalion arrived home in March 1945. Sailed into Prince's Dock on the Clyde, all of us in our starched uniforms, crammed onto the deck of the boat like we were readying for a mass tap dance, peering around the crowd to find our people. As we disembarked, the flood of men spilled through the waiting crowd, children being hoisted, wives and girlfriends being kissed, mothers with tears of gratitude. And dads. Dads clapping sons on their backs, dads giving strong handshakes, dads gazing with pride at their sons. And these fully grown men who had hiked through foreign forests and fields and towns and cities with great hulking packs, slept in barns, built bridges, crouched in sodden trenches whilst body parts and shrapnel and smoke surrounded them like a hug from the reaper, here were these men revelling in the pride of their fathers - 'you done good son' - boys wanting and getting their fathers' approval, revelling in it, men still rejuvenated by a nod and a wink from their dads. That hit me somewhere down here. Ach, my mum was there, and my sisters, and that was lovely. I appreciated them so much. But right then, I would have liked a dad. Just that one time. If he could've been lifted and resurrected for that fine March afternoon. Just once. That would have hit the mark alright.'

Outside a troupe of chaffinches were singing shrilly in the chestnut tree that grew close to the house. Their excitable chirruping punctured the silence in the room. Walter was tapping his forefingers against his thumb in a 6/8 rhythm.

'So that was an emotional time. For everyone. The stuff that doesn't matter, well it really didn't matter then. For a wee while we had our priorities just right. And for me, at that time especially, I wanted to know what my dad had been like. All these men around me, they'd been willing to die in that stupid war. Willing to take the hit for the sake of others. At that time especially, I desperately wanted to know if my dad had some gumption, some guts, hoping he hadn't given up on a pregnant young girl.'

'And that he hadn't given up on you,' Joe added.

'Yep, and that too, I guess.'

'So, what did you do?'

'Och, ultimately, nothing. Like always. I took the stone to a blacksmith in the village. Felt like a right eejit. I asked him if he could crack it open. I told him I'd found it in a river and I was curious about what was in it. I asked him if he'd ever seen anything like it but he hadn't. He took out these dirty huge bolt-cutters, looked like they'd cut through your leg in one go. He was all ready to go, had the stone locked in the vice, and he looked strong enough to do the deed, a thick bloody steak of a man. But before he did I looked around at this dark shed with chains and strips of leather hanging from the walls, oil spilled on the floor, brutal looking tools and the lit oven, and I can't explain it but all of a sudden I didn't want the stone cracked open in this alien and dirty place, with a stranger who didn't really care what was inside it or why it had been crafted into this enigma in the first place, and whatever tumbled out of the stone, if it got me emotional or confused, or it disappointed me, I'd be standin there with this guy wondering what I'm all about, and...'

Walter seemed to run out of steam as his warm embarrassment

was reignited.

'I changed my mind. Couldn't go through with it. It felt wrong somehow. Like burying a beloved dog in a peat bog. I told him I'd changed my mind. He looked at me like I was soft in the head as I fumbled the stone out of the vice and disappeared.'

Walter's head was low and shaking slowly, the shame heavy on his old shoulders. Joe wanted to lift him somehow from his acrid pit.

'I have to admit to feeling disappointed, on your behalf perhaps. But it does sound like you learned something important there. About your true feelings about the mystery. That the stone deserved greater dignity, respect, as did your feelings about it and about your dad.'

'But is that not a bit stupid, the way I avoided the tough decision? It's like a metaphor for the way I don't quite take the final step when it comes to big decisions.'

'What else do you have in mind when you say that?'

Walter rubbed at his bad leg, which was becoming a giveaway gesture of discomfort that was more than physical.

'Aye, well, … I don't know. Naw that's garbage - I do know. There I go, trying to avoid it again. Well, like the girlfriend I told you about before. Leaving her when it got serious, worried the men in my family just don't have what it takes to commit. Or when I got sent to Spain to repair the Lady Delilah.'

Walter must have clocked Joe's blank look.

'She was a clipper, built on the Clyde in 1875. She'd been all round the world, passed from the British Navy to the Americans and then to the Spanish who'd used her as a training vessel. Some of us working in John Brown's were asked to travel over to Arsenal de la Carraca, in San Fernando, to repair her in preparation for bringing her back to the UK. It was a fantastic adventure. Six young guys who'd never left Scotland getting whisked over to the most exotic place we'd ever been. We were there for three weeks, repairing big gashes in the hull, replacing crank shafts and pistons in the engines, re-hoisting the masts. There were local tradesmen as well but the guy who'd bought it was a Scot and he insisted on bringing over genuine Clyde shipbuilders to restore this wreck he'd bought from the Spanish navy. In fact, I'm sure there's a photo in amongst this lot.'

Walter picked up the pile of photos and shuffled through them.

'Aye, here we are.'

He handed Joe a small black and white photo. Six pasty white men in grey trousers and white vests stood against a promenade railing, smiling broadly, the pale sea behind them stretching out forever.

'Is this you on the end?' Joe asked, thinking he recognised Walter's round temples and flat nose.

'Aye, that's me. The cat that got the cream. Anyway, we got the basic repairs done and the Lady Delilah was ready to sail back to the Clyde for the final re-fit. The owner, Sir Richard Melrose, he was this larger than life character. Plenty of money - just don't ask where he got it. He had schemes and plans coming out of his ears. So, a couple of days before we finish he takes me and Georgie Mackintosh aside and says he wants to race the Transatlantic Race a month later, then maybe some others – the Transpac, the Newport Bermuda, the Fastnet. He's got a yacht, top of the range, and a pilot. He asked us if we'd join his team, all expenses paid, great wages, for the next 6 months at least, maybe longer.

'You have to understand, I was just a young guy from Auchinairn. Before that trip I'd never been further than Millport. Going to Spain was like falling off the side of the earth. And then here was this wacky raconteur offering to take me on boat races all round the world. And I knew a bit about hulking great ships – I didn't know hee-haw about racing yachts. George, he was in the same boat, if you'll pardon the pun, but he jumped at the chance, told himself a boat's a boat, he'll figure it out. Sent a telegram to the gaffer at the yard to quit his job. But me? I hesitated. I asked for a couple of days to think about it. That night I wandered around the Bay of Cádiz, thinking, homesick, paralysed by this ridiculous offer, remembering my safe life and job back in Glasgow. From Cádiz you could look out over the endless Atlantic, nothing but the blue water merging into blue sky. I wandered into this lovely old cathedral. The priest was there, pottering about the sanctuary. He tried to talk to me in Spanish, which didn't get very far. His smile and his big Mediterranean gestures said more than enough to both welcome me and unsettle me. But he managed to show me where you could climb up the bell tower, and he stood at the bottom and beckoned me to go up. Man, the view from the top of that. This dry red coast stretching around to the Strait of Gibraltar. And then, I realised, I could see Algiers – Africa, by God! Within touching distance! I'd never seen anything like that view, and all of a sudden I was detached from this wee life and its roots. I was a stranger there, no-one in the whole world knew where I was at that moment, I was just a man, floating above the earth. And here I was, on the edge of one continent, peering into another, and everything was different, the feel of the air on your skin, the smells of the plants and the dry earth, the foreign words and the foreign ways. And the great mystery of the ocean. Imagine the first men to cross that. Imagine leaving dry dependable land behind, no way of knowing what you'd find, if anything - if you'd live or if you'd die. The Atlantic had this ghostly magnetism, daring you to cast your life and your wits upon it, or against it! It was beautiful and terrifying. And there was me with this choice. The safety of dry land or the risk of the ocean.'

Though Joe knew Walter's decision, he still found himself wishing he'd taken the adventurous choice, wishing Walter could tell him the further stories, no doubt colourful, of the boat races with Melrose, of near misses with death and delight.

'But I said no, and that was that. Made my choice. Took the sensible option. I was already half-way there but I turned back.'

Walter's face, for the first time in Joe's experience, looked grey and old. His eyes were angry as he glared out the window, picturing perhaps the blue sky over the Bay of Cádiz, trying in vain to recapture the pregnant potential of that moment. And though he did not want to admit it to himself, Joe was frustrated with Walter, frustrated that he hadn't taken his chances, frustrated that fear had held him back, frustrated that he had not investigated the stone or cracked it open, frustrated at Walter's timidity, frustrated at any man's timidity.

A minute passed by in unproductive silence, and then another. Eventually Joe's exasperation leaked out.

'Walter, why did you not just break open the stone as soon as you got it? Or ask around? Why so avoidant? My goodness, I'm more curious about it than you are.' They sighed in unison, an uneasy truce of disappointment. The clock ticked on and the warm sun streamed through the window, illuminating the specks of dust that hung in mid air.

'Don't be like me, Joe,' said Walter eventually. 'Don't stand in the shadows of the platform watching the train pull away without you on it. It did me no good. Same time next Tuesday?'

'Sure. Sure.' It was all still percolating in Joe's thoughts, and he was stilted. 'Sorry Walter. Sorry for getting impatient with you.'

'Ach it's not surprising. It's how I'd feel if I was in your chair.' He put the stone and the photos back in the bag, rose slowly and left the room, leaning heavily on his walking stick as he went.

12

In Meg Miller's simple, pretty semi at the old end of Cambuslang there was a long narrow attic space where headroom was limited by the long jutting rafters where many a head had bounced in pain when haste and forgetfulness met. In one of the dark dusty corners beneath the eaves there sat a haphazard pile of shoe boxes with frayed corners and sagging bulges, half covered with a UCS flag - 'Upper Clyde Shipbuilders – Unity Creates Strength – Forward Together!.'In the grey-white box second from the bottom (which had once contained Alastair's Umbro running shoes before he wore them to death on the tarmac of Bellahouston Park) there were letters (many from the cousins in Canada), birthday cards (sixteen, twenty-one, thirty, forty and the rest), faded grey telegrams, school reports for Alastair and his sister Elizabeth, a dull football medal, and a fridge magnet from Dunoon Pier. One of the letters in the box had lain there undisturbed for many years. It had been written by Alastair's mother, Margaret ('Meg' to everyone but the government) on a wet night in August 1968. The envelope was ordinary enough, six by four, white, a little smudging on the ink of the address, the saliva-powered adhesive still gripping on the stamp despite the years, but no post office date stamp.

In the spare bedroom below, Ingrid surveyed the contents of a wide and wild built in wardrobe, facing, in a way her mother in law never did, the perennial need to throw away. The hanging rail sagged precariously with thick wool overcoats, silk dresses, assorted dressing gowns, an ivory wedding dress, Charlie's old kilt outfit and his funeral suit. On the floor, if there even was a floor, were boxes of shoes, bags with blue overalls and green gardening cords, stacks of Good Housekeeping and Sunday Heralds and Knitting Weekly, a chair with one leg missing, a dusty tartan suitcase, an ironing board with a bent leg. Ingrid tried on a couple of wool winter coats, settling on the burgundy of the two, which a lint roller would freshen up nicely.

In the kitchen downstairs, Isobel was sorting through the ancient crockery for anything salvageable. The Denby had a few chips and cracks but wasn't bad for fifty years of Sunday use and the occasional mid-week visit from the vicar. Isobel mentally ticked it off for herself. She also had her eye on granny's cookbooks, written by wide-busted 1950's women in aprons and stocked with plenty of classic recipes and domestic agony-aunt wisdom.

Joe was in the garage, which had lain pretty unchanged since his grandpa Charlie had died in 1968. Only the space around the lawnmower looked stepped in – everything else was covered in a fine layer of moistening dust. Joe did not have a garden to tend, and his parents and Isobel had what they needed, so Joe hoped most of this could go straight to the dump. He rummaged amongst it though, as all humans are wont to do, scavenging for useable scraps. There were car parts, bottles of engine oil and antifreeze, a Raleigh bicycle with the chain hanging limply off the gear cogs and the air long since leached from the tyres, a red metal toolbox that looked like it weighed a ton. Joe noticed on a high shelf a handsome looking wooden case with two brass fasteners. He took it down gingerly, wary of what might be on top of it. Laying it flat on an ancient chest freezer, Joe opened the case to reveal a fine set of wood-carving tools. They looked barely used and the steel blades felt smooth and sharp, the bases of the oak handles barely dented by a mallet head. Joe thought of Grant, how he might caress and yield them like the brushes of an artist. Something in them glinted for Joe, and he set the case aside for himself.

In the attic, Alastair was sat amongst the detritus of his parents' life. They had divvied up the rooms, and under some duress Alastair had been assigned the attic. He did not know why he dreaded clearing the house, or the attic especially. He had begun well. The empty suitcases, the broken lampshades, the spare bedding, the bedside tables that never made it to the charity shop, all of these he took without fanfare to the van he'd borrowed from a pal, and he would cast them to the dump with no emotional wrench. Soon he began to falter as the objects took on greater emotional friction, rubbing away the years, seizing him back to tender times - football trophies, photo albums, a school blazer, the dart board that had hung on the back of his bedroom door, leaving a perfect circle of tiny holes in the gloss white when it was removed. He sat transfixed by the LP's of his teenage years - Bing Crosby, The Andrews Sisters, The Ink Spots. Just enough light fell through the cobwebbed skylight to read the first few pages of Moby Dick and Huckleberry Finn. Nostalgia was creeping over him like a seductive fog. He carefully laid these things in the undecided pile.

The stack of boxes under the eaves was next. Alastair looked through a few, but there was little in them to snag his curiosity. He opened the Umbro box and saw that here was the personal and maybe poetic. The birthday cards were just words and pictures. The school reports sounded quaint and understated, belying the brutality of the teachers that wrote them. *Alastair has maths ability, but requires some encouragement to stick to a task. Alastair responds well to discipline when it is required, which is all too often.* He found a postcard sent by his sister soon after she arrived in Canada, intoxicated with the new country, breathing the sweet air of novelty and discovery. She had been there so long it felt like another life when she'd been here in this house. Alastair thumbed half-heartedly through the letters. His mother's inky cursive caught his eye, looping elegantly through the name and address of his mother in law. He turned it over and saw that the envelope was sealed. This struck him as strange and he paused. Perhaps private should be private, even in death. But no-one would know. And if he chose to bin it now, he might be doing someone a disservice. Ingrid might want to keep some of the sentimental garbage. Leave the analysing to Joe, he decided, and opened the envelope.

Dear Mari,

Thank you so much for your letter. I received it a few days ago. It popped through the letterbox and broke the silence that feels so strange now that Charlie has gone. I appreciated a great deal that you came down for the funeral. Such a long trek from Kirkwall! Your kindness has always meant so much to me. You've been in the widows club for much longer – I am just starting to get used to it.

Your letter gives me permission to say that part of me is relieved that Charlie is gone! For his sake, yes, with the illness over and the aching body now at peace. But also for myself. As you know better than most, his harshness was made worse by the illness but it was there for a long time before that. I couldn't do anything without thinking about how I would justify it to him if he questioned me. Everything I spent on groceries, every night out with the girls, where I was going, why? when? the endless questions! Made me doubt my motives and my wits all the time. I was so glad that he didn't subject Alastair and Elizabeth to that. But I was jealous too, I must confess. Even as children he seemed to trust and respect them more than he did me. I was so glad they grew up able to stand up to people if they had to. I never mastered that skill. Though I worry that Alastair can be too tough and rusty with your Ingrid. And with young Joe. Isobel has the measure of him though!

I wonder, did you ever talk to Ingrid about how her dad was towards you? I was always torn about that. Now that Charlie's gone, I suppose there's no point telling Alastair and Fiona. What good would it do? Maybe they know a bit, but not the full extent of the quiet terror I felt for so long. And not the way I kept secrets from him, just for a quieter life. Some of the youngsters get

107

divorced for less these days. But you know what it's like for our generation. If your man isn't knocking you about (and maybe even if he is) you stick by him. Maybe I should have left him years ago. But to go where? And on a dinner lady's wages?

I really hope that Alastair treats your Ingrid better than his dad treated me. I think he does, but you never know what goes on behind closed doors, do you? Anyway, I'm rambling now. Stay in touch. And maybe now that I'm a free woman I could travel up to Orkney on my own to visit! It would be lovely to see the land that shaped you and your family.

Kind regards,

Meg

Downstairs Alastair could hear muffled moving and clinking and creaking. He put the letter back in the envelope as if he might undo the reading of it and leave its secret words there. A rolling grey cloud charged with electricity had embroiled itself around his gut, and his jaw was pushing hard against itself. He glanced furtively towards the hatch, needing that no-one should come through. He had been holding his breath, he exhaled, he held his breath again, all the while his mind shifting and slipping like his little bit of the earth's crust was fracturing and moving on magma.

An image bubbled up to his consciousness: his father's funeral, a church, spartan and simply decorated, the black-cloth minister in the pulpit. Beside Alastair his mum, standing stock still but for her singing lips, the red hymn book in her hands, face turned up towards the stained glass above the chancel, white sunlight falling through the strawberry red of the tunic of the holy one, through the blond-yellow halo behind him, through the sandy skin of his transfigured face, middle east brown refracted through pale

Scottish imagination, all the soft coloured light on his mother's still face as she let go her husband, grieving yes, but also, what he now knew, breathing out freely as if for the first time, letting taut shoulders drop, letting tired anxiety drift slowly to ground like the ceremonial soil cast upon the sunken coffin. And further back, the grey silence of a rainy afternoon when the house held its breath because Charlie was in a mood. Alastair saw his mother washing quietly in the kitchenette, treading carefully, and there was fear in her work, more fear than Alastair had realised. Perhaps if he'd looked harder, perhaps if he'd not stuck his head under the pillow at night.

'It's all gone a bit quiet up there!' Ingrid's voice cracked open the silence. 'How you gettin' on?'

Alastair shuffled noisily across the attic and looked down through the hatch. Ingrid was peering up, one foot on the ladder. A couple of locks of grey-brown hair had escaped from her braid and swung free.

'Naw, naw, don't start your bleating. I'm gettin' on with it. Got a whole pile of stuff for the dump. It's just, some of it's a bit more bitty, odds and ends, letters and stuff.'

'You alright?'

'Aye, I'm fine. Why?' he asked, then regretted it.

'You just look a bit strained or somethin.'

'Naw, I'm fine. Thanks. How you gettin' on?'

'Same. Some stuff's easy, some stuff's hard.'

Alastair clambered down the stairs and they both sat down on the double bed in the main bedroom. Clothes were laid across most of the bed and ramshackle boxes were piled beside the low window.

'What was the phone call this morning?' Ingrid asked.

'What phone call?'

'Alastair.'

'Oh, aye, it was, em, Michelle.'

A few seconds passed and down the hall came chinks of

crockery being gathered.

'Was she askin' for more money?'

'I've told you before. She doesn't ask for it – I give it to her. Freely. She's had a hard time.'

'So what's happened this time? He beat her again?'

'No, and he won't be. For a while at least. He got the jail.'

That put her gas at a peep, Alastair noted with grim satisfaction. 'What for?'

'Beating her up of course.'

'So now she won't even have his unemployment benefit?'

'No. That's true.'

Isobel padded up from the kitchen.

'Do either of you want a cup of tea?'

Both nodded their assent and their thanks. Isobel retreated to the kitchen.

'How long you gonnie keep giving her money?' Ingrid asked when they were alone again.

'As long as she needs it.' It came out like asking permission and he wished it hadn't.

'Alastair. It wasn't your fault. Would you let it go?'

'You don't get it though. It's like the army. You look after your workmate's family when they need it. I was the gaffer.' Alastair sipped at his tea and got up, mooching among the clothes and boxes Ingrid had pulled from the wardrobe. When he moved out to the hallway and climbed the ladder Ingrid knew the conversation was over, at least for now.

Alastair humphed another load of boxes out to the van. Tomorrow's stiffness and pain would remind him that he no longer had a body for lugging boxes but for today his denial was intact. Joe emerged from the garage, blinking in the low sunlight.

'Can I add some of this stuff to the load for the dump?' Joe asked.

'Aye.'

Joe lifted a decrepit lawnmower into the van, then a wooden

crate of kindling.

'Not the kindling, surely someone could use that?'

'Well, do you know anyone with a real fire these days?' Joe asked.

Alastair rubbed at a callous on his thumb and stared at the wood for a few moments.

'Well, no, I can't think of anyone. But surely someone could use it? Seems an awful waste to just throw it away.'

'I suppose that's true. But if there's nowhere for it to go, there's nowhere for it go. It could be of use, but we can't use it.' Joe turned away from his dad to collect more detritus from the garage.

'Is that all you've got?' Alastair asked.

'Uhuh, for now.' Joe squeezed a few paint pots in the remaining spaces in the van.

Alastair closed the doors.

'I'll come with you' Joe said.

'Sorry, the front seat's full of junk as well. I'll manage on my own.'

13

An hour later, Alastair had dumped a van load of his parents stuff at Polmadie dump. He had planned to return to the house for another couple of hours of clearing. Instead he found himself heading through Govanhill, Pollokshields, Dumbreck, then Ibrox bled into Govan. He parked the van on Golspie Street and fell into his habitual way along Govan Road, past Millie's bakery where flour and sugar were folded a hundred different ways, past McKenzie's hardware shop where a tower of coloured buckets and a stand of mops interrupted the pavement. At Elder Park he crossed away from the sounds of children in the play park and mothers barking warnings against greed on the swings. He was then on the north side of the road where the shipyard building swallowed the sky. Past the old gate, locked now and rusting. Past brick walls, ripe now for bill posters, for Simple Minds at the Barras, for The Police at the Apollo. Past the windowed offices where the management had kept their dainty hands clean, far from the shop floor.

Alastair passed the end of the building and turned right down a dirty alleyway between the two yards, past pallets propped against the wall, bags of rubbish covered with dust, an old sleeping bag and three empty cans of McEwans. The walls on either side were windowless and blackened with exhaust grime. A few yards in, a fence stretched across the alley, with a single flimsy gate in it, padlocked. He stood at the gate and glanced up the alley. He took out a pen-knife and snapped open the mini flat-head screwdriver. He pulled back a loose corner of mesh, snaked his hand through, and fumbled the screwdriver into place on the back plate. A few turns and the bolt was slackened. He smacked the lock with an elbow, twice, three times, and with a creak the gate opened.

Alastair replaced the screw from the inside and made the lock look as feebly secure as it had before.

Further down the alley, Alastair came to a tall fence on his right, but the barrenness of the yard inside and the lack of meaningful ownership meant that the woven metal was easily ripped from an upright to squeeze even a man's body through. Alastair climbed through, keeping his coat away from the stray wire ends.

Inside he stood still, tall and upright, surveying the derelict yard. The bulking hangar was rust red, a hundred feet tall and double that long. He walked towards the hangar and through the huge entrance. His footfalls resonated loud and lonely in the vast space. On his right, workstations stretched along the length of the wall.

Alastair sat down on a cobwebbed wooden sleeper. He took a can of irn-bru from the inside pocket of his coat, tugged the ring pull and listened to the fizz.

Break-time. Ten-thirty. Cans of irn-bru. Four-sugared milky tea from the canteen. Grainy coffee. Tunnocks caramel wafers. Cigarettes and roll-ups. The ten man squad, tools downed. Quieter in the corner. Calluses on thumb balls rubbed hard. Stinging oil wiped from minor cuts. The growing ship assessed and admired. Its finish feared. 'It might be the last.' Football results reviewed. Players' performances dissected on the autopsy table. Yard managers' decisions pored over. Shop stewards asserting the union stance. Young cocky apprentices flexing their muscles of rhetoric and bravado. Older journeymen less cocksure. One eye on the order book. Or what they knew of it. Talk of the politicians. Distant in body. Bloody close in decisions.

The bell. Back to work. Last swigs and puffs. Muscles, ligaments, sinews, tightening up for lifting, pulling, twisting. The clock ticking. Back to work.

Alastair got up, his left knee complaining as his bulk pressed down on the joint. He wandered to the back of the shed where the supervisors hut still stood, its door hanging on one hinge. He stepped inside looking for something to reconnect with. Rotas, work plans, sick notes, anything. But there had been none of that here the last time he came - why should he find anything now? Then came the memory he'd come here to examine, safer to cradle in its place of origin.

A November day 1979. Winter champing at the bit. The yards quietly anxious as the Tories settled into government. Working on a navy frigate. 1600 tonnes and long as the Clyde was wide. Alastair's team working below deck on the internal walls.

'Aaah! Ah! Ah! Fuck sake! Aaah! Gie's some fuckin help!' Under the deck, Tommy's voice. Alastair's heart sped but his mind said it sounded worse than it was. The young guys were all talk and squealed like pigs when they got hurt. Alastair dropped a wrench and ran to the hole in the deck, climbed down the steep stairs. The closest men followed him down.

Tommy was kneeling on the floor, his right hand spurting blood from at least two mangled fingers. He was gripping his right wrist with his other hand and gurning, strained moans escaping from him, the muscles of his face taut and grimaced. Alastair was at his side quick. He pulled an oily rag from his overalls and wrapped it around Tommy's decimated hand. He could feel the loose broken fingers.

'Ah! Fuck! It's too tight – it's too tight!'

'Got to slow down the bleeding Tommy. I know it's sore. Stevie! First aid kit! Up on the deck. Don't worry wee man. We'll get ye sorted.'

The first aid kit arrived. Alastair took out a bandage and wrapped it as best he could round Tommy's mangled hand, red stains already seeping through the layers. He had no more first aid training than anyone else.

'Gaffer' said Stevie, and motioned with his eyes to Tommy's face. Alastair looked up just as Tommy's eyelids closed woozily and his head slumped down, his chin coming to rest on his chest.

'Ah, for fuck sake' muttered Alastair, pity and exasperation mingled. He held Tommy's head as they laid him flat on the floor. Tommy's hair left a film of sweat on Alastair's hand. He scanned around the gathered men. 'George, go an' phone an ambulance, would ye? Shouldnae take long from the Southern. Tell em he's badly damaged his fingers, lost a bit a blood, and tell em he's fainted.'

Alastair looked again at the unconscious man and listened at his gaping mouth for breathing. He seemed reassured. He looked around. An angle grinder lay carelessly on the floor, some drops of blood on the blade.

Two of the bystanders were muttering to each other. One elbowed the other in the ribs and told him to shoosh.

'Whit is it?' Alastair spat.

Willie Brown stood with his fists jammed in his overall pockets, giving his mate the evil eye as he spoke.

'Maybe we should gie him a wee drink. My grannie faints a' the time and a wee lick of brandy does the trick.' The others tittered, glad of the distraction.

'Aye, well, that might work if anyone was stupid enough to bring a drink into work, wouldn't it?' Alastair said, not sure himself if it was a question or not. A few seconds passed. Another elbow in the ribs for Willie.

'Ah might have accidentally left a quarter bottle in my coat, accidentally you understand.' Willie's gallusness was tempered. A few more seconds passed. Alastair sighed.

'Awright. Go'n get it. But not a word to anyone else.'

Willie turned tail and took the ladder two steps at a time and his footfalls tripped away.

'Think he'll lose the fingers, gaffer?' Stevie asked quietly.

Alastair grimaced and rubbed his temples. He watched the

blood stain widening on the makeshift bandage.

'Well I wouldnae be putting my money on him winning the darts from here on in.'

The clanging and shouts from the rest of the ship continued to ricochet around them whilst the group of men stood loosely around Tommy and Alastair. A set of footfalls grew louder and Willie Brown came jangling back down the stairs. He pulled a quarter bottle of Bells from his pocket and pushed it towards Alastair. Alastair looked at it a moment then took it from Willie's hand and removed the cap.

'Sit him up a wee bit, would you?' Alastair said. Stevie sat down, got Tommy's head and shoulders off the floor and squeezed his knees under him. Tommy's head lolled to one side. Alastair held the bottle right under Tommy's nose. No response. He tipped a few drops between the closed lips. He pulled Tommy's chin down to open the mouth and the amber liquid dribbled in. He poured more in, a measure, and then another. Tommy's head jolted as he gagged on the drink, and the men got a fright. His body started to move as he came slowly out of the faint, and Stevie held his shoulders while he tried to come to. Alastair moved Tommy's injured hand behind his own knee so Tommy wouldn't see it, lest he pass out again.

The pain was returning to Tommy's consciousness and he started to moan.

'Stevie, you stay here. Willie, go'n look out for the paramedics. The rest of you might as well get back to work.' The rest of the men trudged off, casting glances back.

Tommy was fully awake now and shifting uncomfortably. Alastair and Stevie propped him up with his back against the wall. He tried to lift his mangled hand and yelled with pain again.

'Just leave it where it is Tommy. No need to look at it just now. The ambulance is on its way.'

Tommy banged his head back against the metal wall.

'Idiot. Frickin idiot. It was my fault, gaffer.'

Tommy stopped to groan as a wave of pain pulsed from his

hand up the nerves to his brain.

'I was clumsy with it. I'm sorry. I'm sorry. I've buggered it up for myself haven't I?'

'Naw, naw, son, you'll be fine. Don't worry about all that. Let's just get you mended and rested. The doctors work miracles these days. You'll be finger-pickin like Dick Gaughan in no time.'

'I bloody hate Dick Gaughan,' Tommy replied. 'And I couldnae play guitar before this happened so I think you're talkin garbage on a couple of counts.'

Alastair looked at Stevie. 'Well, I'm glad to see breakin some fingers hasnae stemmed his cheek.'

'Michelle's gonnie be right pissed aff. Probably break my other fingers.'

They stopped talking and Tommy's heavy breathing and groans were loud in the small corridor. After a couple of minutes the paramedics arrived and took charge. They could not stretcher him out but they gave him enough morphine to numb the worst of it, and Tommy walked up and out of the ship leaning as little as he could on one of the paramedics. The work had stopped all round the ship now, and the men stood by watching as Tommy and his support act left the ship, descending down the long wooden gangplank. As he was escorted to the ambulance in the lane, the men went back to work with their drills and mallets and ratchets and pulleys, the humming and whirring and banging and scraping building again like an industrial symphony, a graceless and unconducted crescendo. The sounds slowly faded for Tommy as he left the shed, the cold wind whipping his clammy skin and drowning the yard sounds as they walked across the tarmac, into the back of the ambulance whose doors shut out for the last time the familiar soundtrack of the work.

Tommy never got back to work of course. They stitched up his fingers as best they could but the damage was done. Alastair remembered visiting him in hospital the next day. Telling him a job could be found at the yard for a man with one working hand. Knowing it wasn't true and knowing Tommy knew it. Promising to help in any way he could. Promising to pin the blame on management. Bringing best wishes from the crew. Easy for them to say sympathetic things.

Two weeks down the line. Tommy paid off and already getting too drunk too often on the redundancy money. Management deciding the accident wasn't their fault. Wasn't wearing the right protective gear. Saying the nurses smelt alcohol on his breath when he was admitted.

Four weeks down the line. Telling Alastair he'll get another job. Won't be on the brew for long. Won't let his wife and kids go hungry. The young wife hovering in the kitchen, one eye purple and swollen. Alastair not knowing what to say.

A year down the line. Alastair sending a bit of money each month. Scared to know what Tommy was doing with it. Saw Tommy's kids around Elder Park sometimes. Thin and angry looking.

Finally, today's phone call. Tommy's wife Michelle. Telling him that Tommy has been jailed for two years for kicking the crap out of her and their eldest son after Rangers were solidly humped by Aberdeen.

Alastair jolted upright. A noise had broken his trance. Footsteps out in the shed. Three boys were running fast from the great opening towards the back of the shed. They yelled some noises, enjoying the echo thrown around them in the cavernous space. Alastair watched them through the grime and cobwebs on the small square window. Two of them stopped in the corner, kicking some bricks and cardboard about, looking for some kind of treasure. The third wandered towards the hut, staring up at the old hoist rails and chains that hung from the dark ceiling. Alastair stared at the boy, unsure what to do. The boy's gaze fell slowly down the walls, taking in their size. His gaze came down onto the hut, to the window, where he registered Alastair's angry face through the cobwebs.

'Shit!'

The boy jerked back, stumbled over a crate, feel awkwardly on one knee, scrambled up and shouted, 'Come on!' to his friends. Alastair followed through on his role in the drama, emerging through the doorway just to scare them. The two other boys saw him and scarpered after their friend. As they rounded the wall of the shed Alastair heard their laughter.

'Aw, you pure wet yersel, didn't ye?!' one shouted to another.

In a moment, the place was dead quiet again.

Alastair returned to the chair in the hut. He thought again of how things had worked out for Tommy and rummaged around inside himself for the curious gravitational pull of self-flagellation. Honest guilt and sadness mixed with indulgent self-shaming. But Alastair knew sometimes you couldn't prevent accidents. Dangerous jobs, dangerous tools. One wee slip of concentration – bang, your fingers are hanging on by a red thread and your job for life is dead. Mind you, he thought, these weren't jobs for life any more. No such thing now. But Tommy, sitting at home drinking, spitting out his disappointment at his woman and his kids. That stuck in the gullet. Why did it always have to work its way into anger? Do all roads lead to Rome? Do we all end up angry men eventually?

Alastair was pulled, irritated, from his sour reverie by more footsteps. He was gearing up to give the boys an earful when he saw that it was a security guard, or as close as it got to one round here. The old man walked with a slight limp and wore a cheap blue jacket over dirty blue jeans. He carried a polystyrene cup which likely had more than just coffee in it. Alastair walked towards him and the man eyed him warily.

'Did you see they boys?' the guard asked.

'Aye. Scared them away I think. Did your job for you.'

'Well. Maybe so. But whit are you doing here?'

'That's a very good question.' Alastair shifted his weight and shoved his hands deeper in his pockets. 'Used to work here. I like to come back sometimes. I don't do any damage.'

Alastair noticed the guard swaying ever so slightly. Clearly not sober enough to be officially angry.

'No-one's meant to be in here,' said the guard. 'They say it's dangerous.'

'It was a damn sight more dangerous when it was open.'

'Still, though. Got to ask you to leave. I'll get pelters if I don't do my job.'

'Aye, well, I know what that's like,' Alastair replied, and began walking towards the exit. The guard followed, his ill-fitting boots clicking on the concrete.

As they reached the fence, the guard spoke up.

'No hard feelings, eh?'

'Sure.'

'Listen, you said you worked here. When did you leave?'

Alastair breathed out heavily and stared back at the huge building with its gaping mouth that would never spit another ship into the Clyde.

'Not sure I ever really did.'

14

Joe was nearing the end of a session with Pauline. She had been coming to him for many months but progress was painfully slow. Pauline's family was a disaster. Her uncle had sexually abused her from the age of seven. Her mother claimed not to know. Her father found out but did nothing. He told Pauline it would kill her mother to find out so she must keep quiet. In Pauline's eyes, her mother was the only pure and innocent one. Pauline had grown up and married a man who beat her often and cheated on her almost as much. He left after seven years and two children, but she would have put up with more if he hadn't. She didn't come to therapy – she was sent. Other people always seemed to know what was best for her, and more or less made her decisions for her. Pauline was paralysed by choices, and, when presented with one, reverted to a helpless child mode, creating a vacuum which invited the control and dominance of people who were often only too glad to take such control.

Joe felt enormous concern for her and wished she could grow stronger. He had tried to help foster in her a self-respect and self-compassion that had never been encouraged. But with the array of forces stacked against him, he was pissing in the wind.

Time was running out in the session, and Joe was running out of patient concern.

'Pauline, I'm afraid we need to finish fairly soon. I know there's always more to say. But I find myself wondering whether these sessions are making much difference to you. We've talked a lot about the people and events that have influenced you to have so little sense of self-worth. You've said many times that you'd like to develop relationships with better people, people who would treat you better, who would show you that you're a decent, valuable human being. But, when it comes to taking action, attending the women's group for example, something always gets in the way.'

Pauline sat staring at the floor, her body tensed, her fingers folding and re-folding a tissue. It seemed to Joe that she felt criticised, but didn't understand what for. It seemed that she liked the space to talk and someone to listen. She knew that it wasn't right what people had done to her, and she felt Joe had helped her believe that. But when Joe talked about things changing, improving, she felt even more scared. She had trained herself to aim low. To get your hopes up and then to be disappointed, to crash back down to earth with a bang, that was the worst feeling in the world. Safer to stay in the familiar dark pit than to summon the effort and optimism to try climbing up the slippery sides, where an evil hand may grab her ankle and yank her back down, where fresh reminders of her inadequacy would await her.

Joe thought she felt better when he wasn't asking anything of her, wasn't prodding her to change anything. When she felt confused and fearful, as she did now, she became paralysed, and passive. She wanted just to sink into herself, to find a secret corner where no-one would bother her.

When Pauline went into her corner, Joe became more frustrated, for her but, he had to admit, also for himself. His well thought through appeals to hope and self-compassion and the possibility of change simply bounced off her. And then it became a debate, both trying to persuade the other of the rightness of their position. And debates rarely change people's minds. So the debate was futile, but nonetheless Joe found himself at it again.

'I don't know what to say,' Pauline said very quietly. 'I just can't do anything right. You must think I'm pretty pathetic.'

Joe had once seen a documentary about surviving in the wild. If you encounter a bear, it said, you should start beating yourself hard with your fists. Beat yourself and scratch yourself and cry loudly. Then, the theory went, the bear would be confused, then actually take pity on you and instead of attacking you, would try to stop you hitting yourself. Joe wondered if this had become Pauline's default strategy at any sign of conflict because it often worked, at least with kind people. He had seen this response many times, and was working at not taking the bait. Instead he tried to help Pauline notice the dynamic in the room between them.

'Pauline, can we think about what's happening right now, in our interaction? We've noticed this before haven't we? The way you shut down when there's any mention of moving out of the cruel safety of your situation. And you start telling me again that you're useless and pathetic. Why is that? What response are you wanting from me when you do that?'

Pauline looked quietly bamboozled. Perhaps it felt too intense, to look squarely at what she was doing right now. Perhaps she liked it better when Joe just listened. Perhaps when he talked, it felt like a pressure.

'I'm not looking for any response. I'm just saying what I feel,' she said miserably.

Joe hesitated. He usually took the easy way out in these moments – back down, give up on the effort to get into the brass tacks of their relating, into meta-communication. He questioned again whether Pauline was simply unable to think reflectively enough to observe her own mode shifts and their function. This time he gambled that she was able, just not willing.

'No, I disagree. Because I care about you and your well-being, I'm challenging that. I don't think you're just saying what you feel. I think that usually when you repeat those tired old self-critical messages, other people give you sympathy. I certainly feel sympathetic towards you when you say those things. But then, nothing changes. The sympathy doesn't actually get through to you – you can't receive it appreciatively. You bat it away. So I don't think sympathy is what you're looking for in those moments. And I know I'm being really direct here, but I think when I offer you sympathy, I'm no longer pushing you to make changes. And so then you're off the hook, you don't need to do anything, you don't need to try, you don't need to be pro-active.'

Joe stopped speaking, and steeled himself to not rescue her from the awkward silence. He was glad he'd made the effort to drill down into process issues, taking the risk of upsetting her. He was more determined this time to push her to wrestle with his words. His buttocks were starting to go numb, but he did not want to disturb his determination by shifting position. The clock ticked on quietly. One minute passed. He kept his gaze mostly on the floor, to let her think without his eyes on her. The hour had passed but Joe held his silence. Pauline was sniffling but if she was to solidify herself Joe had to trust her to handle her own emotions. Two minutes passed. Pauline rigidly stared at the floor. She rubbed aggressively at a sore place of skin on her left wrist. Joe did not bite. Three minutes passed. Joe began to wonder with some bemusement how long this stalemate might last before Pauline would do anything. Joe rubbed his hands over his face, fanning out from his brow, over his forehead, down his cheeks, and stared up at the ceiling. He was tense, and some sweat was seeping into his thin shirt under his armpits. The urge to back down was still there, but weakening. There was something strangely liberating about pushing further than he'd pushed before. Five minutes passed and the air in the room had grown heavy and warm.

'I need to go,' Pauline said abruptly, and stood up. 'My dad's waiting for me.' She grabbed her coat and without looking at Joe, opened the door and walked out. Joe was caught so off guard that he didn't even rise to walk her out. She knew the way out, and besides, his gut told him to stay put, rather than try to make it all better.

He heard the main door to the department open and close. Only then did he rise from his chair and look out the window. A few yards away, Pauline was standing with an older man. Her shoulders were drooped and she looked at the ground. Even through the window, Joe could hear him berating her for keeping him waiting. He grabbed her by the elbow, glaring into her frightened face as he called her stupid, time-waster, a snivelling wreck. He started walking towards Craigpark, his hand firmly clenched on Pauline's arm, though she was walking in step with him and not resisting. Joe's mixed feelings towards her became subsumed by malice towards her dad, and his held-in tension became a deep growl in his throat.

Joe stayed late, dictating letters and writing up notes. He tried not to notice that he was doing this more these days, or sitting in the cafes and bars of Duke Street to shorten his evenings. Thankfully Oliver had left early for his weekly open-water swim at Loch Lomond. The rumour went that he swam naked, which wouldn't have surprised Joe in the slightest. Zara was on holiday and Bernie left bang on 5pm, rain or shine, probably the only one of them with healthy boundaries. Around half seven Joe called it a night. He checked all the cabinets in the office were locked, windows were closed, the kettle and toaster unplugged. He turned off the lights, went out, and locked the inner door and the wooden storm doors. It was raining fat wet drops as he walked along Oakley Terrace, down Craigpark past the library and left onto Duke Street where sandstone tenements sat on bookies, newsagents and greasy cafes. Cars and buses emptied puddles onto the pavements and white headlights and red rear lights were kaleidoscopes through the rain.

Joe stayed close to the buildings, his collar upturned uselessly against savage bucketfuls of rain. The weather meant Coia's was quieter than it might otherwise have been, and Joe could see a free table through the window beyond the ice cream display case. Ten minutes later he was drying out, a house white and a bowl of glistening Contadina on the table. It was half cafe, half chippy, half local gossip shop. The cafe was in the hands of the second generation of Coia's, and the patriarch held court from behind the counter. It was a beloved institution of the east end, and its bright lights spilling onto the wet pavement were a compelling magnet to passers-by who, up until then, had not realised how hungry they really were. The take away counter served out portions and portions of fish, chips, black pudding, smoked sausage, haggis, pies, potato fritters, and for the more indulgent, thin base pizzas and stodgy lasagne. Joe liked the bustle, and the call and response of customers and staff, which was musical and warm. The hard intensity of therapeutic work could be dissolved and softened by wine, olive oil, and comfortable patter in the background. The tightness around his neck and shoulders slowly began to melt, and the food and the wine laid a velvet blanket over his bristling nerves.

Joe was almost at the end of his pasta when a familiar face appeared at the counter. He recognised Pauline's dad from earlier in the day. He looked like he was on his own and pretty drunk. He ordered a fish supper, and stood swaying slightly while he waited. Joe could watch him pretty freely without being noticed, though a small voice suggested he should ignore him.

Two young women came in behind Harry, teetering on high heels, both wearing leather jackets, black miniskirts and neon green tights. They stood close together, looking at the backlit menu high on the back wall. Joe noticed Harry looking at the girls, a lecherous half-smile on his face. Joe was often astounded at the self-delusion of men, thinking these young women would be charmed by some witless banter.

'Awright ladies,' Harry announced himself. They had learned without being told that as a woman, you had no choice but to put up with men like this, to humour them, throw them a bone, let them think they're Cary Grant and Sean Connery all rolled into one. They smiled at Harry momentarily, but that was more than enough encouragement for him.

'Oot on the swalley are ye? Doon to the Louden perhaps?'

One of the girls forced a half-smile whilst the other willed their order to hurry up.

'Whit, are no chatting to yer auld pal Harry? Where's yer manners? Aye, yer skirts are no long enough for manners.' Harry moved over closer to the girls, who looked pleadingly to Roberto Coia, the patriarch, standing behind the sweet counter. Joe, knowing what he'd heard from Pauline, felt his tension returning.

'Come on, Mr Wilson, leave the girls alone' Mr Coia called out with good humour in his voice. 'Let them get their chips in peace.'

'Who're you talking to? Ye sticking up for they tarts? C'mon wi' me ladies, I'll shout ye a spritzer in the pub.' By now, the atmosphere was thick with awkwardness, but really no-one wanted to have to talk a drunk out of the place. Mercifully, the girls were given their carry-out and hurried towards the door. As they did, Harry tried to grab one of them on her bum. His aim was off, but his effort was obvious enough as they rushed out the door. He stood a few moments longer, a languid smile on his face, until they gave him his sausage supper. He swayed out the door, muttering to himself, and headed left along Duke Street.

Joe went to the counter and handed over £10, telling them to keep the change. He went out the door and turned left to the corner. He could see the waddling figure of Harry heading up the hill. Pauline lived up that way. If Harry was heading to hers in that state, she'd be a convenient piece of soft flesh for his fists and his impotent rage. Joe could not bear the thought of her taking another beating, turning up at her session again with purple skin fading red, claiming a fall. Joe turned up Whitehill Street, ignoring the voice in his head asking him what the hell he was planning. Harry was slow going up the hill. He stopped at a corner, laid his take-away on a garden wall and lit a cigarette, his drunk hands taking three jerky attempts to get the thing lit. Joe stopped as well, ten yards behind him, shouldering a dripping hedge. Harry set off again and Joe followed at a distance. Eventually Harry reached Onslow Drive and turned right towards where Pauline lived. Joe sped up. He caught up with him as they came to a tenement with high hedges either side of the entrance path.

'Get in here you bastard' Joe hissed, and bundled Harry into the path where they were hidden from most of the tenement windows.

'Whit? Whit are you doing? Who're you?' Harry protested.

Joe was finally released from his self-control. His emotions sang a shrill tone inside him. He pushed Harry into the hedge, the thin sharp branches scraping Harry's red and frightened face. Joe grabbed him by his jacket, their faces close, Harry's breath stinking of stale hops. Joe pushed him towards the building, dragging against the hedge, and Harry stumbled into the small garden. Joe pushed him again and he fell back hard on the pebbles. Joe felt his height and his power as anger surged freely in him.

'What the hell gives you the right to treat women like that?' Joe's voice was venomous and metallic. 'You're scum, you're a pathetic piece of shit.'

Harry was still on the ground, wide eyed and scared to get up.

'Who the hell are you?' he asked.

'I'm a man who doesn't need to mistreat women to feel like a man. I'm a man who watches while dicks like you make life miserable for other people. You're a bloody insult to masculinity!'

Joe leaned over Harry, his muscles twitching and a freedom pulsing through him. He pointed a finger in Harry's face and spoke slowly,

'Stop treating people like that! Especially your family! What a disgrace.'

And with that Joe stepped away, kicking Harry's legs out of his way as he strode out of the garden and out the path to the street.

The rain kept pelting the buildings and the roads and the pavements and it bounced off the cars and bubbled into rivers that whirl-pooled around the drains. Colours were obliterated and all was wet grey. Joe trudged up the hill away from Harry, away from Pauline's flat, breaking through the curtains of sweeping rain. He walked and walked, pushing through the onslaught of stinging pellets. He came soon to Alexandra Parade, his blood pumping hard, the food and drink in his belly starting to churn. At the Parade he thought fleetingly of the park and found himself headed that way. With no pubs, the Parade was quiet, and he hardly passed a

128

soul. He vaguely thought his face and his body might betray the rolling anger, the creeping fear, and the disorientation he was feeling. The rain started to register and it began to cool the hot blush on his face. It splashed into his eyes, ran in rivulets down either side of his nose, fell around his neck, seeped into his collar, and spread through his coat and into his shirt which clung to his skin.

He reached Alexandra Park. The wrought iron gates were open and isolated street lamps gave enough light to walk by but not enough to feel safe by. It looked deserted and Joe blundered in. He walked past the flower beds, up to the cast iron fountain. He sat down on a bench and his head fell into his hands and he heaved huge breaths. The rain battered on the back of his neck and ran around his jaw.

Joe stared into the darkness of the trees, hoping his emotions might right themselves if he sat sit still long enough. He sat back and tried to see the sky. The sky was not there because it was all falling, melting into liquid form, seeping and dropping and rushing blue and grey and black. Finally Joe's heart began to slow down, his flesh was cooling, and his sodden clothes gripped like a wetsuit to his skin. He heard the echo of Mrs Selby's voice - 'you're a good boy.' He stood up, and began heading home.

By the time Joe arrived home, he was utterly freezing, though the rain had now stopped. Walking had been hard with his clothes clinging fiercely to his body. His mind had been playing over it all, relentlessly. He felt again and again the surge of freedom when his temper exploded, an almost sweet feeling. But creeping into his awareness had been the realisation that he had attacked the father of one of his patients. Harry might go to the police. Joe might have breached Pauline's confidentiality, if Harry found out who he was. Harry might take out his hurt pride on Pauline, making things even worse for her. For this reason, more than the cold and wet, Joe was shivering and nauseous when he got home. He set the shower lukewarm, squeezed himself out of the sodden clothes, and climbed wearily into the water. As he began to warm up, he turned the dial hotter. His muscles were grateful for the soothing patter of the water, and he felt cut loose from the outside world, safer to take stock and assess. Safer also to take some satisfaction from what he had done, but it was a fragile and guilty satisfaction. In the glut of sour feelings, Joe thought of Walter's stone and the thought of it glinted like flint sparks in a dark cave. Here was an intrigue, a possibility, the chance of a precious piece of life hidden in its secret womb. In the growing darkness and weariness of Joe's life, the stone and Walter's untold story took on the weight of Joe's hopes of re-enchantment, but the bright hope was fading. For now, the deadweight of his own stupidity and recklessness and weariness was winning.

15

Later that same night, outside Baxter House, a tall roe deer nuzzled for food amongst the thickets of nettles and wild grass. The night was silent and secure around her. She had seen that the place was dark, that the reflective spaces in the building were dark at last. She knew there was food to be found here. She came often, when the place was dark. She sniffed around some pungent toadstools that sprouted around the wide roots of a weeping willow. Her wet nose prodded a bramble bush but the berries were not yet ripe so she left it be. She stopped moving, eyes alert to the house. Her breath rose ghost-grey from moist nostrils and dissipated into the cool air. She saw no movement in the human place and carried on searching. She stepped forward with long spindly legs and her hooves pressed on fallen branches that cracked crisply. She stepped onto the cut grass, and bent low her long neck. She chewed on some fresh cut grass. Not as exciting as berries or nuts, but plentiful in the warm times.

The deer froze again. She raised her eyes to the human place. The curtains were open in a window and a figure was there. The deer stared at the figure and the figure stared at the deer and neither moved. All the deer's muscles were primed for motion. The sinews and ligaments tingled with electrical readiness just as the eyes kept watch for any threat movements. The curtains closed slowly and the figure was gone. The deer stood watching, primed but patient. Eventually the signals of her hunger overrode those of her fear, and she returned to her forage, ambling quietly in the cover of the old trees.

Inside, Adam moved softly away from the window. He had risen from bed to drink in the sky, and the image of a thousand stars kept reverberating in his vision. His mind sang loudly to him as he marvelled at the thought of the stars screaming outwards from each other, viciously burning up their nitrogen, their helium, their oxygen. The great supernova seedbeds where glowing neon gas clouds gave birth to fledgling yet mighty stars. The turning, twisting pairs of dancing binary systems. The unique package of light in mystical particle-waves streaming headlong from a distant galaxy to land slap bang in the middle of his retina only. The light carrying its life story of the moons and asteroids and black holes it skirted and dashed between on its soundless journey from there to here. Adam's mind whirred in delight at the wonder of it all and he worried that the sounds of his cartwheeling brain might wake his fellow patients.

In the room, the three other men were asleep. Peter was a brute of a man and his white sheets barely covered the rolling hillocks of his sleeping body and he snored in long, rasping exhalations. Gregor's sleep was fitful and filled with heroic and violent dreams and he contorted his body into balletic and angular poses around the bed. Sammy was racked with fears day and night so he stuffed his head under two pillows and wrapped his sheets close around him like the straight jacket he'd once been forced into by an over-zealous nurse with a twisted nostalgia for the old ways of psychiatry.

Adam knew how to move without waking them. He slipped a dressing gown over his pyjamas, lifted his trainers from under the bed, and stuffed a sock in each trainer. The room was off a long corridor with the nurses' station at the far end. Adam opened his door and peeked down the corridor. Nurse Archibald was slouched at a desk at the station, his feet propped up on a chair, reading a copy of NME. If Adam came out of his room, he would be spotted.

Adam stood there a few minutes. A faint voice began to carry from one of the other rooms, rising and falling and keening, like a badly acted pantomime witch. Adam recognised Quintus's voice. He talked often in his sleep. If you caught him at the right moment he would answer questions in his sleep with complete honesty and with no memory of it when he awoke. They had once coaxed from Quintus a detailed account of playing in his room as a child whilst in the next room his mother elicited primal screams and baby talk from her middle class psychotherapy clients.

Nurse Archibald walked towards the room to check on him. Adam pulled back into his room with the door ajar. The nurse listened in at Quintus's room a few moments, then padded back down the hall. Adam sat on his bed and put on his trainers. The window way was dangerous but better than getting caught by Archie-Baldy-Noggin in the middle of the night. Adam pulled up the sash window, envisaging the cast iron weight on the pulley inside the wooden frame, perfectly balancing the weight of the window. He lifted one leg then the other over the edge, and manoeuvred his upper body under the window so that he was sitting on the deep sill, his legs dangling down in mid air. He breathed in the damp cool air and looked left and right for any light spilling from the other windows. Only twelve feet and the grass is spongy with moss, he whispered to himself. He stared at the grass and now his mind was a microscope. He saw through the lens hundreds and thousands of moss and grass hands, standing ready to catch him and absorb his fall. Little green men and women with slick rubbery bodies that would feel no pain when his giant body crushed upon them. Now they were willing him to jump, awaiting their chance to do something heroic, knowing they would return afterwards, eventually, mostly, to their full and sturdy stature.

Adam sniffed the air again, checking for predators or spoilsports. He looked again at the stars for comfort, then pushed himself off the ledge. Gravity grabbed him hard and down he fell, displacing atoms and molecules as he sliced the air, his dressing gown flailing out behind him like it was reaching desperately for help. Down he fell and landed on the outstretched hands of the green rubber army, thousands of them sacrificing themselves to bear his impact, taking the hit, the force vibrating and pulsing through their tiny bodies and down their fierce roots into the packed wet soil. Adam rolled forward out of his fall, his gown and skin and hair slipping through the grass. Millions of droplets of dew were torn from the grass men and women and squashed, obliterated on the surface of this flying giant. An army of droplets were wiped from his face to his hands, and clapped away to fall swiftly back to earth.

Adam stood upright, turned, and admired the distance he'd jumped. It sounded like no-one had stirred in the room. He skipped along the back of the building to the staff entrance. There in the porch was Archie-Baldie-Noggin's bicycle. Adam took the bike, confident he would do his utmost to return it in fair condition. He tucked the ends of his striped pyjamas into his socks, wheeled the bike through the grass, through the thicket of shrubs, and onto the rough path that looped around the hospital grounds. He boarded the bike and set off, wobbling over roots and brushing past nettles. The moon cast only a fragile light on his path.

He reached the main road. It was not lit but the surface was smooth and wide. He turned left, north-west, towards the Campsies. Now he was free to pick up some speed. Now the tyres began to sing as the rubber kissed and fled from the road. Now his feet pushed hard into the metal of the pedals, his ankles and knees and hips flexing with pent up energy and his heart responding to the demands of his body as it guzzled freshly oxygenated blood and his lungs began to heave in gulpfuls of cool air. Now Adam watched as the spokes became a blur but for brief flashes of reflected moonlight zinging outwards and disappearing. Now his eyes became attuned to the road ten feet ahead, scanning for bumps and broken glass. On either side of the road trees stood to attention and parted politely to give him passage. He pictured the frogs and hedgehogs and deer of the night watching with awe as he flew past their homes and their hideouts. He pedalled hard, the rising steepness of the road burrowing itself into his firing muscles, the hill tugging at his stretching ligaments.

Where the stars met the horizon Adam could see the ragged

ridge of the Campsies. The hill rose at first gently in the east, the face becoming steeper towards the west, until it reached the jagged glen where he knew the river split the mound and dropped unevenly towards Clachan. West of the glen the long ridge turned north-west and Adam's vision could not catch the Lomond Hills beyond. But he could see enough by the midnight murk to head for the inviting hills. Past a couple of small towns he rode, their few street lights blaringly bright and exposing until he lapsed again into the comforting darkness of the unlit country road. Past farms he rode, where the fine rich stink of manure hung stagnant in the air. The cold air met his clammy warm skin and drove beads of sweat slowly around his face. His pyjamas began to dampen with sweat as his feet drove around and around in mindless, hypnotic motion.

His reverie was broken by the sight of twin headlights streaming over the trees ahead of him. He gripped his brakes tight, feeling the thrill of a skid as he came to a stop. He lifted the bike up the grass embankment on his left and hid amongst a cluster of white birch. The car lit up his spot as it rounded a corner but carried on past, and he was safe from curious scrutiny again. He got back on the bike and rode more slowly, looking out for a familiar but faint sign. A few minutes later he saw it, a dirty white sign for Emerson Wood. Adam hid the bike amongst some gorse bush and began to walk up the stony path on what he knew was ancient volcanic rock. The wood sat on a drumlin of it, spewed up magma from distant past.

To the east of the wood there was a dairy farm, and where the wood met the farmland was an abandoned hut. Adam, still breathing heavily from his ride and his climb, opened the rotting door to the hut. His eyes slowly adjusted to the blackness and he felt with his hand to clear the cobwebs from the doorway. He ducked inside and found the black bag where he had left it last time. He swung it over his shoulder and walked back up the hill to the summit of the little drumlin. By the milky moonlight he came upon the cairn of stones that he was looking for. The sheep had

135

disturbed them only a little. The stones were all a similar size, chalk-grey with little specks of quartz that caught the sallow moonlight. Adam dropped the bag and pulled out a khaki groundsheet. He folded it twice and lay it on the grass. He moved the stones into place, one at a time, deliberately, prayerfully. Gathered around the groundsheet the stones took on the rough shape of a coffin. Adam laid himself down inside the arrangement of stones, easing his flesh against the unforgiving ground. Hard lumps of soil pressed discordantly against his flesh.

He closed his eyes and for him the thin crust of the earth began to ripple and strain and the trees swayed and creaked and swollen shapes bulged amongst the grass and heather, and the dry skin of the country splintered and cracked as the deep impatient reserves of molten lava burst through the fragile ground, sending waves and waves of burning bright red and blood orange into the night sky where the stars were obscured and the ash and smoke billowed and burrowed fast into the troposphere, and forked lightning spat sparks through the rumbling mess and boiling rocks screamed through the electric air, sending demonic light in all directions, and Adam's breath quickened and his soul seared bright with pleasure and he saw it all unfold like a great burning tapestry, the earth's brute force and pent up energy pummelling the night sky. He saw the undulating waves of destructive power and he floated above it so that it spread out below him. He saw the heat of the raw living earth feed the spread and it billowed and swelled and flooded the land. Then, he watched as the eruption of magma began to slow, the white bright lightning began to dissipate, the cloud of ash lost its upward momentum and began to sink outwards and downwards, the fight against gravity lost, and the melted earth started to harden and stiffen. Over seconds and minutes and days and weeks the twisting liquid rock lost its movement and succumbed to cooling lethargy. Years passed patiently, the wind and ice and rain and sunshine sanded the land. And Adam from his narrator's elevation saw how the land changed. Igneous rock was left in grotesque and unnatural silhouettes. In time, the rich minerals gave birth to rich soil which gave birth to wild grass. The wild grass gave off a faint honeyed scent when the dew was upon it and petrichor after rain. Adam breathed in these smells as he lay on his altar and his quickened breath began to return to rest. He felt in himself the rolling history of these hills and the power that had sculpted them, and he claimed this small part as sacred.

16

Walter was standing on an African plain. It was early evening. The air was warm and utterly still around him. There was dry, cracked mud under his feet, a brilliant orange ochre. The ground felt hot and unforgiving on the skin of his feet. On each side of a him a few feet away the ground rose a couple of feet. He saw he was standing in a dried up river bed and it snaked in smooth curves along a wide flood plain. A long drought, he thought. The few trees around were spindly, jagged, Dali-esque. Flies buzzed around three rotting carcasses of what looked like antelope. The sky was turquoise blue, turning mauve and crimson at one horizon. Time had paused at dusk.

There appeared in his awareness a choice. To walk upstream or to walk downstream. Downstream, he could see through the shimmering haze of the ground's heat a village of mud huts. Some smoke rose from the village but no sound. Upstream, there was nothing except the dry plain and some high mountains in the distance. Downstream looked safer, more signs of life. But he turned and began walking upstream. Occasionally he had to step over the crumbling bones of a fish, or a large crack in the dried up river bed. Otherwise, he simply walked. The heat bounced off the ground, emanated from the ground, and distorted light and shapes. After a little time it seemed that through the swithering, rippling air, Walter could see green ahead. He moved out of the river bed onto the dead shore. The green grew larger and stronger. Not just a trick of the heat and light. The distortions began to crystallise and Walter saw he was approaching thick jungle. The dead ground stopped abruptly and live, green, lush vegetation began. Strong trees hung branches and creepers in alien and exotic shapes, and huge broad leaves dripped with moisture. Sounds sprung from the undergrowth, the buzzing of mosquitoes, croaks of a cricket, scurrying, secretive noises. Walter entered the forest in a trance. His lungs breathed in humid air perfumed by sweet orchids and rotting dead wood. He walked on and further on, and no longer felt the ground beneath his feet. Wispy fronds touched his face and he felt the strange, rough textures of tree trunks with his hands. He heard sounds which should have alarmed him but didn't, snakes in the undergrowth, vicious mosquitoes hovering close by.

Walter walked further in. He began to hear a different sound. A man made sound. A rhythmic thud, steady and magnetic. He moved in the direction of the sound. It become louder, and blended with the drumbeat were the sounds of voices. There was a compulsive draw to the sound and Walter moved unquestioningly towards it. Soon, he smelled smoke. The smoke had a piercing, pungent scent within it. He stepped on a branch which broke loudly. The drumming and chanting almost imperceptibly began to quieten. The beating which had been bold and echoed, now started to shrink down, lower, softer, with a quality of anticipation about it. Walter could do no other than continue walking, and now he could see the men. There was a clearing in the forest, perfectly round, man-made perhaps. In the clearing stood about thirty men standing in a circle, stamping their feet and thudding the ground with long ornamental spears. They were black and the darkening dusk made them blacker. But their bodies and faces were coloured with lines and shapes of paint, blood red and tangerine and chalky white. Walter left the shade of the undergrowth and stepped into the clearing. The circle broke and widened in front of him and he saw that he was to take his appointed place. As with one mind, the circle stopped their beating. The men all turned their heads towards Walter and nodded once in unison. They all then turned their gaze to the centre of the circle.

He saw that in the middle of the circle two men were lying flat on their backs, naked but adorned with many beads and with long thick stripes of red paint diagonally across their torsos. They looked young. Their eyes were fixed on the sky straight above them and their bodies were utterly still. A shout came from the other side of the circle and one of the men stepped out of the circle towards the centre. He wore an elaborate mask of bark, painted like a face with a huge wide grin and his eyes stared through narrow holes. A stringy grey beard hung from below the mask. Strapped to his back were two spears and in his hand he carried a small black sack. The chief walked to the two men. He knelt down at each in turn, and whispered something in their ears. The chief lay down his sack on the hard ground and opened the top. He took out a fistful of pebbles in his right hand. He faced the first man, kneeling at his side. He took a pebble and placed it on the young man's belly button. He took another pebble and placed it on the young man's left thigh, then another on his right thigh. He placed pebbles on his thighs and shins, on his belly and chest, on his arms and on his forehead. The chief stood up, and took from a small pouch at his groin a flat piece of flint. He held the flint in his bony left hand and raised it in salute to the circle of men. He knelt down again beside the young man. The chief took hold of the man's foreskin and stretched it out. The young man let out a rumbling growl. The flint flashed quickly through the skin and a soaring howl flew to the sky. But the young man stayed still. His muscles twitched and were taut with the brutal effort but he remained still. The pebbles on every part of his body stayed. The chief stood, took a spear from his back, and began shaking it in the air. The chant began again and the other men shook their spears. A perplexed smile came onto the face of the wounded man. One of those in the circle approached the initiate, took his hand and helped him by to his feet. He held a rag to the man's wound. The wounded man held the rag in place and they both walked to where the circle had now opened. The wounded men was led off into the shadows.

Now that Walter had seen what would happen, he stared with intensity at the other initiate still lying on the ground. As before, the chief approached the young man. Each step was slow and measured. Walter felt something pounding and a morbid astonishment at what was to happen. The chief began placing the pebbles on the appointed places of the man's body. Walter could almost feel the touch of stone on his skin, the muscles held tense, the desire to remain strong. The chief took again his flint and raised it to the circle of men. Walter felt pain and fear emanating from his groin. The chief bent down beside the initiate. A thread, an umbilical cord of fear ran between Walter and the initiate. Now, the initiate turned his head sideways and looked directly at Walter, sparks in his eyes and furious intensity in his face and as the flint scythed through the air, the initiate contorted his face and howled and Walter was falling, tumbling, through darkness and green leaves and the bites of mosquitoes and awoke, violently, straining for breath and dripping with sweat.

17

It was now early in October and the crispness of autumn was biting at the heels of the departing summer as Joe arrived at Hunter House for his weekly session with Walter. The day would warm up but it was the mornings that foretold the coming season. It was a day to be outside, to use the palatable conditions before they died. It was Walter who suggested a walk in the park for their session, and the idea resonated with Joe.

'I don't know why things trigger me sometimes,' Walter began when they were safe amongst the muffling greenery of Tollcross Park. 'Feel like a big soft marshmallow or something. I was at the swimming pool the other day. Did my lengths. Got out, got dressed. I was standing in the cafe where it overlooks the pool. I was speaking to a couple of the other old timers. Talking about who's had what replaced recently. Between the three of us we've got about three good hips, two good knees, and half a dozen original teeth.

'Anyway, we were watching a young boy with Down's Syndrome. He was there with his dad, I guess. Maybe thirteen or fourteen. He was havin a whale of a time. Doing belly flops til his skin was red as an apple. I was watching his dad. He was just enjoying watching his son. Laughing with him. No self-consciousness from either of them. And I thought about what it might be like to have a kid who...' Walter stared at the ground, his eyes scanning for the right word.

'I thought of the hopes that dad might have had for his son. And then... Realising his son had, I don't know, what's the right word these days?'

'A disability?' Joe offered.

'Aye, that's it. And him realising that his child was ... different to how he'd expected. Realising his son wouldn't do all the things that might be expected of him.

'Anyway, I was thinking about all that. But mostly I was watching this boy canter around. Not a care in the world. Totally free and innocent. At one point, he was about to run and jump in and he saw me and my buddies watching him. I guess we must all have been smiling at him. Well, what does he do but come over to us, a huge grin on his face, and he hugs me. Just me. Not the others. And I'm dressed and he's soaking wet. It caught me totally off guard. Hugged me like he'd known me all his life. And it seemed so ... so natural and normal for him. And at the time, I just thought it was a bit funny. Touching, you know? The other guys, they just got smiles. Me, I got a hug. And I don't know why, why me? And then, he ran down the side of the pool, waved to us, and jumped about a mile in the air and into the water. The whole place was watching.'

Walter's face was tight from keeping back tears. They both watched as a grey squirrel scurried across the grass on the other side of the path and scrambled up a white birch whose bark was peeling away like ancient manuscript.

'And it keeps coming back to me. I've thought about that boy every day. I don't know why it gets me so much. It just feels ... emotional.'

'What is it you feel when you think about it now?'

The lines were deeply etched on Walter's face and his mouth was shut tight.

'Like a big barrel of water filling up, threatening to overflow. Like fear and love and envy and gratitude all tangled up in each other.' Walter stared hard at the ground and gripped his stick and suddenly choked up, tears coming now and his shoulders shaking and the powerful silence of inhaling just enough breath to feed the cry, and then sobbing loudly, as Joe looked on, shocked and feeling much of the emotion as well, feeling saltwater well in his own tired eyes too. Walter cried freely, his head almost nodding, seconding the motion, surrendering. He reached for his handkerchief and covered his face, covered his emotional nakedness. Then soon the two men were quiet in a tender sorrow neither of them really understood, letting Walter's waves of feeling break on the shore as they needed to, quietening, drawing down as his breath slowed and lengthened.

'Ah for Pete's sake! The one time I cry is the one time we're out in public.'

'Ach never mind the stoic West of Scotland male thing,' Joe replied. 'It's all good. Nobody around anyway. And the squirrels don't judge.'

Walter continued to dab at his face and his breathing deepened further. Somewhere in the park a dog was yelping excitedly and closer by the undergrowth rustled with scavenging birds.

'What about you Joe? Don't ye ever cry?'

Joe was grateful Walter's gaze was not upon him as he mulled his answer.

'Is that … relevant, important?'

'Well, aye, I think so. You encourage this kind of thing, don't you? Your generation, they say they're getting more 'sensitive', 'enlightened' and all that. Don't do that skirting round the question with smart-alec tangents and bamboozlin me with psycho-babble.'

Joe was on the spot but curiously glad of Walter's uncharacteristic prodding.

'Well, sometimes, yes. Not as often as I should.' A fractured image cut into his awareness, of Sarah's arm in the grip of the dog's teeth. No tears that day. Nor on the night when the woman got attacked and spurned his offer of help. Nor when he'd attacked Harry on that dark, rainy night, and half-drowned in fear and confusion. Joe's dam of tears had yet to burst, despite the strain and pressure building against it. Perhaps Walter was the wiser one for giving in to it.

'It's hard to know, isn't it?' Walter continued. 'How much attention to give to your own problems, and how much to give to the wider world's. Your own stuff feels so big to you but it's tiny in the big scheme of things. I sometimes worry I'm just indulging myself, blowing it up so it obscures my view of what's really important out there. Maybe this is self-centred. Maybe I'd be better if my focus was out there more than in here. What do you think?'

They paused as a woman walked by with a spaniel straining at his leash, jittering and leaping towards the undergrowth. Walter nodded hello as she passed.

'Honestly Walter, I worry about that too. Sometimes. This process can seem indulgent. We can get lost in the nitty-gritty and lose sight of the bigger tasks and priorities of life. You remember when I came over and you were out at the shed with Grant? I meant what I said that day. Sometimes working with more tangible practical stuff is a welcome balancing to the abstract, invisible matters of psychological work. But I also know this is important too. It's valid and it's necessary. Sometimes we need to do the tiny stuff to enable the big stuff. And lots of people need to know that their individual private struggles are important, and can't just be written off because someone else's suffering is worse. Telling yourself it doesn't matter doesn't ring true, doesn't work.'

The wind whispered around them and played with the crisp leaves on the ground.

'I was at a protest a few months ago,' Walter continued. 'Anti-nuclear weapons. Peaceful, you know, properly planned and civil and all that. But what if your convictions tell you to break the law, to break the rules, for a good cause? How far should you go in trusting your own instincts? Do you ever break the rules for a good cause Joe? Maybe I've toed the line too much. Maybe I should have been stronger.

'After I got drafted during the war I swore I'd never do that again. Swore I'd never march into my brother's land with a gun in my hands. Swore I'd go the extra mile to avoid bloodshed. Sure, the war was a tricky one, morally. Maybe we had to defend ourselves. And the others. It was all mayhem. But violence always begets more violence, doesn't it? We might be part of the solution and part of the problem all at the same time. Nobody ever truly backs down. The rage just goes underground for a time. Unless it's actually transformed. And that doesn't happen much.'

'What about you Walter? Is there anything in you that you still wish could be transformed?'

'I had another dream. I was in a jungle - who knows where. Must be watchin' too many Vietnam movies. I found this big clearing right in the thick of it. There were all these standing stones, arranged in a circle. They were all different heights, but all tall and thin. As I got closer, I realised they were arranged in a spiral, all leading into a point in the centre where the biggest one stood, a beast of a thing. I walked around them and between them – I can remember how the surfaces felt warm and smooth. The place was so quiet, like the buzzing jungle was miles away.

'As I walked around the stones, I found a space. On the outside of the spiral, there was a space where another rock should have been. There was a flat slate on the ground, like a plinth, ready and waiting. So, of course, I stood on it, like I was testing it out, was this my place to fill? I stood there and looked up to the sky – it was grey, like a thunderstorm was gathering. I can remember the soft flesh of my feet against the hard ragged rock. As I stood there, the other stones began to, I don't know how to describe it, they began to change. They stayed still and just as they were but at the same time, below the surface, like it was stretched granite skin, I could see grey shapes developing. It was subtle, so subtle I could've been imagining it. But it was like the grey rock was revealing shapes. Like a thick belly, gnarled legs, a breathing chest, a hairy head, bulgy cheeks, closed eyes. And it was like they were old, they had once been men, great men perhaps, the elders of a tribe. It made me sad that I wasn't one of them, and wanted to be. And it tantalised me that maybe, just maybe, that could be my place one day, that I might earn that dignity.'

Silence sank over them again like purple velvet. Joe looked up through the trees. Dark clouds were sneaking towards them from the west.

'I wish I had found out more about my dad. I do wish that now. And I wish I'd cracked open that bloody stone. Have it done with either way.'

'Maybe it's not too late?'

'No, I think it is too late Joe. I missed my chance. Don't miss yours.'

18

Later that day, Joe and Pauline were nearing the end of the session. The approaching limit was often a catalyst for the kind of self-disclosure that deserved further time to explore, just when time was running out.

Pauline spoke.

'I want to tell my dad to stop bullying me. I've had enough. I'm tired of him slagging me off, putting me down, all that shit. He's been a right pain in the arse recently. I'd love to tell him that.'

Joe hid his surprise but not his pleasure.

'Go on. Say more.'

'Well, it's all that stuff we've been talking about here. Me moaning about him here, and then I go back out there and let him do it again. I'm getting pissed aff at myself now.'

'As you talk about this, you're sounding stronger, more in tune with your own needs and rights. There's a kind of compassionate self-respect there.'

'Aye, well, that too. You know, Joe, sometimes you take normal talk and you dress it up in your psycho-lingo. Like sticking Samantha Fox in an evening dress. But, I know you mean well.'

Joe let himself be bashful for a moment.

'Alright, fair point. Bring me back down to earth why don't you.'

'Anyway. I was thinkin.' About speaking to my dad. I remember you saying, 'sometimes you need a pal.' Some back up, you know. Someone else to keep you on track when you're tempted to back down.'

Pauline was indeed quoting Joe back to himself. And there was a click in his head and then he knew with terrible certainty where she was going with this. His mind fell out of gear and whirred uselessly in neutral as he tried to think of a way to head this off.

'I wondered whether I could bring my dad to one of these sessions. Just once. To tell him what I really think.'

Joe realised now he had managed to convince himself that he'd gotten away with it. Convinced himself there would be no real consequences. Now his stupidity had come back to bite him, and bit him hard it did. To his shame, he dissembled, stalled for time.

'Well, I'm happy to consider that, and talk over the potential pros and cons. Why do you think it might help to bring him here?'

Pauline responded but Joe was lost in a frantic analysis of self-protective problem-solving. It was a sign of real progress that Pauline wanted to confront her dad. It was a sign of her success and Joe's success. And she had no-one as supportive in her life as Joe, so of course she would think to ask Joe to be her witness and her back up. But even without Joe's clumsy fight with Harry, her idea of bringing him to a session was loaded with potential pitfalls and questions. What if he refused to come? What if he came and listened, then waited until they were safely home before tearing into her again? Perhaps nothing would change. Perhaps it would make things worse.

But add in Joe's history with Harry. Would Harry recognise him? He had been pretty drunk. It had been dark and wet. But perhaps Joe was kidding himself. Maybe you'd remember the face of someone standing over you and shouting in your face, even with a few pints under your belt. If Harry did come, and did recognise Joe, what then? Would he attack Joe there and then? Wait for him outside one night with a hammer? Follow him home? Tell Joe's boss and get him fired? Perhaps even charged with assault? He had played out all these nightmare scenarios in the hours and days after the attack. They had been slowly receding into unlikelihood as days passed without consequences. Indeed Joe confronting Harry seemed to have emboldened Pauline. She knew something had happened because Harry wasn't as cocky and rough after it. Now, quite healthily, she wanted to stand up to him. Joe's therapeutic patience and his un-therapeutic recklessness had helped move Pauline to this point, which then threatened his very career and his safety and his liberty. It was like the Ouroboros snake devouring its own tail.

He realised Pauline had stopped talking and was looking at him expectantly. He needed time to think, to strategize, to figure this out. The pressure to make a decision in this moment was too much and he didn't trust himself right now.

'Pauline, I appreciate where you're coming from. I'm glad you want to stand up to your dad. But I need a bit of time to think about this, to figure out what to do. We need to think about the best way to handle this. I don't want to risk making things worse. Can you leave this with me til next week and we can talk about it further then?'

Pauline looked disappointed but had no choice. Joe hoped she wouldn't chalk this up as yet another person not taking her seriously. More than that he hoped the ground would open up and swallow the whole impossible situation, because he saw no good way out of it. Pauline left him alone, unaware of the horn of a dilemma upon which she had just impaled him.

The northern half of the earth tilted further and further from the dear warm sun and the people of Glasgow began to quietly brace for the winter. The trees shed their summer finery, the grass took a break from growing, the animals that could began to grow their extra fur, and people began to rummage in the bottoms of their drawers for woolly jumpers and those thick ugly socks the kids bought them three Christmases ago. The visitors to the city became a trickle as they left the city to its winter endurance. The greens of the parks became a little less green and the clouds cast a grey wetness over the office blocks and schools and high-rises and factories. Joe took the bus from Dennistoun to Parkhead, getting off at Parkhead Cross. He walked wearily down Springfield Road to the social work offices. They were housed in one of the many

150

Victorian school buildings which had fallen out of use as the new wave of schools were built in the seventies and eighties. The ceilings were too high for heating to be efficient, and the playgrounds were all concrete. The old school had been put back into use as the social work base for the east end.

Joe was there to attend a meeting about the children of one of his clients. Mary had a serious alcohol problem, though she'd been sober for nine weeks now. The social workers had put her two kids into the care of their father Sajid, who had split from Mary a year ago. His family had been less than pleased at him going out with a western girl, but he had already been pulling away from their generation before he met Mary. His family were first generation immigrants from Pakistan but he had grown up in Scotland, absorbing its accent, its clothes and its football.

The two boys were four and two and Mary saw them under social work supervision twice a week, on the condition she was sober. She dearly wanted to be a good enough mum and she talked in her sessions with Joe about wanting a better family for her kids than she had had growing up. But great damage had been done already in her life and it would take more than sheer willpower to unravel the knotted messages she'd received. It was too easy for her to drink, especially with the kids not there, and she was hanging onto sobriety by her fingertips. After previous lapses, the social workers had temporarily stopped her contact for the kids' sake, and the children were confused and scared. She had almost exhausted her second chances.

This particular meeting had been called to discuss the care arrangements, with everyone present. Joe was attending as Mary's therapist. Mary and Sajid would be there, the social workers, and the health visitor. Joe hated these meetings, necessary as they were, though no doubt Mary hated them more. He was the person most on her side, but he knew there had to be limits where the children's welfare was concerned. He did not envy the social workers who had to make these decisions, and he believed they usually did their best in horrible situations.

As he entered the building, Joe was acutely aware that Mary had missed his last appointment with him three days before, at which they had planned to prepare for the meeting. She had not phoned and he feared the worst. Joe signed in at the front desk and sat down to wait to be called in. He felt again a creeping sense of fatigue and futility and the whole sordid business with Pauline and her dad had moved him closer to the edge, like another ten pence piece dropped into the penny falls machine, the pressure building. He had entered the helping profession to help but increasingly he felt the hard limits of what could be done. Like others, he tried to enter empathically into the subjective world of the other, though it was delusion to think you were living it like the client was living it. To care was a risk, and in Mary's case Joe feared the risk was about to backfire.

A tall grey man with a manila folder under his arm approached Joe.

'Joe Miller?' he asked.

'Yes, that's me.'

'Hi. I'm Graeme White, senior social worker. D'you want to come through?'

He led the way through double doors and up wide stairs. Joe followed the social worker into a large room lit with harsh fluorescents, with a lacquered wooden floor and tall sash windows. Around a rectangular table were grey plastic chairs. Two women sat on the opposite side of the table. One introduced herself as Olivia, the family's social worker. She wore the vibrant summer colours of her native Malawi and her wide beam of a smile pushed fulsome cheeks high on her face. She greeted Joe with a handshake. The other woman was introduced as Sarah McAllister, the boys' nursery teacher. Her face was open and kind, though there were lines of worry around her eyes.

One by one the others arrived. The health visitor, and then the GP. It must be serious if the GP has come, thought Joe with a

152

shiver. Lastly Mary and Sajid arrived. Mary made little eye contact with anyone. She was dressed okay but her makeup looked desperate and her hair was ragged. Her face failed to hide a desperate fear, and she sat hugging her arms against her chest, shaking ever so slightly.

The social workers took the lead

'Thank you everyone for coming,' said Graeme. 'Mary, I'm especially glad you're here as we make some decisions about the care arrangements for Marcus and Ben. As you know, each of the professionals here will give a short report about their involvement with the boys, or with yourself. Mary and Sajid, you'll also have the opportunity to give your views about where we go from here. At the end of the meeting, Olivia and I will make a decision about that. Perhaps we can start with some introductions.'

The meeting progressed routinely. The nursery teacher and health visitor agreed that the boys were doing pretty well, all things considered. They both worried that the ups and downs of Mary's contact with her sons could be confusing and upsetting for the boys. The GP had little to say, except some comment about Mary's liver damage and the likely effect that her drinking would continue to have on her physical and mental health. When it came to Joe, he spoke as hopefully as he could.

'As you all know, Mary has been attending therapy sessions with me for around three months, and she was aware that I would have to share some information from those sessions in these kinds of meetings. Mary, I guess in our sessions, we have been trying to better understand the reasons for your drinking. I'm not going to go into detail about those here, but I think it's right to say that your own family background has played a significant role in your lack of confidence in yourself, and in your need for escapism. I know from our discussions how much you want to be there for your boys, and how they've become a really important motivation for you. Graeme, Olivia, I know it's your job to make decisions about the boys' care. For my part, I would be hopeful that Mary could make further progress in our sessions, especially in finding healthier coping strategies, so that drinking becomes easier to resist. I do have to add, though, that we were due to meet on Tuesday and Mary didn't attend that session. I don't know what happened there.'

Mary looked like she was about to vomit as Olivia spoke up.

'I can say something about that. Mary, as you know, you were due to see the boys for supervised contact here on Monday. The boys were really looking forward to seeing you.' Tears were now streaming down Mary's face, her black mascara running badly. Joe's guts started to churn.

'When you arrived here, you were clearly under the influence of alcohol. When I met you at reception, I explained that you wouldn't be able to see the boys in that state.'

Olivia addressed the other professionals.

'Mary began shouting at me and demanding to see the boys. We had to keep the main door locked because she starting kicking and punching it. Unfortunately, down the corridor the boys heard what was going on. They thought someone was hurting their mum. They didn't understand what was happening. We had to escort Mary out of the building. We called her mum to make sure someone could take her home and make sure she was safe.'

Mary was crying loudly now, sniffing wetly between intakes of breath. Sajid sitting beside her had one hand on her back, his head in the other hand. No-one knew where to look. Joe was tensed all over, sweating uncomfortably. The senior social worker took over.

'We have to make a decision based on the best interests of the boys. In an ideal world, that would include positive time with both parents. But Mary, when you turn up to see the boys when you've been drinking, it puts all the progress back by months. We've spoken separately to Sajid and he is willing to care for the boys full-time. Mary, we need to suspend all contact between you and the boys.' Graeme almost had to shout to make himself heard over Mary's crying.

'We will review your case in a year. If you have remained sober during that time, we will re-consider some supervised contact at that time. For now, the boys are in the sole custody of their dad, and they're to have no contact with you. Mary, Sajid, do either of you want to say anything?' Sajid shook his head, Mary was just lost.

'Well I think we should bring this meeting to a close,' Graeme said finally.

Mary was in a world of her own now, her arms wrapped around her head in desolation. Sajid, normally languid, was shaking slightly. He was beside Mary but the distance between them was palpable. Olivia had to stay with Mary whether she wanted to or not. Joe put away his papers, stood slowly, put on his jacket, and nodded to the others as they left. He moved a few steps towards Mary then faltered, not knowing what to do. He was acutely aware of being one of the professionals, one of those with power, one of those who could go home to his own life at 5 o'clock. He hoped she did not blame him and yet he felt he'd failed her. He didn't know what to say. It could not possibly be right to talk to her just now about further sessions but neither did it feel right to leave her in limbo.

'I'm sorry Mary' he said. His voice was quiet and pinched. He did not know exactly what his sorry was for. She did not lift her head to him, perhaps did not even hear him. Sajid stood, came away from the table and said thank you to Joe, shaking his hand. Joe felt some relief at this acknowledgement that he had at least tried. But he knew it was a gratitude pierced through with pity, disappointment politely concealed. It felt wrong, Joe and Sajid, two men standing, functioning, accentuating Mary's inability to function.

Words were Joe's only real tool, and in that moment he could find none to salve, to restore, to bring hope. He was rooted to the spot. He could not work out when or where to move. In his silence was sympathy and concern and sorrow, but he was unable to make that silence known to Mary. For all she knew it was a silence of cowardice or callousness.

19

Joe left the room, and was mercifully alone in the bright corridor. He was desperate to get out of the building and ashamed of how unable he was to tolerate or communicate his discomfort. He moved in a trance through the double glass doors, through reception, and out into a dark grey humidity. He turned instinctively north, needing simply to walk somewhere. His face was red with awkwardness. His back and shoulders and neck and jaw were taut and his movements jarred against the stiffness. He strode painfully and tears congregated behind his eyes.

Joe crossed London Road, running over the tarmac as a bus blared a horn at him. He marched up Duke Street, past the empty barren site of the old steelworks. The works had shrunk over many years and finally closed in 1981. He walked past fenced walls, the empty red brick buildings and steel black cranes still visible over the fences. The desolate emptiness of the giant site seemed to sigh in great sympathy with Mary, as Joe replayed and replayed how she crumbled in that meeting. He remembered the shine in her eyes just a few weeks before as she began to hope that she might be leaving her drinking behind. She had raised her hopes – and he had raised her hopes, he realised now. He had colluded with a risky venture, and perhaps he ought to have known better. He berated himself viciously. He told himself he should have used more structure in the sessions, not let it flow so organically. He imagined other therapists doing it better. And he couldn't just back out and lick his wounds. He would have to be the one to sit with her in her bleakness. There would be little incentive for sobriety now. Would she even want to keep working with Joe after this? This was not a game, he scolded himself. The stakes are high, real people going through real dramas.

He was almost talking out loud to himself as he reached Duke Street and slunk under the railway bridge towards Dennistoun. The weariness which had been building for months started to creep heavier over his body. The feeling, becoming familiar, that perhaps he had made a mistake. Perhaps he was not right for this work. Perhaps he had pushed too far beyond his abilities and temperament, pushed further than he was equipped to go. Perhaps it had been presumptuous to hope he might overcome his basic shyness about emotions and a mistake to choose a profession where his only tool was himself. His frailty hung heavily on him as he trudged west along Duke Street, past bookies and pubs, newsagents and barbers. He walked past Coia's and remembered with nausea the business with Pauline's dad, terrible possibilities still hanging over him.

By the time he got to Oakley Terrace Joe's sweat had become stale, a headache was building in his temples, and he was thirsting for escape and absolution. His thighs shimmered with sore fatigue as he climbed the steps to the front door. In the department, he went into the office to let Bernie know he was back. She sat behind her typewriter and looked concerned. He opened his mouth to tell her what had happened but what little energy he had left was finally sucked out of him when he saw Oliver sitting on the armchair opposite Bernie.

'How did it go?' Bernie asked.

Joe took a few breaths. 'It was bloody awful. You remember I'd said she missed her last session with me? Well, she'd been drinking. And she turned up drunk for a supervised visit at social work. They've banned her from seeing the kids for the next year. The dad's got full custody.'

'Was she there, at the meeting?' Bernie asked.

Joe looked Bernie in the eye and nodded quickly. He rubbed the thumb and middle finger of his right hand hard on his forehead. Then he scratched up and down on the back of his head sharply, sighing loudly.

Oliver piped up in his favourite tone of resigned but superior knowledge. 'Well that's how it usually goes with that type.'

Joe's jaw clenched and a faint rumble came from his throat as he breathed out.

'And what 'type' do you think she is?'

'Well, borderlines of course. They *thrive* on drama. Probably best the kids are with their dad.' Oliver spoke as if he was enlightening Joe. 'I've seen it so many times. You can try your best with them but they're basically untreatable. The illness is too ingrained. And it works for them, in roundabout ways. Secondary gains, you know?'

'Oliver, you hardly know anything about her. What are you basing this opinion on?'

Joe had folded his arms and turned so he was facing Oliver directly. Bernie tried to focus on a pile of papers on her desk. She had never seen Joe challenge Oliver, and Oliver seemed oblivious to the reaction he was inducing.

'I read your report on her. Very compassionate and all but the clinical indicators are all there. She's probably got you believing in her innocent victim persona.' A note of imperiousness came into Oliver's speech.

Joe stared at Oliver for an excruciating few seconds. He looked out the window for restraint, found none, and returned his attention to Oliver.

'What gives you the right to sit there casting diagnostic insults at someone you barely know? This is one of our patients! Someone we're meant to be helping. Have you any idea what you sound like?' Joe's voice was building in strength. He could feel the same exhilarating and frightening release of pent up anger as when he confronted Pauline's dad. The wave was hitting the shore and nothing would stop it breaking now. Oliver looked utterly confused.

'I'm sick of your condescending, know it all, self-aggrandising, pretentious grandstanding. Have you never looked at your own stuff? Do you think anyone around here cares about your egocentric ramblings? I'm sick of it, sick of it!' Oliver was staring, his hands gripping the chair, his face losing colour. Bernie was paralysed and cringing.

'These patients, yes, of course some of them confuse us and irritate us. But we're the ones who need to make the effort to rise above those reactions, get beneath them, beyond them, whatever. But it suits you, doesn't it, to stick them in one of your pigeonholes. That way you're still in control, they're unwell and you're alright. Well, Oliver, I'm sorry to be the one to tell you but it just isn't that simple. Go and get your own therapy and maybe then you'll have something useful to offer these patients. Honest to God, the crap we have to listen to from you.'

Oliver was staring at Joe, silently enraged but almost impotent to speak. He recovered belatedly.

'How dare you speak to me like that!'

'How dare you call yourself a therapist!' The malignancy of Joe's attack sucked the air out of the room.

'I'm taking my annual leave now.' Joe turned, opened the door, closed it behind him and they heard the front door slam.

Oliver stood immediately and swept out of the office, his studied neutral expression painfully distorted and his long limbs rigid and brittle. Bernie heard him enter his office and close the door quietly. Bernie realised she'd been holding her breath. She put her head back, opened her mouth widely, and pushed air out through pursed lips. She put a hand over her mouth, and looked around, suddenly alone with the conversation reverberating in the room and a low whine in her ears. She rose from her desk, straightened her skirt, and went to make a cup of tea.

Joe's train ride home was torture. Everybody that squeezed into the carriage exuded warm air and bad breath and meaningless chatter that pounded like a cracked snare in his throbbing head. The bumps and wobbles of the train jarred discordantly against his steel-tense

160

body. Elephant-grey clouds spat heavy lumps of rain at the city, and it cast a blurred curtain of water over the window Joe stared dumbly through. The strength he harvested from silence was used and crumpled, and now his quietness was a prison. He jammed his fingers under his thighs but still they kept on shaking, shaking out, releasing nothing, useless gesture of the body's shock. By the time Joe arrived home his stomach was cramping and his head was pounding but somehow mush as well. Patches of sweat were spreading under his arms, and even he could not miss the acrid smell. He felt assailed by his own stupidity, and a restless terror was creeping over him. When he closed the front door of the tenement, he no longer had the comforting noise of the outside world to interfere with his internal babbling, and in the quietness of his kitchen where he finally lay his head in his hands, the tumult and folly bellowed in his head. He breathed quicker and quicker, his stomach roiling in spasm, heat rising through his chest, his neck, his burning face. The words he had fired at Oliver repeated and repeated in his ears, the crumpling expression on Oliver's face hung in front of him like a pathetic grey piñata. Acid bile bubbled inside him and he stumbled to the bathroom and gripped the toilet until his body heaved and he was sick, not copious and restorative but thin and stingy, leaving him no better off. As he limped out of the bathroom, he saw his copy of Psychotherapy Monthly lying behind the front door, a picture of wise old Carl Jung on the cover, serene and apparently unfazeable. Joe snatched it up and threw it down the toilet. Emboldened by his gesture, he ran to the cupboard under the sink and ripped out a black bag. He stumbled to the living room, to the bookcase in the alcove and grabbed his therapy books from their pretentiously arranged places and flung them into the black bag, fine white paper bending and creasing and ripping, back page bearded faces lost to the plastic darkness. He yanked open a window, threw the bag into the back court, and closed the curtains on the world.

20

There is a strangely liminal space you enter when your stupidity or your errant emotions knock you from your pedestal and your future spins sickeningly off-balance. The train has careened off its tracks and is ripping clumsily through pretty fields, trailing destruction, embarrassingly visible. For once Joe had no idea what would or should happen next. His dependence on calm had deserted him. The building crisis of confidence and his flagging compassion had reached a zenith. Again he tasted a dangerous liberation amongst the sour shame and regret, as if he had secretly enjoyed the loss of his patience and the running dry of his ability to hold his tongue. His life-long avoidance of conflict had not stopped his outburst with Oliver, nor his fumbling attack on Harry. What further control might ebb away slowly or disintegrate in a moment's heat?

He lay in bed for two days punishing himself by not eating, not washing, not coping. In the days he dozed on and off, fitful sleep blurring with the torture of consciousness. The bedclothes writhed and twisted about him, determined to entrap him, wrapping their warm tentacles round his restless limbs, soaked with fevered sweat then irritatingly dry, tucked in clumsily then pulled loose again, every bump and loose spring choosing part of his aching body to prod and pester, the embossed squares of the papered ceiling swimming in endless kaleidoscopic Escher trips through dim eyes into an even dimmer brain. Images formed slowly from fragments, swathed in the sad colours of pale dusk. Jackie entering the bomb shelter that bright day at the hospital, that brick house limbo, cocooned against falling destruction, the darkness swallowing her up. Adam high up in the tree, out of Joe's reach, achieving something Joe couldn't, the tree twisting and tangling around Joe's helpless limbs, ants and spiders and wasps crawling around him.

The dog that savaged Sarah's arm, its drooling bloody jaw snapping hideously again and again in Joe's hands and its limp body lying pathetic on sweet green grass. He fantasised about some kind of suitable punishment, a way to do penance, to neutralise the guilt. At some point the doorbell buzzed but it only filtered into Joe's dulled awareness through a thick layer of mental sludge.

And the thought now of having to attend to another client's story, to find within himself compassion, empathy, patience, or curiosity, felt like razor blades under his finger nails. Lost was the desire to help, the desire to co-understand, the desire to unravel knotted problems, and in their place only the desire to rest, to be left alone, to be salved and shriven. Stories which once had moved and enlivened him now felt cold and empty, hard work rather than good work.

On the third day, the rain pummelled the city all day whilst Joe nursed a black coffee at his kitchen table and forced some limp toast down. It rained whilst he sat in his armchair failing to read even the simplest of books. It rained whilst he lay in the bath until the water cooled and his body shivered. As the day wore on, and the sun began to die, Joe decided something must be done, anything, to break the paralysis. He got dressed, loose jeans and loose shirt, a thick red lumberjack jacket bought second hand in Flip, the collar turned up. He left the flat in its ruffled state and headed towards Albert Drive. In the newsagent, he bought coke and chewing gum, and headed for the Clyde. From the peak of Shields Road Joe looked over the city to his north and beyond to the Campsies. He walked what once had been the freight railroad to the docks at Kingston, now long gone along with Kingston itself, a whole neighbourhood razed to make way for the motorway that cracked open the city like a fault line. He passed under the motorway, where the coo-ing of pigeons bounced hypnotically around the concrete pillars. The thick road rumbled and shook above him. In Kinning Park, he passed the Grand Ole Opry where grey-faced men and overweight women danced in squares whilst the corn-sweet end of the country and western spectrum blared. Down he walked past the dying infrastructure of the shipyards.

Eventually he stood at the side of the Clyde. Far below him the gathered white scum and detritus of the river slapped against the river wall, broken tree limbs, Irn Bru bottles, crisp packets, a ripped bicycle tyre. The shipyards had been ripped from their roots leaving gaping concrete wounds that nature was struggling to re-colonise. The riverfront was ragged and ugly, abandoned and unloved.

Now, with the fresh air around him, he could stare hard in the face his predicament and his options. He could continue for only so long in anxious rumination. He saw clearly for the first time that he was fatigued of compassion. His interest in people and his care for their wellbeing was badly unwell. But what can a helper do when they are meant to help and cannot? Joe stared down at the river. He remember a painting he'd seen at the Kelvingrove, of the river at this very point two hundred years ago when the shore was fields and meadows, leading softly down to the water's edge, where horses drank and children paddled. That was before they dredged it and deepened it and cast walls at its sides for shipyards and piers and streets and commerce. How simple and inexorable was the flow of the river, going blindly where gravity allowed it.

He thought of casting himself upon the river and letting it carry him without question or judgement down its widening course, past Partick, past Clydebank, spilling eventually into the firth of Clyde where eddies and strange currents flustered the water, and floating further, if the tide was kind, out past Dunoon, past Great Cumbrae and its pretty town, past Little Cumbrae with its colonies of oystercatchers and curlews, past Arran and Kintyre, the mainland shrinking into insignificance, and on out into the mighty Atlantic where swells of deep dark water would lift him like an offering to the sky, a sacrifice to the gods, then lay him down low again in the space between swells, hidden momentarily amongst the protective waves, entombed, then up, up again, the muscular power of the water utterly in control, his own body willingly limp and useless, at the mercy of the great other, devoid of will or agency.

Joe leaned on the rusty railing and aimed rocks at a football floating slowly past where he stood. The rocks missed, inevitably, and the ball bobbed happily on the ripples they left. It took him some time to register the voice shouting into his consciousness.

'Hey mister! Hey! Gonnie gie us a hon?'

Joe looked round, his head heavy and his movement forced. Whilst he had been staring at the water, the day had darkened further, but the slate grey clouds were pierced through here and there by sharp shafts of marble-white sunlight and the air was drying. Against the grey cityscape behind him a boy under a tree was waving wildly at him. The clump of trees had marked the edge of the tenement backcourts where they met the shipyard. The yard and the flats were gone, leaving only crumpled waste ground and the trees, shocking bursts of verdant green against the bones and ashes of the demolished buildings.

Joe's mind was sluggish and he could not tell what the boy wanted but he walked in a trance towards the trees. His legs felt like sandbags. Closer he could see there were three boys gathered under one tree. Closer still he saw they were poking unsuccessfully at something with their sticks.

'Hey big man, can y' help us get that frisbee doon?'

The boys were all in variations of grey tracksuits and it was the smallest who had shouted for his help.

'Can you not climb up and get it?' Joe asked.

'D'ye no think we'd huv tried that? The branches here are too high.'

Joe looked up to the frisbee then looked around him.

'Give me that stick, the long one,' Joe said. With the crooked branch in his hand, Joe stretched. He slapped at the branch but the frisbee was just out of reach and wedged well into a crook of branches. He did not have the energy to jump.

'Just put me up on your shoulders,' said the boy. So the boy took the stick in his hand and Joe knelt while the boy clambered onto his shoulders. He was light enough, Joe noticed (thank God for Glaswegian malnourishment) and he hoiked him upwards. Finally they dislodged the frisbee and it tumbled down into the waiting arms of another of the boys.

'Cheers very much,' said the boy as Joe lowered him back to ground. 'Good thing you were here.' He seemed to be the only one that talked.

'Aye, no problem,' Joe replied.

'At least we got this back,' the boy grinned. 'We lost our football in the river!'

'Is it not a bit daft playing football beside the river and frisbee near the trees? What are you doing down here anyway?'

'Just havin' fun,' said the boy with an expression on his face as if Joe had asked him what two plus two was. 'What are you doing here?' the boy asked back.

Joe looked at his questioning face. The two other boys were watching too. Joe thought about the question and stared at the boy and could not answer. The gears had stopped turning in his brain. He turned his head to look at where he had stood by the river, as if the answer might be there, or he might see his real self leaning against the railing. And for no rational reason he could ever later find, Joe began to laugh. A snicker at first, escaping through his clenched mouth, then a giggle, reluctant and embarrassed, then a torrent of nervous energy sent laughter rippling up through his rib cage and exploding from his face and he lost it completely.

The boys caught the bug without knowing why and began laughing at this strange creature. Joe's eyes streamed with tears and his head was in his hands, and he laughed so hard he was silent and his body shook with the remorseless tumbling of the laughter inside him. The boys now were safe to let go and they too began bellowing with laughter, mostly at him, not with him, and the sound echoed off the near tenements and drifted across the dirty river and reached the ears of the drunks on the Broomielaw. The fit of mirth began to burn itself out and Joe gradually calmed down, heaving deep breaths and feeling something old and welcome return a little to pulse through his tired body, and the jagged lines of blue sky and the sweet warm wash of dying sunshine was right there around him, immediate and huge and visceral, pulling at his senses like a magnet.

And now Joe could see what had been there in the boys faces all along, their eagerness to preserve the day, to play as long as they could, to defy the dipping of the sun and the dying light, for the night was like death. And they are right and I am wrong, he whispered to himself as he walked away, the irrational laughter still singing somewhere in the air around him.

21

The next day, Joe arrived at Hunter House. On this occasion Grant let him in.

'Hi Grant. How are you doing?'

'I'm grand, thanks. How are you?'

'Aye, okay. Been a bit unwell. Tired. The dreaded lurgy. How did you get on with that bench you were working on?'

'It's finished. It's out in the back garden. You should go and have a look if you have a chance. You can tell me if there's any rough edges left.'

'Ah, fantastic, well done. I will do that. Though I doubt I would notice if there was anything wrong with it. What are you working on now?'

'Ach just tidying up the garden before winter. Nothing artistic, but it needs done.'

'Do you know where Walter is by any chance? I'm here to see him.'

'I'm not sure. Most the residents are in the lounge watching Casablanca. He might be in there. He loves his old black and white movies.'

'Alright, thanks, I'll have a look there. And I'll have a look at your bench while I'm here.'

Joe went down the hallway to access the lounge through the dining room. Between the dining room and the lounge was a glass door. Joe stood at the door and looked through the glass to see if Walter was in there. He saw Walter, sitting in a high backed armchair, glued to the screen. Joe could see that Walter knew the words off by heart and was mouthing them along with the characters on screen. He looked content.

He opted to leave him be and enjoy his film. Perhaps it had

been a foolish idea to come and see him like this. Joe was just about to leave quietly when he remembered Grant's bench. He walked out of the dining room and down the corridor that would take him to the back door. He passed a room with W. McLellan marked on the door. He'd never noticed it before. Joe headed outside and peered around the garden blinking in the sunlight. Grant's bench was on the other side of the lawn in a neat little sun trap enclosed with honey suckle and clematis, though their flowers were now gone for the winter and the stems were spindly and bare. Joe admired the bench as he approached. Here was real tangible proof of work done well, work that could be seen and touched and smelled and tested. Something physical to show for the hours of skilled work. It hung together solid and dependable, with wood that was sawn and sanded and varnished well by bare hands. And strewn from work that could be solitary, work that did not hinge on the fragile and mercurial collaboration with another human.

Joe sat on the bench and surveyed the wide garden. A vegetable patch was rimmed with smooth grey stones. The stones sparked like flint a memory of the last time he'd seen Adam. Joe had listened as Adam recounted his night time escape, scared and impressed and envious at Adam's chutzpah. To listen to Adam was to be infected a little with his ability to revel wholeheartedly in the magic of the present moment. It was Adam's unwillingness to be ground down by the grinding weight of the mundane that left him sometimes vulnerable and unconventional. But he thought of Adam lying on the hillside in his mystical tomb of stones, symbolically dead but utterly alive under the yawning chasm of the night sky, and he found himself yearning for a dose of Adam's spirit, to make him choke and splutter but liven up, like a shot of good whisky would.

Again, Joe noticed himself ruminating on his work, on his yearning to hear clients' stories but re-tell those stories back to the clients, transformed somehow. To perform some kind of alchemy, to recycle, to re-imagine. Sometimes that couldn't be done, and all he could do was witness attentively to their stories. And he only ever had the raw material of what they told him. No magical new information he could bring to them, no way to fill in any of their blanks for certain.

Joe crossed back over the garden and into the house. He turned along the short corridor and past Walter's room. The house was still quiet, everyone watching the film. He stopped in his tracks. Or, more accurately, he *was* stopped in his tracks. He looked around, self-conscious but also gripped by an idea. He felt momentarily disjointed from the world, travelling a parallel path like a train that had abruptly jumped track at a junction. Was it even possible? He took three steps backwards, eyes trained on the opening at the end of the hall. A thudding looped around his chest and up his spine. His hand found the handle of the door, half-hoping it would be locked.

To his fright the door opened. It would have looked bad to be seen now, half in the room. He stepped in quickly. He felt a swirling of giddy and fearful confusion, and a strange white lightness of hope and exhilaration. He scanned quickly and found the bookshelves. Books were piled messily on each other, and half a shelf was filled with photos of Walter's sisters and their families. He could not see the stone, and his stupidity loomed large in front of him. He thought of his own crowded bookshelves and the quest for new spaces. He snaked a hand into the space behind the books on the top shelf. Nothing. Second shelf, nothing. On the third shelf his fingers found something hard behind a framed photo of the four grandchildren, and he watched himself pulling the stone out, cradling it carefully like the egg of an exotic bird. Joe left the room, his heart pounding, walked quickly down the hall, and left the house without a word to anyone.

22

The day was cold and biting and a wet snarling wind huffed and griped. There was little left of Jelly Hill but the white cottages that bracketed the main road as it crossed the dirty canal. Joe squelched down a sodden track to the narrow canal path, impractical loafers and corduroy flares gathering wet mud splodges. The banks of the canal were deserted of people yet thick with meadow fescue and Japanese knotweed, bare hazel and wild bramble, the last few fruits shrivelled and hard. Some way along the canal path the rotting bones of the wooden rail bridge stuck out the water, a wilting skeletal monument to forgotten trade. A wide and weather-worn breeze block marked the old path where once Mavis Valley had nestled amongst idyllic meadows and dangerous pits. Joe followed the faint path, carrying a damp stick as if it might divine some artefacts of the forgotten history of the place. A gap between gnarly trees suggested where the old road had once been.

From an old map Joe had found in the Mitchell Library, he knew there must have been a row of houses each side, heading north from the canal. The village had been deserted in the fifties. Joe hoped something might still be standing, some remnants, some testament. Alongside the road lay a parallel dip, an old burn perhaps? Joe poked amongst the damp weeds, shrivelling nettles and knots of thick grass, looking for some sign of life - bricks, rotting wood that once had been a chair or a bed, a rusty copper wire, ripped rags of bed sheets, anything. His cords caught on grabbing thorns as he thwacked a stick amongst the growth. Nothing.

Further up the road that once was the layout was harder to discern – perhaps here had been larger houses, perhaps another small road? Here also was nothing of the bittersweet history he sought. Some rubbled stones lay amongst tree roots, once laid in walls and coalescing into cottages, but now they were lost fragments, the stones rejected when others were scavenged for farm walls and rock gardens. In one place Joe saw the rough outline of a room where enough stones still lay where they had once been stacked and mortared. He tried to conjure an image of a family here, the coal-blackened husband, the wife tending the home, the community to the left and the right. He tried to fit Walter's story like a jigsaw piece into this place that once was, to make a spark fly between two times, to tie two loose ends in a ragged but sturdy knot. But too much time had passed, and too much weathering by man and by nature's relentless reclaiming of its own, and Joe's feeble imagination could not colour in the blank spaces. He stood in the quiet while rain gathered in the trees.

That morning he had done his very best to figure out what might be inside the stone. Under the glare of the angle poise lamp, using one of the wood carving knives he'd taken from his grandparents' garage, he tried to prise apart the two halves. Although there was a millimetre or two of give, he could barely get the knife between the two halves. Even when he did, and even when the crack took some light into it, there was no way to see what lay inside. For his trouble he got only a stinging cut between his thumb and forefinger when the knife scythed out of the stone. He had even phoned the x-ray department at Glasgow Royal, awkward and blushing, to ask if an x-ray could see inside a stone, knowing, really, what the answer would be. His fatigue told him this wasn't going to work.

From the ghost of Mavis Valley he walked to the nearest library. In the bookish hush he danced the library shuffle around the other shufflers, hoping their eyes did not stray from the texts of crime thrillers and penny romances to the embarrassment of the drying crusts around his trouser hems, looking like they'd been dipped in a mud fondue. In *Strathkelvin by Canal,* he found old photos of the canal, details about the myriad coal mines in the area, one grainy photo of Mavis Valley in its short-lived hey-day. There was a sign advertising a new book for sale by a local historian all about the Mavis Valley mining disaster, but apparently no copies of the book. He went to the counter.

'Excuse me, do you happen to have any more copies of the book about the Mavis Valley mining disaster? I was hoping to buy one.'

The librarian looked unsure.

'Em, I don't think we have any left. I'll have a look around. Bear with me.' The librarian shuffled around books and forms under the counter.

'I'm sorry. We don't seem to have any more. There are some on loan. I can put a hold on one for you if you like?'

'Oh, that's a shame. I'm not from round here so I'm not a member of the library. I just came over to do some research on this very topic. Is there anywhere else local I could buy a copy?'

The librarian looked pained.

'The author actually lives nearby. I'm sure she could bring in some more copies in the next few days.'

Joe played his trump card.

'I'm actually looking for a copy for a friend whose dad was one of the miners who died in the fire. He doesn't know much about it and when I saw you have a book all about it, I thought that would be wonderful for him.'

The librarian wilted further.

'Hold on, let me speak to a colleague.' She hurried towards the back of the room and into the offices in the rear of the building. Joe hung about, looking again at the local interest section. A fine sculpture of Thomas Muir stared sternly at Joe from an alcove, and posters listed community events for Bishopbriggs, Auchinairn and Cadder. The librarian was hurrying back, looking happier.

'Excuse me sir? Yes, I think you're in luck. I spoke to a colleague and she actually phoned the author to see when she might bring some more copies. The author sounded pleased that the

173

books had sold out and that someone was in asking for one. She's going to pop in soon with some copies, and you can perhaps meet her as well if you like?'

'Oh, that's great. Thanks a lot. I guess I'll just browse for a while until she arrives?'

'Yes, of course, please do. I'll come and find you when she arrives.'

A short while later, the librarian found Joe and introduced him to Christa Weber. Joe learned that she was originally from Munich but had been living in Scotland since fleeing Hitler's regime just before the invasion of Poland. Christa looked about sixty and had dyed purple hair. Her German accent was mild and the odd word was pronounced in a distinctly Scottish brogue. She was a keen amateur historian and had gotten interested in the lost village of Mavis Valley and the fire in the mine. Her father had worked in a mine outside Munich and she had remained fascinated by these subterranean worlds ever since. Joe made up a story about Walter being a friend of his father's, and told Christa about Walter's father. She excitedly pulled a copy of her book from a large holdall and turned to the opening pages. At the dedication were the names of all the men who died in the fire. For a moment, Joe was confused. There was no Michael McLennan in the list. There was one Michael, though, a Michael Simpson. Joe saw his mistake. Walter was McLennan because he had been given his step-father's name.

'Did you find out anything much about Michael when you were researching this book?'

'Let me see, I can't remember offhand.' Christa flicked ahead through the pages. Her fingers were thin and wrinkled but nimble.

'Ah, here we are. Michael Simpson. No, there wasn't really much recorded about him. In the official report into the fire, he must have been listed as being single. But that wouldn't fit with what your friend is saying, would it?'

'Well, single in the sense of not being married, I guess?'

Joe looked up to the domed ceiling for a few moments. A muffled sunshine fell through the windows and illuminated tiny wafting specks of dust.

'Neither of their families wanted them to be together. One was Catholic, the other was Protestant. Before he died, Michael and Maggie had been told to stay apart.'

'That would fit with the spirit of the times,' said Christa. 'The sectarian divide was strong then. The Catholic and Protestant miners had separate funerals, and were buried in separate graveyards.'

'Really?'

'Yes. Look. I'll show you the photographs of the funerals.' Christa turned in the book to some sepia photographs. In one, the protestant dead were carried along the canal path amongst crowds of people, a mingling of black blotches against grey meadows. In another, the Catholics were being mourned at the chapel at Lambhill, the sad crowd spilled out onto the steps outside.

'So, let's assume that was him, even though he was listed as single. Was there any other information about him?'

'I don't think so, not that I could find, I'm afraid. He was young, nineteen we think. Hadn't amassed much life or reputation by that age. We know he was a driller.'

'Only nineteen. Were they all that young?'

'No, I think that was at the lower end of the range. Let me check the list again. No, there was no-one else that age amongst the victims. He was the youngest. But I think there was one other man that young who survived the fire. Let me see. Fergus McAllister, a brusher.' Her face came to life again.

'Ah, now, I remember him. He's the only one who's still alive. Or at least he was when I wrote the book last year.'

'He's still alive? I don't …' Joe started doing the sums in his head. 'He must be, what, 90?'

Christa did the sum too. 'Yep, I guess that's about right. A miserly old sod too.'

'What? You've met him?'

'Yes, but only very briefly and not in very amicable circumstances. When I was researching the book I assumed all the miners who'd been involved in the disaster would be dead by now. Especially with the black lung and all manner of brutal illnesses that chew up and hollow out these mining men. But I was desperate to talk to anyone who might have been there at the time. And, with a lot of perseverance, I might point out, I found out Mr McAllister was still alive.'

She could see Joe was taken aback.

'I really wanted to meet him, to hear about his experiences. He was on shift in the mine when the fire happened. There was only him and three others who survived. They took a different route out of the mine and they avoided the fire. Everyone could have survived if they'd followed that route. So sad. It would have been amazing to hear about it directly from him. So I tracked down where he was living. A place called Spean Bridge, up in the Highlands. He doesn't have a phone,' Christa raised her eyebrows, 'so I wrote to him. Three times. He didn't respond to my letters. So I decided to go and see him. It's three and a half hours away,' she emphasised.

'When I got to his house, he refused to talk to me. My goodness, he was cantankerous. What was it he called me? Boche, kraut, a bride of Hitler - that was the best one. I tried to tell him about the book but he was adamant he didn't want to discuss it. Wouldn't surprise me if he has some kind of PTSD or suchlike.'

Joe was still processing the fact that someone from the fire was still alive. The possibility had not even occurred to him. And, coming quickly on the back of that realisation, the fanciful idea that he could find this Fergus and get him to talk. To find out if he knew Walter's dad. To find out if he had anything that might help Walter fill in some blanks.

Joe realised he'd have to ask for Christa's help.

'I'm sorry to hear that Fergus was so rude to you. Especially as you travelled all that way.' Christa nodded and gave a wry smile.

'I know this will sound a bit unconventional, but I'm excited by the possibility of trying to meet this man, to see if he can give my friend Walter even a little bit of insight into life in the mines, the fire, perhaps about Mavis Valley, firsthand accounts, you know? Perhaps he knew Michael. Would you be willing to give me Fergus's address?'

Christa was quiet whilst she chewed this one over. She stared Joe in the eye. He tried to look trustworthy and deserving of her compassion.

'I shouldn't, you know? He probably wouldn't appreciate me giving someone else his address. However,' she paused for dramatic effect, and Joe's heart leapt, 'he was cheeky and impudent when I met him, and with worse manners than Hitler himself! So, I kind of *like* the idea of someone else hassling him and pushing him to do something for someone else. And I feel for your friend, with his absence of knowledge. And I admire you trying to help him. So I *will* give you the address for Fergus McAllister. And I hope you have better success than I did!'

With that, she concluded her speech and arranged to phone Joe once she had checked her notes back home. He thanked her profusely, gladly paid for a signed copy of her book, and tried not to think too rationally about what he was embarking upon.

23

The next morning Joe was awake early, his mind whirring and his body alive with anticipation. After a quick breakfast of scrambled eggs and black coffee, he finished packing his rucksack – clothes, whiskey, tapes for the walkman, Christa's book. With Murmur playing on his headphones he set off for the subway. Joe enjoyed the old rattle and clatter of the train as it sped through black tunnels. He emerged from the underground world into sweet light and the bustle of the west end.

The Book Den, hidden off Gibson Street, was the business and the symptom of a great hoarder. There had once been shelves smartly filled with books. Over the years, the books had split like amoeba to multiply and multiply and had begun forming themselves into small forgivable piles on the floor which had grown like gangly teenagers into precarious and awkward towers, held up only by other dusty towers of the same dyspraxic dimensions. In one typically eclectic pile, Joe found a book he'd heard of and filed away in his mental wish-list. Hero With A Thousand Faces by Joseph Campbell was about half-way down, or half-way up depending on one's outlook. He faced the perennial dilemma of everyone who browsed the shop, whether the book was important enough to try pulling it out from its supporting role and risk the whole thing collapsing, Buckaroo-style, books thudding and shattering the contented silence, and then needing to rebuild the precious structure in the same (dis)order. Joe took the plunge, laid down his rucksack and leaned his shoulder against the upper half of the pile while slowly inching the desired book out of its place. At the last moment he whisked it out, and the upper pile sank clumsily down an inch and miraculously no books were harmed in the making of this extraction.

The price, written in pencil, was 50 pence, and Joe thought wryly that he might have to stick to 50 pence books for a while if Oliver sacked him. But the thought tumbled away into the 'deal with later' segment of his mind that he had been cultivating lately.

The book acquired, Joe headed back towards the city centre. He decided he had time to walk it. He came to Charing Cross where he took the footbridge that leaped the wide and noisy road. Where the footbridge rose out of the pavement, someone had written in green graffiti on the tarmac 'O city you are mighty yet tender.' And at that moment, his gaze was lifted and the simple great blue sky with a few scattered white clouds cracked his heart open a little and his soul's flood rose like an arterian well bursting up from a deep aquifer, the briefest cup of painful joy brimming over. It was the same wide sky that had always been there, consistent and unchanged since the day of his birth, the same fond colour of bubblegum blue it had always been, the same impenetrable view of black space and nothingness, yet coloured and lit as if it were something rather than nothing, coloured and lit for the cover and protection of the earth and everything that is in it. The feeling sweetened and revived him, a long-lost friend passing quickly through on her adventurous way.

The Mallaig train rumbled contentedly at platform 4, blue grey smoke drifting and dissipating towards the high arched roof. The train was quiet when Joe came on board. Ticket stubs stuck out of the booked seats dotted around the carriage. Two young couples sat with cups of steaming coffee, hunched over a map like generals planning their conquests. A mother tried to read The Daily Record whilst a young boy entertained and asserted himself by stomping stubbornly to the furthest end of the carriage. A young man checked nervously with the conductor that he was on the right carriage, checked the train would split at Crianlarich, checked he could get home on Sunday. Joe eased his tired body into the seat and rubbed his fingers along its heavy fabric, a half-hearted tartan of green, red and yellow which more or less concealed a thousand spills of tea and Irn Bru.

At 11:07 the conductor in blue blazer blew a long shrill whistle. The engine flared, sending rough vibrations through the train, and the great iron wheels began to turn. For Joe, the sensation of movement was delicious, the sense of escape and of someone else making the decisions. On a train no-one could contact you. On a train you could slip into self-centred absorption, a holiday from your work and obligations, time not for productivity but for staring out of windows, watching the land change, watching for snippets of life like a voyeur, quotidian scenes like an overweight woman smoking at her back door or a farmer in a lush green field feeding his cows for the thousandth time or a pretty young woman getting dressed in her bedroom - a flash of skin then lost from view. The train gathered pace and one open window let in buffeting air.

They passed a plot of allotments. Small ramshackle huts bore the individuality and quirks of their tenants. The vegetable patches were winter-barren and around the huts overflowing racks and crates resembled unsuccessful jumble sales. They passed the epic cranes of Browns Shipyard, derelict but charged with grandeur. Beautifully kept grass football pitches heralded the shift into sparser parts of the urban sprawl before the hulking mass of the Erskine Bridge passed over the track and seemed to float above the mist of the river. The wooded hills to the north disappeared slowly into the mist and the river widened. An old harbour was decaying and sinking slowly into the oblivion of the Clyde. The train passed silver birch peeling thin bark like sunburnt skin. Copper brown wild grass gave way to mint green with frosted icing. Dumbarton Rock rose on the left, the site of many a Viking plunder – who would have thought Dumbarton was a prize worth invading three times for?

On Joe's Walkman, the resonant voice of Stan Rogers was singing of sunken ships and heartbreak. Frankie had introduced Stan Rogers to him a few months earlier when the folk singer had died in a plane crash. They passed the Lomond Hills, the first hint of the highlands. Snow jags on the peaks lit up against slate grey sky. A long muddy sandy beach ran alongside the track. Wading birds picked at the sand for juicy sea worms. The towns out here aspired less to be urban, and the farmland began to dominate. At Helensburgh Upper, another gang of serious walkers boarded, with waterproofs of luminous greens and yellows, bright red Carrrimor rucksacks and walking poles. This was the day's only train to the north, the one chance for walkers and climbers to make their pilgrimage for a hit of wildness.

The track was rising now, level with the snow line on the hills to the west. The sun was fully up, the sky frozen in glacial white and blue. The track burrowed through undisturbed land, deep dark forests, the hiding place of a thousand burrowing and pecking creatures hunkering down for the winter. White burns of melted frost slipped down the slopes in channels carved out over slow millennia. Again the lushness of wild, thick rhododendron and russet dogwood in cold November shocked Joe, his city ignorance a little embarrassing in this place.

Joe thought about his plan to find the prickly Fergus and extract from his story any crumbs of consolation and enlightenment for Walter. He held up the urge like a mineral, peering briefly through its opaque colours, to see what lay in its centre. And yet, he let it remain opaque and didn't wish to examine it too long or too closely. Already the distance had taken him further from work, from the crisis with Oliver, from the longer story of his father's slow defeat, and from Joe's own confident walk in his work slowing to a weary stumble.

Now, from where he sat, Joe could not see any ground on his left – he felt like they were floating above the thick hazy cloud. Passengers got out their cameras in a rush, drinking it in, flashbulbs popping. The peaks of the hills began to look more daunting, asserting their growing power and grandeur, challenging mere humans to take them on. The village below was heartbreakingly cosy and romantic in the midst of such inhospitable land. Thin tall evergreens, sturdy but delicately thin, pointed like arrows to the sky that feeds them.

The sun cast light on the tops of the peaks, the valleys remaining in slate grey shadow. Daffodil light filled the valley. The train swept into another valley, the strong pull of a mechanical body straining with grunt and whine and rumble against the incline of the land. Here drystone dykes carved fields into ownership and sheep bore the daubed colours of their herd. Pleasure boats, fishing boats, bright orange buoys and the icy water lay beautifully still at Ardlui. Joe's neck was beginning to hurt from twisting hungrily towards the scenery but happily so.

Further on the frost disappeared. Joe savoured the moments when a gap appeared in the dips of valleys and distant mountains came into view, ever more mighty, covered in snow, Lord what a beautiful country. Precarious roads wrapped around harsh hills. There came fairy glens, where the imaginations of many had conjured gothic tales of elfs and goblins and sprites. Each house now was a landmark, an expression of love for the landscape and stubborn defiance and longing for solitude. Yet, Joe reflected, it would have been common in years gone by for many more to live in these isolated places, to build communities which did not depend on electricity, on running water, on gas, on telephone lines, on smooth roads to the cities. For many, seeing this terrain would not usually have been with a sense of wanderlust, but with survival and daily routines in mind. But then the highlands had been half emptied in the clearances, a genocide of sorts, an imposed fast-forward to modernity.

It seemed almost indulgent for one country to have so much space un-colonised. Joe felt chills of satisfaction as the winter land pierced into him. He thought maybe cities and great buildings grow up as a defence against the creeping fear of our insignificance. Even the grandest man-made structures are puny from a distance yet we must marvel at our stature and our cleverness and our hard work. In the expanse of wilderness we sit more easily with our littleness, where an isolated cottage is dwarfed by even the smallest of hills, and we don't need the desperate height and exhibitionist facades of our great buildings.

Despite the hour, a big group of climbers were sharing swigs of cheap whisky at the other end of the carriage. The ringleader stood in the aisle, orchestrating the distribution of the dram and the conversation it lubricated.

Joe wondered again what on earth he was doing. Fergus had refused to talk to Christa. What on earth made Joe think he could persuade him to talk by turning up? It was a fool's errand, a wasteful hop. He was going north regardless. He told himself it was what he needed, the break, the distance, the clean air. But he knew he would be crestfallen if he didn't get Fergus to talk. Even just some morsels, to connect Walter with the world his dad had inhabited. To know more concretely in his soul that his dad had been real, had real friends, had really worked in the mine. It was almost as if Walter wasn't quite convinced his dad had ever truly existed. Now that the family and friends who'd known his dad were all gone, it was easier for Walter's mind to conjure up the fantasy that it was all a bluff, a cruel joke.

And Joe felt again Walter's anguish. Believing his father had given up on his sweetheart and his unborn child. From what kind of masculine quarry was he strewn if his father gave up on his young family without a fight? He felt for the deep uncertainty in Walter. Joe was disappointed in his dad at times, but at least he could see and touch what his dad was. He could rage quietly against his dad. Walter did not know who or what to rage against, if indeed it was rage that was needed.

Joe wondered what was different this time. He had heard many stories where women and men longed for a stronger sense of connection with someone or somewhere they didn't have any more. They could form and reform their story in the absence of tangible real life connections. Why was he traipsing a hundred miles north in search, a futile search most likely, of a sliver of a thread of connection for Walter?

He fondled the question and stared dumbly out of the window. The smooth curve of the golden grassy hills drew the eyes upwards to the steeper jagged outcrops where white powder snow coated bald stony ground. The stop at Bridge of Orchy came and went. On Joe's Walkman, Stan Rogers and his band of men were singing "Northwest Passage".

Something caught in Joe's mind at the idea of the explorer tracing the steps of John Franklin, finding a connection with a journey long gone. An idea was wriggling like a worm somewhere under the mud of his awareness. What was it?

The worm wriggled to the surface, smiling triumphantly. Here Joe could actually find a real live link for Walter. He had always had to be content with historical reconstruction, psychological archaeology and reshaping of the narrative. Here, now, he might just uncover something real and still living for Walter. Fergus might be the only man alive who had known Michael. And, hope against all hope, maybe he would know about the stone. Maybe speculation could give way to bare fact, to certainty, in the process of therapy when certainty is almost impossible. That was what was different this time. That was the hook. Joe pounded his fist on the seat. He could bring some true, new information to the client, something that really changes things, that really shifts reality.

Up into Rannoch Moor now, a plateau after the long climb. The wide moor was ringed by jagged hills, a crown of sorts. Small lochs were frozen solid. The harsher peaks of Binnein Mor and the beast of Ben Nevis rose further to the west. What a job to lay a railway line through this.

Before Walter died, before Fergus died, Joe was the only one who might be able to transmit a spark of knowledge between these two men – two men who had probably never met and probably never would. Joe was perhaps the only person alive who knew how one man might feed another man. Walter was not starving, but he had missed a crucial nutrient his whole life. And at some level Walter knew it. His poignant and dramatic dreams betrayed a child still thirsting for 'dad.' In the privacy of a face turned towards the window, whilst the other passengers sat spell-bound by the moor, Joe cried for the first time in years, quietly, unashamedly.

The country was almost showing off now. At Corrour, the magnetic pull of the hills took two young women off the train and pacing immediately out along a path, their faces bright and alive under warm hats, their bones and muscles eager for movement.

Joe took a break from pure thought and pulled out the dog-eared copy of Hero With A Thousand Faces. For a few minutes he read of the belly of the whale, of liminal spaces, of Oriental myths. He glanced involuntarily out of the window again and swore out loud. The land had changed again. A fearsome slope met the train track, the hill threatening to keel over on top of the train. Trees grew out above the train, a wild and magical tunnel of sorts. A moment later cloud enveloped the train completely and it might as well have been a plane flying high above the earth. The cloud began to break. Joe marvelled at the splendid isolation of a croft house perched on the sunny side of the craggy valley. The valley widened and the hills receded again, taunting with their grandeur then taking pity by falling away just as quickly. He thought of Adam as his mind somersaulted in excited freedom.

In this alien country the city and its travails became faded and forgotten. In the valley approaching Roybridge the land changed again, becoming pastoral and giving. The snow and ice had disappeared. It was a lull before the true wilderness of the Cairngorms would soon appear to the north east.

Eventually, the train arrived at Spean Bridge, another elegant Victorian station, where Joe got off. He pulled out a grainy photocopy of a map he'd found in the library. He had booked a cheap bed and breakfast, a single room to boot - his father's frugality had sunk deep into Joe's decision making. The owners of the bed and breakfast, an elderly couple, were welcoming and gracious. They were polite enough not to ask further when Joe explained he was here to find someone he'd never met. They gave Joe a map of the town and marked an X roughly where Fergus's house must be.

Back in his room, Joe flaked on the bed. The private exhilaration of the journey had tired him, though his mind was still conjuring up pictures of the hoped for encounter with Fergus. Nevertheless, his body sank towards sleep, eventually taking his mind with it.

24

The next morning Joe opted uncharacteristically for a full cooked breakfast. He packed his rucksack with a notepad and pen, the directions for the house, and a bottle of Speyside whisky in the hope that he'd have something for which to thank Fergus.

Past the Highland Hotel he found the shortcut he'd been told about and followed the path down the short hill. Ahead of him loomed the grey mass of Annoch Mor and to the right, the Nevis range. Where the path met a dirt track, there was a wooden sign for Annoch Mor house staked in the ground. Down a stony driveway was a house, handsome but worn in. Joe looked around, suddenly nervous and unsure and self-conscious again about his bizarre quest.

The house was old, mostly on one level but with one dormer window set into the roof at the front. The house was stone and probably three times as old as Fergus. The window frames were shedding old paint and the garden was colonised more than kept. There was an old green army jeep parked in front of the house. Through frosted glass panels he could see the blurred shapes of the hall and its doorways.

Joe knocked on the wooden door. Nothing happened. Recalling what he'd been told about Fergus's age and hermit lifestyle, Joe considered that it was possible the old man was dead and rotting inside.

A shuffling figure came down the hall and opened the door, which creaked obnoxiously as it swung open. Fergus looked his eighty-nine years and he stared at Joe with small bloodshot eyes.

'Yes?'

'Hi. I'm very sorry to bother you -'

'If it makes you sorry, why are you doing it?'

' - but are you Fergus McAllister?'

'Who's asking?'

Joe put on his best voice of calm reasonableness.

'My name is Joe Miller I've come up from Glasgow. I have a friend whose dad worked in the Cadder mine in 1913 when there was the fire. I understand you worked there as well.'

Fergus's eyes narrowed. His hand stayed put on the door.

'My friend, Walter, his dad was Michael Simpson. Michael died in the fire before Walter was born. I hoped you might tell me a bit about life back then, and about Michael if you knew him.'

Fergus just kept glaring. Joe was accustomed to talking to people who wanted to talk. This wasn't in his skill-set.

'No, no, no!' Fergus finally responded. 'I cannae be bothered talking about all that. It wis a long time ago. I don't remember much. Leave me alone! I keep to myself. Why can't others do the same?' And with that he slammed the door.

Although Joe had known hypothetically this might happen, he realised now he had assumed the best. What the hell was he to do now? Out of habitual politeness and self-consciousness he started walking back up the driveway. Walking was better for thinking anyway.

Joe soon found himself back on the main road. He passed a red phone box and felt the need for connection and sympathy. He dialled his sister's number. It rang three times before Sarah answered.

'Who's there?' she called down the phone.

'Hello Sarah. It's Uncle Joe. How are you getting on?'

'I'm great! We're making paper mache on balloons. What are you doing?'

'Good question. I'm up in the mountains, on a kind of adventure.'

'Wow. Are you hunting for treasure?'

'Well, kind of, yeah. I haven't found it yet.'

'Well, keep looking. Sometime you have to look really, really hard to find hidden treasure. Once we buried a tin of money in the garden with loads and loads of one pence's and two pence's. And then it took us *ages* to find it again. We had to dig about seven holes!'

Joe chuckled.

'Well Sarah that is very helpful advice. I'll remember that when I'm searching for my treasure. Now, is your mummy there so I can say hello to her?'

'Yep, I'll just get her for you. Bye Uncle Joe!'

'Bye Sarah.'

Isobel came to the phone a little breathless.

'Joe, hello, how are you doing?'

'I'm alright, thanks. Still up north. How's the paper mache going? Is your dining table ruined yet?'

'No, not yet, but they're doing their best. How is it up there? Have you found your grumpy old man?'

'Yes I found him. And he is grumpy. And he won't talk to me.' Joe was relieved to tell someone. 'He's just like I was told he would be. I guess I hoped I might be able to reason with him, man to man, something like that. But I never got the chance.'

'What a dick,' Isobel said with sympathy. 'You've gone all the way up there to see him. What are you going to do now?'

'I don't know. Do you think I should try again?'

'Now you're talking. But maybe … Joe don't take this the wrong way, but did you talk to him in your therapist voice?'

Joe was confused.

'Yes, of course. What other way is there?'

'Well, I was just thinking, if it was me, I'd go back there and stick a thistle up his arse. Maybe he's the kind of guy who just isn't going to play nice. Maybe you should be a bit more bolshy. Imagine you're dad, lecturing to Thatcher on the TV, or arguing with a manager in the shipyards about overtime pay. Your gentle way of talking probably works very well in therapy but if you're determined to get this guy to talk, maybe you need to crank up the

189

testosterone.'

Joe was silent for a few seconds as a lorry thundered by on the road.

'Do you know Isobel, that's probably the best and most insulting piece of advice I've ever had.' She roared with laughter down the phone, hurting his cold ear. 'I might just try that. Thanks very much. And say thanks to Sarah as well.'

'To Sarah? What for?'

'She'll know. See you later.'

Joe set off at a march back towards Fergus's place. He remembered reading about the commandos who trained just down the road at Achnacarry during the second world war. The story went that after arriving at Spean Bridge station, they would quick march the seven miles to the training centre. If they didn't make it in an hour, they were sent back to their regiments - not good enough for the commandos. Joe could feel now how marching could gird your loins and gather up your fight. He marched along the main road and down the dirt track again. He pulled out Walter's stone. He marched on and turned briskly down Fergus's driveway, contemptuous of the mess now. He rapped his knuckles hard on the door.

Fergus opened the door just a little, saw who was there, and tried to shut it again. Joe found himself shoving his foot over the doorway to stop it shutting in his face again.

'Look just hear me out, would you? You could really help us out here.'

'Get yer foot out of there!' Fergus growled. 'This is ma hoose. I'll call the bloody commandos on you!'

'Aye, so you will. And the foreign legion and the Spartans of Greece as well no doubt! Look, do you see this stone?' Joe held up Walter's stone and shook it so the mystery object inside rattled. 'Have you seen this before?'

Fergus kept the door jammed against Joe's toes but he stared quizzically at the stone, his eyes widening and his mouth falling open. He rallied his stubbornness.

'Bugger off. I swore I'd never talk about that.' He pushed a bony hand against Joe's chest. Joe lost this balance, took his foot back to steady himself, and Fergus slammed the door shut.

'Ha!' Fergus's grainy voice was triumphant behind the door.

Joe harrumphed and cursed himself. But now he knew that Fergus recognised the stone. He stood where he was and knocked again and again. He heard noises from the house, the creaking of the stairs perhaps? A few seconds later, a noise came from above him. Joe stepped back and looked up towards the upstairs window. Something whizzed past his head and struck his rucksack. Joe twisted his head round and saw an egg smashed on his rucksack. He looked up quickly and saw Fergus at the window, grinning like a goblin and releasing another egg missile. Joe dodged towards the house as the second egg splattered on the stones behind him.

'What are you doing, you…bampot!' Joe shouted. He took the rucksack from his back and tried to shake some of the viscous white and yolk onto the ground. He was at least sheltered in the overhang of the eaves for now.

'Who gave you my address anyway?' Fergus shouted angrily from the window above.

'The bride of Hitler!' Joe shouted back. 'She warned me about your highland charm!' Joe stroked his chin and considered his options. He opted for the long game. He walked boldly out and climbed onto the truck bed of the jeep. The ancient truck creaked its objection. He sat on one of the splintered wooden bench seats and looked up at Fergus in the window.

'Get off my truck!' Fergus shouted from the window.

'Make me' Joe replied calmly. He was betting Fergus wouldn't want to egg his own truck, and would probably miss from that distance anyway. Joe took the rucksack off his back and sat it at his feet. He took out the whisky from the side pocket. There was no way Fergus was getting it now, even if he did change his mind. Joe took a good swig from the bottle. Fergus stared at him. Out here, in the November cold, in the shadow of Nevis, the whisky was unspeakably good. Thick nectar burned pleasure into his mouth, his throat, his nervous belly. Joe ran his fingers along the contours of the bottle and looked nonchalantly around at the bare trees and browning grass. Minutes passed by. Fergus closed the window and disappeared from sight. Joe took another mouthful from the bottle and swirled it around his mouth. He let it sit in his mouth, numbing his gums, before savouring the smoky after-taste as he swallowed it down. His heart was galloping and he was shivering slightly.

After about ten minutes the front door swung open. The sun was coming up over the mountains now and Joe had to squint through the light to see the doorway.

'Well, are ye gonnae share that or not?' came Fergus's voice, still gruff.

Joe grinned broadly, shocked it had actually worked. He wasted no time getting off the truck. They eyed each other warily as Joe approached the house.

'Let me see that stone again would you?' Fergus asked.

Joe took it from his pocket and handed it to Fergus, who turned it over and around in his hands. He shook it beside his ear, listening to the rattle. He stroked a thumb over its contours. It appeared to be Joe's entrance ticket.

'Come on in' Fergus said. 'I'm sorry about the eggs.'

'Thanks. Apology accepted.'

'No, I didn't mean you. They were for my lunch.' But he was grinning at his own joke and he showed Joe in to the old house.

25

Two hours later, Joe emerged from the house, blinking in the midday brightness. He stepped past the smashed egg, stroked the jeep affectionately, and headed up the driveway. The bed and breakfast owner had told him about a rough path along the River Spean, which passed the remains of Highbridge, where the Jacobite rebellion had kicked off, along General Wade's old military road, and back up towards the Commando Memorial. Joe had time to kill before the next train so he set off on that route. He sighed deeply as he walked. Layers of tired preoccupation fell from his shoulders. For the first time in months, he walked with a spring in his step and his face wore a mystic smile. As he left the woods, he saw properly for the first time the implacable slopes of Ben Nevis and Annoch Mor. Their size, their permanence, their magnetic draw for climbing pilgrims, all of it resonated in the echoing chamber of his body, as they had no doubt done for countless others stretching back through time. Joe breathed in their goodness, and his mind was at last at peace.

The train journey home took Joe through the same stunning route but he was excited and impatient to get back to Glasgow, and could not appreciate it in the same way. He made some notes in his journal from the conversation with Fergus. He read more of Christa's book and a photocopy of the investigation report on the mine disaster. Facts fell into their places and the story shook off its cobwebs and came to life in Joe's imagination. He dozed briefly as the train left the glens and started its final approach along the Clyde.

Joe awoke with a start when the train stopped at Queen Street. The cavernous station and the drunken streets around it were ugly in comparison with the mountains of heaven he had just left behind but Joe did not care. He got in a taxi and headed straight for Hunter House. He was tired but telling Walter his story felt like a privilege he did not want to delay.

At the home, quiet, graceful Mary was on shift and was surprised to see Joe.

'Yes, I'm sorry for turning up unannounced. And at the weekend. But I was really hoping to see Walter. I've got some important information for him. I think he won't mind interrupting his evening.'

Mary's face was falling as Joe spoke. She was more hesitant than usual.

'Hasn't Ruth been in touch with you recently?' she asked.

'No, I've been on annual leave for the last week or so. Why?' An ominous ringing was gathering in Joe's mind. Mary appeared to be looking around for someone else but they were alone in the hall.

'Walter's in hospital. He's had a stroke.' She looked fearful and she watched Joe carefully for his reaction.

'How bad?' Joe asked.

'We're not really sure. He's at the Royal just now. Ruth is with him. You know he's been having TIA's?'

'No, I didn't know that.' Nauseous fear stepped up a few notches in Joe's gut. 'He didn't tell me that. How long's he been having them?'

'A few weeks, I think. I thought he would have told you.'

Joe looked at his watch. It was 7 o'clock.

'Which ward is he in?'

'Ward 14. Intensive care.'

'Can you call me a taxi please?'

'Sure. I'll do it right now.'

'Thank you.'

The taxi ride to the hospital was a short piece of hell for Joe. Thankfully the taxi driver could read enough of Joe's expression not to make small talk. The taxi dropped him at the Castle Street entrance, where the original Victorian building a hundred feet high surveyed Townhead. Joe hurried into the main entrance hall whose grandeur was wasted on anyone who was ill or worried about someone else who was. Joe took the stairs two at a time to the fourth floor. Intensive care was down the corridor to his left and only now did he slow down, fearful of what he may have to face. At the nurses' station he spoke to the matron, and explained who he was.

'Mr McLennan has had a serious stroke,' she told him. 'We don't know at the moment the extent of the damage. The next 24 hours will be crucial. The manager from the care home is here with him just now, though I think she's gone downstairs for a cup of tea.'

'He's got two sisters. Have they been informed, do you know?' Joe asked.

'Yes, they've been phoned but they can't get here until the morning. I believe they were down south on holiday.'

'Can I see him?'

The nurse led Joe down to the last bed on the left of the long ward. The curtain was open enough that Joe could see Walter in his bed as they approached. He forced himself to look.

Walter was wired up to monitoring machines and wearing a hospital gown. Other than that, he looked like he was sleeping. In all the excitement of the last few days, Joe had almost lost sight of Walter as a real human being. Now he was real again. Joe looked longer, forcing himself to take it in. He was relieved Walter was not cut or bruised or emaciated. That would have been even harder, and that was his memory of seeing older people in hospital beds. Joe thanked the nurse and she left him. There were two chairs alongside the bed. He sat on the one furthest away.

The excitement of the last few days, the burgeoning story he was bringing back to Walter, it felt like a cruel build up to a bad punch-line. Joe began to lose hope. He remembered how he'd imagined a touching scene where he would apologise to Walter for stealing the stone. Where he would explain his reasons. Where he would explain that he'd found Fergus and more importantly, found some missing pieces of Walter's story. Where Walter would know he was important enough that Joe had gone on this odyssey. It was all crumbling now and Joe could not help feeling sorry for himself as well as anxious for Walter.

He stood up, panicking, and walked quickly out of the ward, avoiding eye contact with the nurse as he passed the nurses' station. He did not want to spill his emotion here. He had no right. He stumped down the stairs, hoping he wouldn't see Ruth. He got outside, and the freezing air hit him now, when just ten minutes before he'd been oblivious to it. The darkness was merciful for a man who did not want to be watched falling apart. But the car park was busy with comings and goings and did not feel right. Joe turned left, out of the hospital grounds, and left again into the courtyard of the cathedral. It was lit from the ground and proclaimed itself a haven for the troubled soul. But Joe carried on past it. A bridged path took him over the road into the Necropolis, the oldest cemetery in the city. Here at least was proper solitude and a place fit for sadness.

Joe stomped up a steep path. He passed the ornate headstones and tombs of rich Glaswegians. He turned off the path onto frosted grass and snaked between graves. When he was sure he was alone and hidden, he sank to his knees and put his bare hands into the grass. The pain of the cold was oddly welcome. He began to catch his breath, which showed up as big puffs of steam in the cold air. He rubbed his fingers harshly in the hard soil. Flakes of frost fell from the long blades and tumbled onto his skin. He spread his hands flat against the earth then curled them into fists, staring blankly at the shapes. His fingers were turning blue-white. He turned off his knees and sat clumsily on his bum, his head falling between his legs. He rubbed cold hands against the back of his head, scrunching roughly through his hair. His poor skin flared in protest. He took long heaving breaths and began to sound out long low notes of a droning hum. He sat up, straightened his back, crossed his legs, and lay his forearms on his legs, his palms upturned. He closed his eyes and wet his dry lips with his tongue. He sat in the private darkness and let time slowly swirl past him.

When he opened his eyes, the gathered lights of the whole city were laid out before him, twinkling with promise and unconditional giving. The high rise towers were lights and the great round gas tanks were lights and the climbing streets of Castlemilk and Cathkin were lights. Tiny white lights moved slowly on the yellow lit streets. Above the horizon stretching from Airdrie to Paisley, flickering stars cast kaleidoscopic fragments of the sun's light. The tiniest sliver of a moon, almost precarious in its thinness, was the grandfather of the sky. All of this presented itself to Joe's exhausted eyes.

He picked himself up and dusted himself down. He knew what to do. He walked back down the hill, out of the necropolis and back to the metropolis. He walked to the hospital and let himself take the lift this time. Back in the ward, Ruth had returned with her tea.

Joe and Ruth hugged. They had never touched before. It felt natural now.

'What are you doing here Joe? I thought you were on annual leave. How did you find out?'

'I am on annual leave, kind of,' he said awkwardly. 'I might have quit. Or been sacked. I don't know.' He saw Ruth's alarm. 'It's no big deal. I'll explain another time.' Ruth fetched him another chair from behind a curtain. They both sat down beside the bed, Ruth near enough to Walter to hold his hand.

'Did someone phone you about Walter?' Ruth asked.

'No, I went to the house earlier on, and they told me what had happened. I've been researching some of Walter's family history. I'd found out some things I really wanted to tell him. That's why I went there. I just got back from up north. Ruth, how long has Walter been having TIA's?'

It was Ruth's turn to feel awkward.

'A few weeks.'

'Why didn't he tell me?'

'I don't honestly know. I know he asked me not to tell you.'

Joe looked at Walter's face.

'I'm tempted to ask why, but perhaps it's right that I respect his choice. And your choice to keep that private.'

Ruth looked at Joe.

'Thanks,' she said, 'and sorry.'

'I guess that doesn't matter much now' added Joe. 'Have they told you anything more … how bad the damage is?'

'No. We found him unconscious in his room when he didn't come for lunch. He's been unconscious since. They'll do a scan in the morning to see what damage has been done.'

One of the nurses came in. She nodded hello to them both, looked at the displays on the machines, and wrote some notes on a clipboard at the base of the bed before heading to the next patient.

'The nurse told me Walter's sisters can't get here until the morning,' Joe said.

'Yes. I'll stay until the morning then I can go home and get some sleep. I'd rather he sees a familiar face if he wakes up.'

'Okay. Thank you. On his behalf, I mean.'

Machines beeped softly throughout the ward. A car horn resounded outside and they could hear the rumble of traffic from the M8 not a hundred yards away. The nurses padded softly up and down the long room.

'I hope you don't mind me saying Joe, but you've been acting a bit strange. Going above and beyond the call of duty with Walter. You came to see him a few days ago then left soon after, you're turning up here when you're off duty. What's the deal?'

Joe avoided her gaze while he thought about her question. 'I will tell you more about it from my side sometime soon. But for now I think there's something more important, more urgent for me to do. I know Walter thinks highly of you so I hope he won't mind

198

me telling you.'

Joe took a deep breath.

'His father died before he was born, in a mining disaster in 1913. At that time, his father and mother were young, in love, and had been warned by their families not to see each other. A protestant-catholic thing. When his father Michael died, he and Maggie hadn't seen each for weeks. His mum Maggie believed that Michael had given up on her, and wasn't prepared to fight their families to be with her and their child.

'After Michael died, Maggie met and married someone else. Walter's step-dad loved him as his own, but Walter's mum told him, when he was old enough to understand, who his real father had been. So Walter never knew his dad. But he also believed his dad had given up on his true love *and* had given up on him, his son. And that's the main reason Walter has never married. He believed that he would be his father's son, that he was unfit to marry and raise a family, that he wouldn't stick it out if the going got tough, because his father had given up when it really counted. He's had this deep insecurity about his masculine heritage all his life.

'On top of that, he never felt like he should ask his mum too many questions, lest it upset her. Now he actually wishes he'd found out more about his dad, rather than keeping silent all his questions all these years. He's been having all these dreams about maleness and initiation and about his dad. Now, all the people who knew his dad are dead. Or so we believed. But I'll come back to that. You know the stone Walter has?'

Ruth looked blank.

'You've not seen it?' he asked.

'Not seen what?'

Joe took the stone from his rucksack and handed it to Ruth. Her blank look remained.

'Walter showed this to me a few sessions ago. He told me that he found it when he was 14. Somebody had left it on his windowsill. It had a note wrapped around it saying it had belonged

199

to his dad when he died. Well, this freaked him out no end, as you can imagine. He never saw who'd left it there, and never knew why. But if the note was true, it was a connection to his dad, the only physical connection he had. Which explains why he showed it to me in our sessions, when we were talking about all this. So, he kept the stone all these years. But he never spoke to anyone about it, least of all his mum. She seemed to have moved on. And you know us men, we like to meditate on such things in the privacy of our own thoughts.'

Ruth did not disagree.

'I admit I have been especially moved by Walter's plight and the themes in our sessions. I started researching the fire in which his dad died, the mine, the village they lived in, all that stuff. But, you know, I'm getting ahead of myself here. Just recently I've found out some stuff that I think Walter needs and deserves to hear. That's why I came straight to the home when I got back from up north. I was desperately looking forward to telling him what I found out. The whole train ride home, I'd been picturing his face when I told him what I've found out.'

Joe paused for a few moments to let Ruth catch up. She had a quizzical look on her face and then it was sad.

'And now you're wondering whether you'll get to tell Walter what you've found?'

'Yes. And no. I didn't tell you. I arrived here earlier when you were down getting a cuppa. I was pretty upset. I'd been so excited about reporting back to Walter. And, here, it looked like history was going to repeat itself. I'd have this knowledge that could help someone else but it would be too late to pass it on. So, I'm going to tell Walter the story now. I know doctors and nurses probably think that someone unconscious can't hear what's being said around them. I know it might be a waste of my breath. But bloody hell, I've gone to some lengths to do this for him, and I'm not going to let a stupid stroke stop me now.'

Ruth had never seen Joe like this.

'Okay,' she said slowly. 'I think I understand. Here, take my seat. I'll leave you to it. I'll go and get another cuppa.' She went to stand.

'No, no, it's okay. I'd like you to stay.'

She looked sceptical.

'Honestly, Ruth, please stay. I think Walter would be glad of that.'

'Okay, okay.'

'Better get comfy. This might take some time.'

26

Joe sat on the chair nearest to Walter and took out his notepad. He poured some water into a plastic cup from the jug on the bedside cabinet and drank deeply. Ruth subtly moved her chair further back still.

Joe found it hard to start. Even now he seriously doubted whether Walter could hear him. But the die was cast.

'Walter. I'm so sorry this has happened to you. I really hope you'll pull through. I believe you will. But, just in case you don't, I have some stuff to tell you. I've done a lot of listening to you over these past months. Now you've got to listen to me, whether you want to or not. You're a captive audience.

'I know that you've had a tough time, going your whole life without your dad. It sounds like your step-dad did a good job and cared for you deeply. And your mum must have been a resilient and loving woman. They did a good job and I think those who know you would credit you with a great deal of goodness and kindness. But, I know you've always had doubts about your ability to be a husband and father. You believed that your dad gave up on your mum. And gave up on you. And, I guess that added to your angst about your dad and about being a man. I really appreciate how open you've been about all this, and it's been a privilege to journey with you so far.

'But I confess, I've become more emotionally involved in your story than I normally do. The themes of fathers and maleness and the stuff we *don't* talk about – that's all resonated very deeply with me. So I hope you don't mind that I've taken this further. I think also I never quite believed your story. What I mean is this. You're such a fatherly figure, to others in the home, to your grand-nieces and grand-nephew. I couldn't quite believe that your own father didn't pass some of that on to you. Maybe that's naïve, or idealistic. I don't know. But I hoped that maybe there was more to the story about your dad. And that stone! I can't believe you've never cracked it open to find out what's inside! I'm all for preserving some mystery, but man, the trouble you could have saved yourself!

'Well, here's the brunt of it. I found the guy that put that stone on your windowsill in 1927. I found the one man who survived the fire and is still alive today. I found the one man who remembers your dad. And I met him this morning.'

Joe looked closely at Walter's face for any signs of response. There was nothing. A memory flashed through his mind of himself at six, telling his dad about winning a race at the school sports day.

'His name is Fergus McAllister. He and your dad were friends. They both lived in Mavis Valley and both worked in the mine. They were both nineteen when the fire happened. He escaped - your father didn't. After the fire, as you know, your mum Maggie moved with her family to Auchinairn and more or less started a new life with your step-dad. Fergus never saw Maggie again.

'He told me about what it was like in the mine that night. I hope this isn't too upsetting for you. I'm taking a gamble that you'd rather know.'

Joe opened his notebook and flicked through some pages. He found the right place in his scrawled notes.

'The fire happened on Sunday August 3rd 1913. Your dad Michael was on the backshift along with Fergus. The men were split into three teams. Michael was in the team working a coal cutter. Halfway along the main passage there was a wooden cabin where the miners would leave their belongings. Above the cabin there were layers of wood, holding up an old collapsed roof. They reckon the fire started somewhere round there. The alarm was first raised when smoke was rising out of the mine head. This much you can find out from the written records.

'I said that Michael and Fergus were friends, though how that man Fergus ever kept a single friend I cannot imagine. I guess he was different then. Anyway, Michael had told Fergus all about Maggie, about her being pregnant, and about the families being against the relationship. Now, listen carefully. What Fergus told me was this. Michael, before he died, had no intention of giving up on Maggie, or you. It broke his heart that he couldn't see Maggie, and that she might be thinking he'd given up. Michael confided to Fergus that he planned to run away with the pregnant Maggie to Millport and get married without the families knowing. He had almost saved up enough money for the train fares. Michael had also bought her a Luckenbooth brooch. You'll maybe have heard of them – I hadn't. They were silver brooches, fairly cheap. They were originally sold out of wee booths on the royal mile in Edinburgh. The booths were locked at night, thus the name, Lockin' Booth. The brooches had many symbolic meanings. Most of all though, they were traditionally given as a sign of betrothal from a groom to his bride. And, they were considered to bring good luck to a nursing mother, so she would produce plenty of milk for the baby.

'Michael had bought a Luckenbooth brooch for Maggie, his sweetheart. But he was half-convinced her family might rough him up and he didn't want them to find the brooch in his possession. So, he'd put it in a rock he'd found that had split down the middle. He got a blacksmith to weld the rings of copper around it. That way he could keep it secret until he was ready to defy the families and take your mother to Millport to marry. Apparently your father had a sense of humour. He said putting the brooch in the stone symbolised their love being between a rock and a hard place. Michael had this whole romantic scheme all worked out. I couldn't believe this young miner had such a romantic soul. He always planned to break open the stone and retrieve the brooch to give it to Maggie. I wish you'd done the same at some point. You might have figured this out yourself had you done so.

'Anyway, that was Michael's plan. And he'd told Fergus all about it. And then the fire happened. During the fire, the miners obviously tried desperately to escape. But parts of the structure of the mine were starting to collapse. Michael got trapped under a falling beam as things got out of hand. He couldn't move, he was trapped. Fergus and his crew found Michael and tried to rescue him. They tried desperately hard. Fergus got badly hurt trying to shift the beam. He's got a big scar down his left arm to show for it. But they couldn't get Michael out. Michael ordered them to save themselves, to get out whilst they still had the chance. But Michael said something else to Fergus. He knew by this point he was probably going to die down there. He told Fergus not to tell anyone about his plan to marry Maggie. It was his dying wish that Maggie find someone else, so she wouldn't waste time mourning for him. Michael wanted Maggie to move on and find a good man who'd be a father to you. Now, that Fergus has a pretty hard heart but even he had a tear in his eye when he was telling me all this.

'With the fire growing and the situation getting more and more desperate, Fergus offered to take the stone, to give the brooch to Maggie. He thought Michael would want her to have it as a sign of his love to comfort her in her grief. But Michael said it would be easier on Maggie if she didn't know his plan. That it would be easier for her to find another man if she believed that her relationship with Michael was over.

'So, there you go Walter. Your dad was a brave, romantic man. He loved your mother and planned to marry her with or without the families' blessing. But when he realised he was going to die, he wanted Maggie to suffer as little as possible so he swore Fergus to secrecy so that Maggie could move on and build a new family for you.'

Joe was spent from giving Walter's story back to him. Walter remained utterly still, almost a sense of strain on his face, and the machines kept mindlessly monitoring his heart rate and the display kept its running graph. Joe turned to look at Ruth. Her eyes were red with tears and she was shaking her head in disbelief. She lay a hand on Joe's shoulder for a moment. Joe took another deep gulp of water. Ruth turned her head to him sharply.

'What about the stone?' she asked. 'You said Michael kept it to himself. How did Fergus get it to give it to Walter fourteen years later?'

'Ah,' said Joe. 'Yes, of course. I forgot about that bit. Well, if you'd met Fergus you would hardly believe this. I had to drag it out of him. The day after the fire, the rescue teams finally found all the bodies and brought them to the surface. Fergus said they were all laid out on the ground near the pit head. A terrible sight it must have been. Fergus looked for Michael's body, and found him. Michael still had his wee satchel round his neck. Fergus looked inside the bag, found the stone, and took it.'

'So he stole it from a dead man?' Ruth's face was scandalised but amused.

'Aye, I guess you could say that,' said Joe. 'But I'm not really one to judge.'

'But why did he take it?' she asked.

'I asked him the very same thing. He said he still didn't understand it himself. He said, despite his promise to Michael, he thought that something that precious shouldn't be lost. He never gave it to Maggie, or told her anything about it. He kept it, for fourteen years, not knowing what to do with it. But when he was about to move up north, he hatched this strange idea of secretly giving it to Michael's son. He thought Walter should have it. A kind of emblem, and a connection for Walter to his dad.'

'Augh,' Ruth groaned. 'The trouble it might have saved if Walter had broken open the stone sooner. Or if Fergus had just told Walter this story himself fifty or sixty years ago, rather than sneakily leaving him the stone without a word of explanation.'

'I know,' Joe replied. 'The things we're too shy to say. The questions we're too scared to ask.'

Joe turned again to Walter.

'Walter, I don't want this to be about regrets, about what could have been different. It is what it is. But I want you to know that you have already graced many lives with your fatherly and grandfatherly presence. I hope you continue to do so. Sure, you took some safe decisions out of fear – who doesn't? But you went to Spain to restore the Lady Delilah when you could have stayed at home. And maybe Richard Melrose crashed his boat on his first race – who knows? But you're right, we've got to take some risks. And not be held back by what we think our heritage is. But rest now in the knowledge that you are a good man and have always been a good man. I just wanted you to know that your father was a good man too.'

'Here, this is yours,' and he laid the stone gently on the bedside table. 'Sorry for taking it without asking. At least I didn't break it open. And, this way, you didn't have to take the risk of killing the mystery. If I had found out there was nothing significant about this stone, I wouldn't have told you. So I stole from you and I was willing to lie to you. Not exactly straight out of the therapy manual.'

In the city's only all-night cafe, Ruth and Joe sat at a window table looking out from time to time at the taxis and occasional ambulance breaking the early morning quietness of the street outside. Nearly finished coffee cooled in thick yellow mugs and only crumbs remained on their shared plate of toast and bacon. In the quiet moments, they could hear the goldfish breaking the surface of their makeshift pond, an old bath in the middle of the floor.

'So the stone. Walter didn't ask you to investigate it for him?'

'Not exactly.' Joe grinned sheepishly and stared intently at the menu.

'And you stole it from him?'

'Well he did show it to me in a session. A few weeks back.'

'And?'

'And then, a few days ago, I took it from his room,' Joe said at last.

'You broke into his room? Like, when he was asleep?' Ruth

looked half horrified, half fascinated.

'No, of course not. It was whilst they were all watching a film. I came by unannounced to see Walter. But I saw he was content watching the film and I didn't want to disturb him. Besides I suddenly felt stupid about coming to see him. I went out the back to see the bench Grant had made. On my way back in, I, I don't know what happened. I noticed his room. I suddenly thought I could take the stone, maybe find out more about it, find out what's inside it, get the story for Walter. I was in a weird state of mind. It honestly wasn't pre-planned.'

The coffee machine hissed behind the counter and cutlery chinked as the waitress dropped it into a tray. The only other couple in the cafe spoke in excited tones about whose Hillhead flat was worst for mice and moths.

'How did you get into his room?'

'It was open.'

'That's interesting. They're meant to keep their doors locked. Some folk can wander, you know? Walter's one of the few that remembers.'

'I'm telling you the truth. It was open.'

'And when did you first see the stone?' Ruth asked.

'As I said, Walter brought it to a session, along with some pictures and mementos.'

'Why do you think he brought it to your session?'

'He said ... now, what did he say?' Joe said, confused. 'He said, 'I think you'll be particularly interested in this.' '

'Then what?'

'Then I asked him more about it. As you would. It represented a lot for him. His hesitancy about finding out more about it was just like his hesitancy about himself and his masculine heritage.'

Ruth watched quizzically as an old man with a wheelbarrow full of scrap metal hurried along the pavement outside.

'Hm. So you were intrigued by the stone. You asked Walter about it. At the same time, he was giving you an unsolved mystery.

208

At a time when you needed something. At a time when you needed a good story, something to get your teeth into, something to rekindle your faith in human nature, especially your faith in men.'

'What are you getting at?'

'Well, look at you, you're alive again. You had gone a bit grey before all this. You were ... disenchanted. Your heart had gone cold. You needed something to get your blood flowing again. Searching for this story for Walter has opened you up. Today, coming home, all excited to tell Walter what you'd found out, and then seeing him in that hospital bed, your heart's been wrenched and wrung out. Which means your heart's working again. I love that you did this for Walter. But do you really think this was all your own idea?'

Joe looked flummoxed and felt alarmed at his incomprehension.

'What are you talking about?'

Ruth smiled the smile of the wise woman.

'You figure it out Sherlock,' she replied softly, got up from her chair, gave Joe a brief hug as he sat looking around him dumbly. She dropped a fiver on the table, and walked into the cool night air.

Joe did not sleep that night. With the delicious reverie of the journey up north, the thrill of extracting the story from Fergus, the punch to his gut hearing about Walter, and the spilling out of everything at the hospital bed, he had far too many thoughts pinballing round his head. And now, added into the mix like a pimento chilli, Ruth's words. Joe faced the idea, turned it and twisted it and squeezed it, ran away from it and returned half-defeated to it. It appeared that the thinker had been out-thought. The helper had been helped. A benevolent trick, the rules reversed. Eventually he feel into the mystery helplessly, gratefully, with wonderment.

Two days later the phone call came. Joe sat in his armchair by the bay window watching the trees wave off their remaining leaves as Ruth spoke calmly and encouragingly and with tender sadness in her voice. It did not feel to Joe like news, more like the signing off of a long document or the fitting and dignified coda to a piano concerto. He lingered on the phone as they sketched their recollections. The story Walter had given to Joe, and which Joe had given back re-born, was a quiet presence behind their talk, too delicate to be voiced out loud.

27

The day was beautiful and bittersweet autumn as the mourners dispersed slowly from Auchinairn North Parish. They laid Walter to rest in a shady plot near a drystone wall under a cherry blossom tree, where, come the spring, chaffinches and bluebirds and house sparrows would gather amongst the soft fruit and cast their tender melodies like confetti over the silent graves. Joe spoke briefly to Ruth and to Mary and to Grant. Most of the residents were there, some in wheelchairs that crunched roughly over the hard frosted ground. Walter's sisters were there, his nieces and nephew, and one great-nephew, a precocious boy of no more than four who lent a welcome lightness to the whole affair with his loud questions and his chasing around the headstones. Joe had sent a note to Fergus but hadn't really expected him to make the trip. As the crowd moved to cars for the customary tea and cake at Hunter House, Joe slipped away quietly into the church. After a quick change in the toilets, he took off on his bike, his mediocre suit stuffed carelessly into his panniers.

A short while later Joe freewheeled down a shady path into the grounds of Eastfield Royal. He weaved his way through the outer paths which were littered with dying leaves, ochre and flame and auburn. Near the nettle-guarded burn he spotted the tree. As he'd been promised, a length of blue wool was tied twice round the trunk to mark the right one. Joe stashed his bike amongst the wild brambles and gorse. He surveyed the fine tree from his place on the ground. It was clothed in gnarled and speckled bark and it reached fine muscular roots into the cold earth.

At the end of a high branch, the soft stem of one weak and dying leaf finally gave in to gravity's pull, the stalk broke, tiny fibres reached the limits of their strength and let go, and the crisp leaf fell tumbling, careening and bending off branches and landing in Joe's collar as he began to climb the tree.

This time he paid no heed to the lilting fear in his chest. He took strength and security from the old and steady tree and swung himself up, arms for pulling, legs for pushing. And he out-climbed his fear. As he neared the top he heard rustling down below, looked, and there was Adam, shinnying up towards him. The leaves nearest the top were the last to die, drinking in the weak sunshine while those below suffered the shade. The branches thinned and the foliage became sparse. Joe and Adam manoeuvred, grinning, around the remaining branches that wobbled and swayed with their weight but never threatened to break.

Adam reached out his hand and Joe shook it. For then, at least, the moment was as fine as it needed to be. Joe and Adam surveyed the pastoral land, the curving slope of the Campsies, the patchwork of fields, sturdy farmhouses, retired racehorses grazing in fields whose resources would never be exhausted, electricity pylons like steel men holding their burden, strong and silent, and above, the organism of the clouds where behind the illusion of quiet stillness there was movement and chemistry, the basic element of life forming and condensing, individual drops coalescing and taking on weight, to give life by falling. Adam saw the hills in the distance, Joe saw the space in between. And around them both the westerly wind rustled crisp leaves and whispered its mysteries.

www.lewisblairstories.com

Printed in Great Britain
by Amazon